The Lynching

The Lynching

Bennie Lee Sinclair

Walker and Company
New York

First published in the United States of America in 1992
by Walker Publishing Company, Inc.

Published simultaneously in Canada by Thomas Allen & Son
Canada, Limited, Markham, Ontario

Library of Congress Cataloging-in-Publication Data
Sinclair, Bennie Lee, 1939–
The lynching / Bennie Lee Sinclair.
p.   cm.
ISBN 0-8027-3201-1
I. Title.
PS3569.I5198L96   1991
813'.54—dc20   91-23605
                                CIP

Printed in the United States of America
2 4 6 8 10 9 7 5 3 1

for Steve, and in memory of Zim

Riddle Poem

If I return
        to my father's land
If I dig deep
      in my father's grave
If I reconstruct
        my father's bones
If I discover
        my father's sins
If I retrace
        my father's steps
If I erase
        my father's voice

Where will it end
What will I find
Who will appear
Who will forgive
Who shall sing

And what of me
Who will I be?

Lynching, like revolution, is actually quite seldom merely the inevitable result of spontaneous public reaction; instead, it is usually well orchestrated and grows out of personal or political conflicts.

—E. DON HERD, JR.,
The South Carolina Upcountry, 1540–1980

Part I

▽

The White Man's Daughter

$\triangledown$

1

WAS IT JUSTYN'S IMAGINATION, or did the passenger who took the seat beside her on the plane from Washington—a young, somewhat ornately dressed black man—glance at her with a shock of recognition before he pulled a book from his briefcase and began to read? Could he have attended the White House conference? He might remember her as one of the few white delegates there—small, with distinctively premature gray hair—but no, she was positive he was a stranger. She would have noticed such a face. He was handsome, with a serious furrow across his high forehead balanced by deep laugh lines around his powerful dark eyes. Puzzled, she searched in her shoulder bag for something to occupy her own time, but the light was not good for needle-work, and she had neglected to pick up a paperback at the airport. Should she ask for a magazine? Most likely she had read them all. There seemed nothing to do except stare out the window at the darkness or study her interesting companion obliquely, which she did.

She had no sense of foreboding.

Despite his flashiness, there was something in the man's style that impressed Justyn. Verve? He was dressed in a gray vested suit that carried the promise of bright silk lining, and wore several distinctive handmade silver rings, one of which, emblazoned with tiny bells, jingled emphatically each time he turned a page. She stared at his long bejeweled fingers, at the span of his hands much greater than the book he held, her thoughts drifting. The sound of his ring reminded her of a horse she had watched that morning from the guest-room window of a farm in Arlington. The animal had stood tethered in a small paddock, and though he did not fight his restraints, he shifted so relentlessly in his impatience that the halter rings rang like music all the way to her window.

Her visit was pleasant to recall, and soon she closed her eyes, almost napping.

Without warning, the plane hit turbulence hard as brick, bounced, then bounced again before shuddering back to a semblance of level flight. Justyn gasped and gripped the seat in front of her. She was trying to breathe deeply when the motion repeated soundly as an aftershock.

"Are you all right?" the man asked.

"I think so. I don't like to fly," she added lamely.

"A little turbulence. Nothing to worry about."

"I know that." She smiled, aware of the scent he wore, more like incense than cologne. Sandalwood? "It doesn't help. But, with my job, I sometimes have to fly."

He looked at her, scowl turning to smile, his forehead lifting with the change. "Is it like this?" Turning back a page or two in the slender book, he read:

The reality of flying
is that some uncut cord
seems to drag me down,
almost as if my soul
had never left the ground.

He read well, in a deep, clear, precise voice, soothingly rhythmical, allowing each word its full weight. She was surprised and pleased—poetry in midflight! Even though the plane still seemed to swing precariously from side to side, she felt better.

"Yes," she said. "That's it exactly."

"Thomas More Levity." He offered his hand.

"Justyn Jones. Thank you for your calming influence. Is that your poem?"

He laughed. "I'm an elementary school teacher. Calming fears is one of the tricks of my trade." The furrow in his brow returned. "A friend of mine from Nam wrote it."

He turned the page resolutely, discussion over.

When finally the stewardess interrupted with dinner, Justyn had mesmerized herself with her own rings; the overly

4

large diamond Frank had given her years before flashed its beguiling rainbow of red-orange-yellow-green-blue-indigo-violet, expanding the warmth of her husband's orderly world to include her again, like a comforting fire. She was embarrassed to find Thomas More Levity smiling at her vainglorious preoccupation. She could feel the color spread across her face.

"No, you misunderstand." He laughed. "I gave my fiancée a diamond before I left California, hoping it would distract her into thinking of me."

A pretty stewardess leaned over him, brushing his arm, straightening his tray.

"Perhaps your fiancée should have given *you* a diamond," Justyn said.

"Touché!" He laughed again, stabbing his fork in the air. "You mentioned that you fly because of your job," he said. "What is your work?"

"I'm an aide to Governor Stan Marston of South Carolina. I don't suppose you've heard of him in California?"

He ate as they talked. "As a matter of fact, I have. He's the one with the limp. The only governor who's served in Nam. He's made the news on the West Coast a couple of times. His red hair lights up the screen unforgettably."

She laughed. "Yes, and what you probably don't know is that his wife is a carrot top too and they've three children so covered with freckles they almost don't photograph. We have to get them to turn sideways, or their features get lost in all the spots. They're a marvelous family."

Her voice lingered on the word *family*.

"A governor's aide. What do you do?"

"I authored a state civil rights study that I presented at the White House yesterday," she said proudly. "That was my major commitment. Now I'm going home 'on leave,' though I don't plan to return to my job."

"And how does one get such a job?"

She laughed, despite the challenge in the question. "One needs to have my particular qualifications, which are eclectic. I've known Stan all my life, and I have a buckshot education."

5

"Buckshot?"

"First, I thought I wanted to be a journalist. Journalism was my undergraduate major. Then I decided I'd rather teach college English, which meant backtracking and a master's. Then the doctoral boom happened when I was *in medias res*, and I got discouraged. I married instead." She sighed. "I got bored with staying home, waiting for babies that didn't happen. Stan's campaign had started and he needed someone articulate to draft and research his stand on complicated issues. My more-or-less useless background suddenly seemed suited for something. . . . I do know how to write a paper and research—sniff out—facts."

"Do you like the work?"

"Some of it, very much. And . . . the White House! That was exciting."

"I imagine so."

"But"—she looked out into the vast starry dark, wondering why she didn't or couldn't stop talking—"I'm not sure I've found my calling. Most of the research I do is from books. I miss the fieldwork I would have done in journalism. My dream was to win a Pulitzer for some extraordinary investigative reporting. And I miss the sense of literature I might have indulged by teaching. Which reminds me—what's the story behind the poem you read a while ago, about flying?"

The stewardess interrupted to reclaim their trays. Justyn asked for white wine, Thomas for coffee. Again the stewardess brushed against him. Her smile when she brought their drinks was dazzling.

"She finds you very attractive," Justyn said.

"I find *you* more interesting." He smiled. "A very classy lady."

"The poem?"

He retrieved the slender book. "This is an anthology of West Coast poetry. The poem I read from is called 'Wind Shear.' Actually, my friend's a pilot who loves to fly. But he has a good deal of empathy for those who don't."

As he turned the pages, she thought she saw his name flare and fade.

6

"Do you write?" she asked.

"Yes, a little poetry."

"Thomas Moore. Wasn't he a poet?"

"Yes. But that's not the spelling of my name. It has only one o."

"Like the Utopians', Thomas More?"

"Yes." He looked at her with raised eyebrow. "You're only the second or third person to make that connection. Actually, it was my father who was given that name—I've never used 'Junior,' since he died before I was born—for the utopian connection, I'm told. My mother thought one of his ancestors had founded a black utopia after he was freed from slavery."

"There were a lot of those utopias," Justyn said, recalling her research. "Near my home, there were several. Happyland and Promiseland, Little Liberia—even the names tell a story." But something else he had said intrigued her. "Never to have known your father . . . There are superstitions about that, where I came from. One is that the child of a dead father is born with the power of healing."

"Really?" He looked at her with interest, the frown settling back on his brow. He cracked his knuckles nervously. "I should tell you how my father died. He was lynched."

Silence settled between them. Justyn looked out the window at the comforting vastness of the night, considering the terrible image his words conjured. She pictured a rural crossroads hamlet in some Deep South state. Mississippi justice. Redneck faces glowing demonically in firelight. She wanted no details. "That must be difficult knowledge to live with," she said finally.

"I'm going back to the town where it happened," he said, "—where I was conceived and my father was lynched. It's a mystery to me, how it happened. My mother ran away to California. I was born and raised there. I didn't know about the lynching until I was eight years old and some cousins came to visit. Mother had said he died from an accident."

Justyn nodded. "My father died violently," she said, something she never voluntarily told anyone, "by his own hand.

I was twelve, but at least I was twelve. I can't imagine never to have known him."

"I apologize for giving a grim twist to our conversation." He smiled wryly.

"I don't mind," she said truthfully. "It feels good to mention him. Back home, he's a forbidden subject. Suicide is a social embarrassment. A failure on everyone's part."

"Well, I want to get my father's death cleared in my own mind, so I can go on with my life. If there are scores to settle, I intend to settle them. I'm ready to marry and have my own son. I want to be able to tell him what happened. What about you? What are you looking forward to?" he asked with interest.

"Oh, my . . . I'll simply be glad to get home. I've seen so little of my husband, Frank, these past months. Most of my research for the study was in Columbia, the state capital, a hundred-mile drive from my home in Green Hills. I took an apartment and commuted home on weekends. Now I just want to stay home, sit for hours over coffee in the mornings, look out the window at my yard, sit on the front steps and pet my dog, cook special meals for Frank, do needlework in the evenings without feeling guilty . . . It may not last, but for a while I want to practice domesticity." This was not entirely true. There was something else she wanted, expansive and unnameable. "Does this sound boring to you?"

"No. As a matter of fact, it sounds familiar, except for the husband and dog. Like my mother, even to the needlework. All that she brought with her from the South, other than her clothes, were quilts—some her handiwork, and some her mother had made. I wish I could show you. I've been told they're fine work." He sighed. His voice became softer. "Mama took such time with her stitches, to make them perfect. When I was a boy doing my homework in the evening, she'd sit by the lamp, sewing. She created harmony in a room. I've always believed that if my father had lived, we would have made a happy family. She said that my father drove a taxi and preached on Sundays. And that he was no 'Tom,' not even back then."

"Is that why he was killed?"

8

"I don't know, but I intend to find out. My mother died this summer. Now that I have her things settled, I've taken a leave from my job. I want to find answers to the questions she wouldn't let me ask."

Justyn wondered how she would sum up her father, her family, in so few sentences? That he was a lawyer who did not make enough money? That he drank a lot? Was morose? That if he had lived, theirs might not have been a happy family? She sipped her wine in silence.

"My mother—Mama—would never admit it, but I think she missed the South. She managed to bring the flowers and food, the music and manners into every conversation, no matter what we were talking about. She said that home had its own sound, its own color, its own sweet smell."

Justyn smiled. "Honeysuckle," she said. "The flower. In warm weather, it's the essence of the South. That's what your mother would have been thinking of. Oh, there are finer, sweeter flowers, roses or tea olive or tuberose, but honeysuckle is everywhere, rich yard or poor, hilltop or field, wherever there has been settlement. Pervasive. It gets into your head and into your blood."

Thomas smiled. "And what about now? How will I know I've come distinctly South, in November?"

It was a poet's question. Justyn meant to attempt to answer, but her thoughts were set adrift by it. She thought of the night air they flew in. From the ground below, the stars would be clearly seen, gleaming in this sky swept clean by cold. The hills would be spicily resonant with autumn: the subtle fecundity of dying leaves, of wood smoke from countless thousands of fires banked against the chill. Ahead lay home. Soon the lights of Green Hills, the town where she had been born and raised, would appear, glittering like a handful of diamonds thrown into the heart of South Carolina's rich, rolling, emerald piedmont.

She had a sudden urge to share this with Thomas More Levity.

"Let me show you my husband's picture," she offered, reaching into her purse. "This is Frank, and this is our

9

house. He built the porch himself. You can just see the corner."

Thomas took it and studied it politely.

"It's a good likeness of Frank," she said. Balding and round-shouldered, he looked happy.

"He looks older than you."

"He is. But it hasn't mattered."

"It's a good picture of you," Thomas said. "It catches your diminutiveness, your sense of style. Who took this picture?" he asked curiously.

"My uncle, Eddie Balantyne. Why? Did you notice his shadow? That struck me, too. I guess that's the reason I prefer to carry *this* picture. When my father died, Eddie—he's my mother's younger brother—was the only male left in either family. He became my substitute father. We lived with him for a while. . . . The irony is, he has all the photography equipment known to man, but this is as good as he gets."

A voice interrupted over the speaker, announcing Green Hills.

"Lord, I'll be glad to get off this plane" Justyn said, "—though it's been interesting, meeting you. I'll be keeping an eye out for your poems. Maybe, when you've learned your father's story, you can write a book about it."

She felt her uneasiness begin to lift. Green Hills. Home. Frank would be waiting, worrying because the flight was a few minutes late. She could depend on him to fold her to his chest and understand her mood before she said a word. He would exult with her in the success of her White House presentation, share her disquieting empathy with Thomas More Levity's mission, and listen sympathetically to her account of the rough flight. She imagined the rush of green-sward turning to runway in the darkness below as the airport lights came into view. She knew that close by in the night the escarpment of Blue Ridge mountains swelled in the black horizon, dark and beckoning and remarkably unsettled. As the plane's wheels touched earth she thought of her bound soul, how correct her seatmate's poet friend had been in his vision.

"In case our paths don't cross again," she said, offering her hand in farewell, "I hope the rest of your flight is pleasant."

"But I'm getting off here, too," he answered quietly. "This is where it happened. My father was lynched in Green Hills."

$\triangledown$

2

I N THE DARKNESS, DRIVING home, Justyn could not be certain, but she thought Frank looked away from her when she asked.

"Yes, I know about the lynching," he said matter-of-factly. "Say, hon, the Garringtons are moving to Atlanta. I'll have their place on the market next week." Green Hills was a realtor's map to him. He knew each house, its square footage.

She sighed. "But why haven't I heard about it? The lynching. It must have happened just a few years before I was born. It's not as if it were ancient history."

"Justyn, why don't you just leave it alone?" he suggested amiably. "It's good to have you home again, hon," he added, reaching across the seat to stroke her shoulder.

"And when I worked on the civil rights study for Stan, I never found reference to a lynching in Green Hills. Why? How in the world could something like that be left out of the news. Or the town's history?"

"Hon, leave it alone. It *is* ancient history. You've been working so hard. I have, too. Let's relax and enjoy ourselves now that you're home."

He turned into the driveway. A welcoming light burned over the front door, another on the screened porch he had built. On each side of the drive baskets of freshly raked leaves testified to his pride in their yard. The bittersweet smell of woodsmoke from their chimney greeted her even before she stepped from the car. Tawny, their aging golden retriever, came yawning from under the hedges and broke into ecstatic barking at sight of her.

"Home!" she said, stooping to pat Tawny's soft forehead. Frank passed them on the narrow walk, carrying Justyn's luggage. She lingered to admire the pyracantha glowing beside the door. Fireplant. Aptly named. If Thomas More Levity were to write a poem about it, would the words explode with color, sing with music, like his rings? When she entered the house, Frank had a glass of wine waiting for her and was pouring bourbon for himself.

"I wonder what Mother remembers about the lynching?" she thought aloud, eyeing the telephone.

"Justyn, *please*," Frank said, "do what I say, and *leave it alone.*"

Justyn couldn't sleep. A lynching in Green Hills? She thought she knew the town's history as well as anyone. Her mother, a Balantyne, came from a founding family. Justyn grew up being friends with or kin to almost everyone, no matter where she went in the town. In the old Balantyne homeplace, where she and her mother lived with Eddie for a few months after her father's death, the library was sufficient as an archives of the town from its earliest days.

She reminded herself that Green Hills wasn't a town anymore, but a city. The past decade of accelerated industrial growth had brought so many new people into the area that she could enter a restaurant or browse through a shopping mall without recognizing a single face—a social phenomenon her mother also experienced and mentioned often, more as lament than commentary.

Still, Green Hills had kept its charm, and after her work away from it, she felt more keenly than ever that she would want to live nowhere else. She liked its gracious melding of old and new. Its industries were clean, the factories streamlined and modern. Mountains were a blue backdrop, the first of them rising just beyond the city limits. The people, by tradition, seemed mannerly and courteous, yet energetic.

There were problems. The local radio, television, and morning and evening newspapers were all owned by the same company, Gargomedia. The crime rate was high. But the media was receptive to her work, Stan Marston being a native son, and crime was centered in the poorer sections— in Fricatown, where a great part of the black population still lived, and in the rawer rural areas, especially the Devil's Heel backside of the county. But in Primavera, where she and Frank lived, doors were left unlocked, the homeowners confident that if some intruder did appear, a neighbor would notice and report it, and the police appear immediately. Here the houses were new enough to be comfortable, the trees old enough to stretch their welcome shade across yards and streets.

When finally she slept, it was poorly. Her unpleasant dreams included a plane crash; Thomas More Levity's handsome, moody face; and the recurring nightmare that visited here only in troubled times.

So close to reality, it was more like memory than dream, a reliving of that morning when, newly turned twelve, she was sent home by her teacher at sign of her first menstruation. She had opened the front hall door to find her father lying just within, gun in palm, skull shattered. At first, she thought an intruder had shot him, but then the even greater enormity of what had happened overcame her. She might have stood there forever if the maid had not arrived. Now it was Frank who wakened her from the nightmare. For a long time he lay holding her, smoothing her hair, whispering comforting words. Finally awake, they lay hand in hand, talking an erratic range of subjects, Frank carefully avoiding the one uppermost in Justyn's mind.

But she could avoid it no longer. What was it about this lynching from the past that made her husband not want to talk about it? How could a whole community have conspired to keep it secret? Why had she not run across any mention of it in her research?

"Tell me about the lynching," she said resolutely.

Frank turned on the light and sat up.

"When it happened—it was a long time ago—it was something everyone talked or whispered about," he said heavily. "I was just a boy. I didn't quite understand the reality of it. The lynching was an awful thing, hon, that touched all sections of this town. The mob wasn't all riffraff, you see. But, before I go any further, Justyn, you need to know that your father was involved. He was assistant to the solicitor who prosecuted the mob. Unsuccessfully, of course. Everyone seemed to hate him for it. Called him a nigger lover, a traitor."

Justyn moaned in astonishment.

"Isn't that enough?" Frank asked gently. "You know there's pain in this for you. Wouldn't it be better to leave it alone?"

"Did this have anything to do with my father's death?"

"I imagine it did. It certainly ruined him with a lot of people in this town. They made it difficult for him from then on. That's what I worry about. I know your moods. I worry that you'll get depressed with the past, your family. Let's face it. Your father was a suicide and your mother's been a lush ever since. I think you should look for sunshine and avoid dark clouds."

"Please, go on and tell me about the lynching," she said.

"It was 1948, thirty years ago," he sighed, "about this time of year. There was a full red moon—a blood moon, they call it. Two little boys in Fricatown found a man, a white man, lying on the railroad tracks, and the midnight Crescent due any minute. They ran to Pear's Place, an all-night black jive joint back then, for help. Pear Plumlee and a half dozen or so patrons went and moved the man . . . only to discover he was dead, throat slashed neat as you please, ear to ear.

"You can imagine how they felt, the Crescent thundering past, several black men standing there with a dead white, and it 1948. Whoever had left him there was clever. If the boys hadn't found him, the train would have decapitated him. It would have seemed like just another drunk gone to sleep on the tracks, especially since the dead man was Stubby Balantyne."

"Mother's cousin Stubby?"

"Yes, the reprobate heir. He was known to frequent Fricatown for its 'pleasures,' and he was certainly known to drink."

"But he was murdered?"

"Yes, and a white man had never been murdered in Fricatown, not since the first freed slaves settled there in the

15

1860s. You can imagine the shock waves it sent through the white community . . . the fear.

"From what I understand, a word-of-mouth case was quickly made against Tom Levity. He had been seen arguing with Stubby earlier that evening—he had accused Stubby of making a pass at his woman—and Stubby had gotten into Tom's cab around ten.

"That was in the days when blacks rode at the back of trolley cars and drank from separate fountains and didn't sass a white man no matter *what* he did. . . . So Levity was arrested. The deputies found him alone and drunk in his house by the tracks, with a bunch of bloody towels on the floor, and he was too drunk to make sense.

"They kept him in jail about a day before Stubby's friends got to him. Stubby had all sorts of friends. He was egalitarian in his choice of drinking buddies—you know, bourbon with Chub Castille at the country club, beer with Buck Stovall, a war buddy, at the Dixie Grill, rotgut with the rednecks who congregated at the dirt track. They all felt they had to avenge 'one of their own.'

"They hung around the back of the courthouse, where the jail was, all afternoon, drinking. My father said some of the lawyers tried to persuade Castille to go home. Castille and Stovall were the ringleaders. But nobody thought it would come to what it did."

"What did it come to?"

"That evening a deputy let someone in to see Tom. He left the door unlocked and some of the mob got through. They dragged Tom out unconscious, formed a caravan, and took him out to the dirt track. They mutilated him and hung him from a chainfall. Someone took a photograph. It was awful. Some of them said they were so drunk they didn't know what they were doing."

"What a terrible story for Thomas to come back to," Justyn said quietly.

"Do you blame the town for wanting to forget it?" Frank asked, pulling her close again.

▽

3

THE NEXT DAY JUSTYN went to meet her mother, Ouida Balantyne Orms, and uncle, Eddie Balantyne, for lunch at the Nullifier.

Her mother made her uncomfortable, but she had to admire her. Despite the whiskey she consumed each day, her fifty years and personal tragedy, Ouida Balantyne Orms was still a beautiful woman. Justyn abhorred her old-style class consciousness, her taste for a pretentious lifestyle, but she couldn't help marveling at her appearance. Though Justyn expected her to metamorphose one day into a harridan, Ouida continued to appear the tiny elegant beauty, teetering on platform heels she ordered especially made. She had the lustrous black Balantyne hair and liquid black eyes and used them to effect, even managing to turn the slight palsy in her hands to charm, appearing shyly startled like a trembling animal. Her voice was gravelly, ruined by too much alcohol and too many cigarettes, but she covered it with a husky, sultry whisper that pulled listeners to her.

Whenever mother and daughter were together, because of their size strangers often mistook them for sisters, which pleased Ouida and didn't bother Justyn. She was proud to favor her father, to have inherited her premature gray from him. But something else about them—perhaps that local air they had of "quality"—turned some men on. Justyn had never been propositioned when she was alone, but she and Ouida had turned down dozens of advances together. Sometimes they could hardly settle into a restaurant before one of the transplanted Northern textile executives appeared, wanting to light Ouida's cigarette.

Eddie did not find it humorous. He took his role of escort-protector seriously. Now, two days after her homecoming, seeing him for the first time in weeks, Justyn noticed that he seemed even more nervous than usual. What a stranger he had become from the Uncle Eddie she first remembered, boyishly curly-haired and handsome, willing to play hide-and-seek or kick-the-can enthusiastically.

"Tell us about the White House," Ouida ordered.

"I talked to the President for a total of about four seconds," Justyn downplayed. "He shook my hand and thanked me for the report. Shake, shake, 'Thanks.' " She mimicked his familiar smile, making them laugh.

"But, you were *there*," Ouida insisted grandly.

"Yes, it *was* beautiful," Justyn admitted, "and they were gracious, it was a gracious place." Ouida and Eddie beamed at having a Southerner affirmed in the White House. "The First Lady showed us the Rose Garden. I'm always amazed," she added, "at how lovely roses are in the fall. They're so fragile, it seems they shouldn't outlast the summer."

"That sounds like poetry, dear," Ouida said sardonically.

"My niece the poet," Eddie added coyly, raising his glass. The Nullifier was crowded and the hum almost drowned out his words. It was not the place Justyn would have chosen for a quiet lunch, but Eddie had selected it for its proximity to Ouida's hairdresser. She had an early-afternoon appointment.

"That reminds me, I want some roses for my dinner party this evening." Ouida turned to Eddie. "May I charge them to you?"

"Oh!" Eddie struck his forehead with his palm. "Do you need some money? Here . . ." He pulled out the checkbook that always rode within easy reach in his breast pocket. "Get what you need, and put something in your account." He scrawled what must have been a generous amount. "Jus, how are you holding out? Could you use a little something, too?"

Justyn hadn't accepted Eddie's money since she was eighteen. "No, but thank you." She smiled, reaching across the table to squeeze his hand. Poor Eddie. He had been sweet as a substitute father, a surrogate brother.

They were finishing lunch, chatting over inconsequentials, when Justyn saw a familiar figure at the bar. Though his back was turned to her, she recognized Thomas More Levity by the cut and thrust of his clothes as he stood restlessly. He turned, and on impulse she motioned to him.

"Mother, Eddie, I want you to meet my seatmate on the flight from Washington," she said when he approached. Eddie rose so quickly to shake hands, he upset his water glass. As he mopped at the spill with his napkin, Ouida said, disbelievingly, forgetting to whisper, "Levity! Why, you're Tom's son!" She paled, but put her hand courteously in his. "Sit down, please join us," she said, still in her gravelly voice. "You'll have to forgive me, " she added, putting her palsied hand to her heart, "but, you gave me such a start! You *are* Tom's son, aren't you? You're his spitting image! Not as dark, but his very image! Even the way your forehead lifts! Eddie, you probably don't remember him, you were just a teenager. Justyn, it was before you were born. This boy's father used to be"—she struggled gallantly for an inoffensive word—" 'affiliated' with us."

"You mean he worked for you?" Thomas asked, sitting down.

"Sis, isn't your appointment at two?" Eddie interrupted nervously.

"Oh, my, yes!" she said, glancing down at her tiny diamond watch. "Well, I can be a little late, can't I? No, he didn't work for us. But Maude, the woman he . . . oh, would Maude be your mother? Of course! Maude worked for close friends of ours. My husband tutored your father, I guess you'd say. They . . ." She searched for words, paused, and did not go on. Justyn was touched by how lost she suddenly looked, as if she had found herself stranded in a frightening place. The past?

"But, I *am* late. I'd better go."

Thomas stood as she rose. "I'd like very much to hear more about my father," he said quietly. Turning to Eddie, he explained, "My father was lynched before I was born."

"Oh!" Eddie put his hand to his mouth in such an exaggerated fashion that it seemed offensive.

Ouida ignored him. "Well, then, we'll have to get together. I'd like that. Will you be in town long?"

"As long as it takes. Thank you, Mrs. Orms. I'd like that very much."

"I don't want to rush you, but you'd better come along," Eddie said, taking her by the arm. "Justyn, aren't you coming?"

"No. I think I'll have another cup of coffee. Won't you join me?" She smiled at Thomas.

"Yes."

"I'll take care of the bill," Eddie said, eyeing Justyn chastisingly. Eddie was not an egalitarian. He was not happy to leave her seated alone in the Nullifier with a handsome young black man.

"So, I *do* look like my father," Thomas said wonderingly. "Mama always said I did, but she knew I wanted to hear it." He sat for a moment, cracking his knuckles. "Your uncle—is he the shadow in that photograph you showed me, of you and your husband?"

"Yes." She sipped scalding coffee as soon as the waiter poured it. "Poor Eddie," she laughed, "he *is* a shadow. A little worse each time I see him. There's only his checkbook to protect him from the world."

"It must be convenient to have such a checkbook."

"Perhaps. For a judicious person. Eddie isn't. He's rotted away his youth alone in that big house, fooling with stocks or bonds or whatever it is he does to make more money. The Balantyne fortune is supposed to have run its course, but he spends money as if . . ." She sighed hopelessly. "The point is, I doubt that much of Eddie's money will outlive him, though woe if it goes before he and Mother do."

Thomas looked puzzled. "Doesn't she have any of her own?"

"No. And it's a fluke that Eddie has it. The Balantynes have practiced the Southern version of primogeniture since my five-greats-grandfather built his holdings here. That's how the fortune stayed intact—no divvying up between younger sons, or daughters, who didn't count. But things have been going downhill for generations. Eddie is the last male Balantyne, and he's turned the downhill run into a race."

"But, your mother certainly appears to be a rich lady."

"It's an appearance, created with what Eddie gives her. Daddy left her modestly, in a middle-class fashion, secure. To have luxuries, she would have had to get a job, which might not have been bad for her. But Mother does *not* have middle-class tastes, and Eddie stepped right in with his checkbook. She can be so grand, so proud, but she grovels for his money. I'm sorry to talk family," she apologized, "but since we met, I've learned that my father was assistant solicitor—prosecutor—at the lynch mob trial."

Something tense in Thomas's face seemed to relax. "Yes. Orms. Balantyne. I've been sitting here putting it together since you introduced me to your mother and uncle."

"And there's more. The man your father allegedly murdered was a relative, Mother's cousin, the Balantyne heir before Eddie. I don't know much about him, and I haven't been able to ask. Have you had any luck collecting information?"

"Bits and pieces. There seems to be more in the courthouse than I would have imagined, but you have to know where to look. I'm cultivating a clerk's acquaintance," he added slyly. "I'm planning on visiting some people later today."

"Be careful."

"What can they be but aging men?"

"Frightened and violent. My husband thinks it's a dangerous subject. He's adamant and he's usually right. I shouldn't pry into it. But, now that I know my father was involved, I have to know what went on. Maybe it's part of the puzzle . . . why he killed himself. I've never understood why he did it."

"Could it be that the truth will set us both free?" he asked, his tone only slightly mocking.

"We could help each other," she answered carefully. "Share information."

"I came here alone," he said. "I didn't even include my fiancée in my plans."

"I won't tell anyone. I won't include my husband. A trade. My information for your information."

21

When he sat down, Thomas had placed his briefcase beneath the table. Now he retrieved it and removed a sheaf of papers. "These are from the Washington-area files," he said, offering them.

"There's a Xerox at the post office around the corner." She could feel her face flush with excitement.

As they rose, Thomas reached in his pocket for a tip.

"Don't." Justyn stopped him. "Eddie will have taken care of *everything*."

Walking down Green Hills's sunlit Main Street beside Thomas More Levity's tall hurrying form, Justyn was warmed by a sudden, personal memory of her father. She remembered men always lighting her mother's cigarettes, and how, when small, she had asked, "Mama, have you never learned to light a cigarette? Would you like me to show you how?"

Now, so many years later, she blushed at her parents' forgotten laughter; at what her father must have meant all those times afterward when he'd amble over to Ouida at the club or a dinner, and leaning his white head down to her, ask in a low voice, "Mama, have you never learned to light a cigarette? Would you like me to show you how?"

It was exactly the sort of memory she had lacked, had wanted, now treasured.

There were errands she hadn't taken care of for weeks. Justyn spent the afternoon at the shopping mall and grocery store, the copies seeming to burn a hole on the front seat of her car. It was her favorite time of day, of year—autumn twilight—when she finally got everything put away and a casserole in the oven. Then she spread the papers across the kitchen table and began to read.

A different generation, a different lifetime. The gap before and after the Civil Rights movement was inconceivable. The "Lucky Thirteen" lynch mob members were so-called because they got away with murder. Though Judge Jonathan Mabry chastised them for saying "nigger" in court and intended, according to at least one out-of-town journalist, to

22

put Chub Castille—"who knew better"—behind bars (Justyn's father was allowed to refer to him as an "animal"), the all-white male jury had been unanimous in its not-guilty verdict. Justyn was proud of the young Zachary Orms she read of, presenting most of the prosecution's case and imposing a sense of dignity for the murdered Tom Levity. His contempt for Castille likewise came through, for a man who would attempt to let social standing be an excuse for his inexcusable actions.

The timer sounded abruptly as a gunshot. Frank was due any moment, but her thoughts were lost in the 1940s. As she set the table in the dining room and lit candles, she imagined those years, her young parents, her mother before the bitterness of her father's death. At least, she reminded herself, she had those memories. Thomas did not.

"Hello, hon," Frank said, standing tiredly in the doorway, Tawny trying to nuzzle her way in beside him.

She kissed him gladly. "You look so tired," she said guiltily.

"I am tired. Damn tired. Of eating TV dinners, watching TV alone. It got old, hon. What happened today? I thought you'd call after your meeting with your mother and Eddie. Didn't they drop the bombshell?"

"Bombshell?" Justyn felt an old, familiar weariness. Her mother often caused trouble.

"That she's planning to sell the condominium and move in with Eddie."

"*What?*"

Frank sat down heavily in a kitchen chair, throwing his coat across the back of another. "She's going to sell her structurally sound, already half-paid-for, appreciating condominium and move into that centuries-old wreck of a mausoleum with Eddie." He got up and fixed himself a bourbon and water and poured a glass of white wine for Justyn.

"I don't believe it."

"Believe it. The papers are drawn up."

"But you know how particular Mama is about her surroundings," Justyn said desperately. "Everything has to be plush and white. The last few times I've been at Eddie's, it's been appalling. Mold and mildew everywhere, the paint peeling, the kitchen dripping grease, the downstairs smelling like garbage . . ."

She served their dinner and ate without tasting. Nothing was turning out as she had planned when she boarded the plane for home.

"I suspect"—Frank chose his words carefully—"that she's worried, really worried, about Eddie. He's gotten to her and made her feel guilty, the older sister who should somehow be protecting him from life."

"Afraid he'll take the same route as my father." She hadn't meant to speak aloud, or so bitterly. "You know as well as I do that if Mother moves in with Eddie she'll drink around the clock. The condominium is the only sensible thing she's done, and that was your doing, finding such a bargain for her when she was about to lose her house. Eddie didn't offer to take her in then, I remember."

"Eddie wasn't hurting for money then. I'm hoping you can dissuade her, Justyn."

"What is she going to do with the money from the sale?"

"Give it to Eddie. Lease a part of the house from him. I suspect that Eddie's about to go under, and hers is the only moola within reach. I suggested she rent the condominium, but she said no, she wanted me to put it on the market, the sooner the better."

"Have you talked to Eddie?"

"I tried. It was like talking to a weasel. He was too busy looking for an egg to suck to listen. He said that he and Beesie need your mother."

"Well, Beesie does, that's true," Justyn said tiredly. Beesie was the Balantyne live-in maid, whose tenancy in the house spanned four generations. Shy and reclusive in her backstairs room, she was fragile as a ninety-year-old shrub. "Well, I know that Mother adores Eddie and would do anything to please him, but I know she adores herself and her own comforts even more. I don't see how he can persuade her to give them up."

Frank got up and mixed himself a second bourbon. "Castles in the air. Eddie has her thinking he'll use all the condo money to fix a fancy suite for her, and he has somebody working on it already. He says he'll have the downstairs redone however she wants. I can't believe they didn't tell you about it. That's what the lunch was for."

"Thomas More Levity appeared," she explained. "He must have distracted them."

"Well, forewarned is forearmed. When Ouida does tell you, you'll be ready to argue the point. It would be ridiculous for her to sell. It would be ruinous. She couldn't buy into a new situation, or even rent, at today's prices, if moving into Balantyne Hall didn't work. And it wouldn't." He stood in the flickering candle glow looking haggard, the second bourbon drained.

If anyone deserved a peaceable kingdom, she knew it was he. She felt empty. "I'll try. Though if those two have made up their minds, there won't be any doing anything about it."

Frank went into the study to go over some papers he had brought home, and Justyn settled in the living room with her needlework. When next she looked up, Frank was dozing in his chair, and a half-moon had appeared in the sky.

$\triangledown$

4

THOMAS MORE LEVITY WALKED away from the Holiday Inn and breathed deeply. Far above the reach of streetlights he saw the half-moon. When he left California the old moon was riding high in the new moon's arms, a mere celestial shadow reflected by arc light. Those same moons rode in an ancient poem about Sir Patrick Spens he had studied in college. An ill-fated Scotsman, Spens had gone to his ocean grave under such a sky.

And what of his own father, he wondered? Where was his resting place? If he could stand there, would he experience some quantum leap, become in his heart a true son, exchange his phantom sire for a flesh-and-blood father? He needed to be near that hunk of flesh and bone moldering beneath the soil, to form a poem. A ballad. An elegy. His father, the old moon. He, the new. Soon to be realized? Now that he was finally beginning the real search, he felt like a child on an adventure, alone in the night in the bracing cold air with a picturesque moon and stars shining.

It was a pleasure driving the rented car, a compact sports model that still smelled of newness, in the light traffic. The desk clerk had given good directions, but even without them Pear's Place was now the most prominently located nightclub in town. Pear Plumlee had come a long way in thirty years, from a rotgut shack by the railroad tracks to a stately midtown plantation-style structure identified by a massive-columned antebellum portico.

Thomas stepped from the car, humming, the moon his champion. It was Pear's night to be closed, and the large parking lot was deserted except for a limousine and service truck. He did not notice two men step from behind the truck. Not until the moon reeled, doubling and quadrupling in upon itself, was he aware how foolish he had been.

A blow to the back of the head and a fist in the kidney brought him down. He was aware of being dragged, of his hands helpless behind his back, of a jagged edge where a smooth tooth had been. He managed a sputtering yell, but there was no one to hear him. One of his attackers kneed him. The two dragged him past the service truck to the back of the building. His breath came in aching gasps.

"That don't sound so good," one of the men said. "Maybe you'd better be quiet, or you won't be breathing at all, black boy."

Thomas spat and coughed, willed himself to silence. The two braced him against what sounded like a hollow metal wall. The odor of garbage was nauseating. A rat leapt near his head, scrambling inches from his face.

"Have you got it ready?"

"I'm getting the cap off."

In a stray shaft of light Thomas saw a hypodermic needle raised. He exploded with all he could summon, yelling, kicking, butting, plunging, screaming. A bone-cracking blow set his chest aflame. He thought he must be dying. Then, suddenly, the parking lot was flooded with light.

Justyn had seen Frank off to work and returned to the kitchen table to savor her morning coffee when the phone rang. The speaker introduced himself as Pear Plumlee. Though he spoke in a strained, weak voice, his message was to the point.

"I'm calling from Memorial Hospital. Thomas Levity is a patient here."

"But what's the matter? How is he?"

"He had an appointment with me, last night, at my club, but he was attacked in the parking lot on the way in." He paused to clear his throat, "I came with him to the hospital. He was semiconscious. He mentioned your name. You do know him, then?"

"Yes." She thought quickly, and decided on candor. After all, hadn't she half expected such a call? "I met him recently.

I asked him to keep me informed concerning his investigation into his father's death, since my own father was involved in its aftermath."

"Well, for a newcomer, Mr. Levity stepped right into high cotton, didn't he?"

She ignored the inference.

"And in over his head, I'm afraid. He could have been killed!" Pear's soft voice made an exclamation of the word.

"How badly is he hurt?"

"A slight concussion. A cracked collarbone. A broken tooth. Assorted cuts and bruises. He's going to be mighty sore for a while. But, frankly, I'm relieved. When I first saw him, I thought it was much worse."

"I'd like to see him."

"Yes. I was hoping you would. You and I must be the only people . . ." He paused and tried to stifle a yawn. "I'm up out of my own sickbed, and I've got to be going home. But I think someone should be with him when he wakes up. Also, I'd like to meet you. Perhaps you'd take care of these few personal items of his. I—"

"I'll be right on down. It will only take me a few minutes to get ready. Is there anything I can bring?"

It was the first time she heard Pear Plumlee laugh, a distinctive, staccato, barking fox laugh. "Considering hospital food, I would say some home cookin'—but, in the shape he's in today, I'm afraid that would be wasted effort."

On the way to the hospital she recalled what she knew of the man. First, that he had cancer, and was dying. Second, that he was wealthy and powerful, and unsavory. There had even been rumors of connections with the Dixie Mafia.

He waited for her beside the reception desk, a small, immaculately dressed man about Eddie's size, with pallid skin, tightly curled hair, and thick sensual lips. They each knew who the other was, though they had never been introduced, and shook hands. His gray eyes were not unlike her own.

"Thomas is still deep asleep. Why don't we have a cup of coffee in the hospital cafeteria, and I'll fill you in on details."

"I'd like that." She had always been curious to meet him,

an enigmatic figure not trusted by either race, but lauded by both for his business leadership and philanthropy. No matter the stories of how his inestimable fortune had been obtained, or that Pear's Place, however elegant its public rooms might appear, had dozens of private suites and salons of unseen traffic and pleasure.

"I called Fred Burroughs in as consulting physician," Pear said as he seated her.

"Yes. He's a fine doctor. Good." The one I would have called myself, she thought, pleased that Pear was taking Thomas seriously.

"I'll get our coffee." There was no one else in line, and he returned quickly with coffee, two small servings of hotcakes, and a dripping pitcher of syrup. "I couldn't resist!" He laughed like a fox again. "I hope you'll join me."

"All I had was juice. This looks wonderful," she admitted, smiling. They sat and ate and talked—about the weather, chilly; about her job, on hold; and, finally, about Thomas.

"I regret you're involved in any way in this 'mission' of young Levity's," Pear said frankly. "Your father wouldn't want you to be involved. This whole business was ugly enough when it happened. It went through the motions if not intent of justice, and your friend Thomas can't rewrite history, no matter how much he wishes. I'm asking you to discourage him, if you can. The point is, you children could get hurt."

"Thomas has already been hurt."

"I mean, much worse. I believe someone intended to kill him."

Justyn stared in disbelief. Worry clouded Pear's face, and a grimace of pain. "He called, and we arranged to meet. I didn't tell anyone. He must have been followed. The police want to think it was a mugging. But he wasn't robbed, and they took him around back. They had a hypodermic. I think they intended to sedate him and stuff him in the garbage dumpster. About now he'd be going through the equipment."

His meaning struck home and she shivered. Recently, in two separate incidents in Green Hills, vagrants who had crawled into similar dumpsters for warmth had been dismembered and crushed when the automated trucks picked up their loads.

"I see by your face that you understand."

"But, why? It's been thirty years!"

Pear smiled. "Young lady, it may have been thirty years, but I'm still scared as hell. Sure, a lot of them are dead, but some aren't, and they have uncles, and brothers, and cousins, and friends. The point is, this business is dangerous. Levity is lucky he escaped with a warning. He ought to give it up."

"Would you?"

"Yes."

Something showed in her face.

"Let me tell you," he said angrily, "though you probably won't understand. I try to tell my daughters, but they don't understand, either. The fact is that I'm alive, they exist, because I had the wisdom to let some things pass. There's courage in that, too."

Courage. It was a word Justyn found unsettling. Because of her father's lack of it, perhaps? Was it courage or cowardice that pulled that trigger? And what of this man? Despite his air of gentility, of forthrightness, something ineffably sinister seemed to tinge her impression of him.

"You don't believe me? You'll learn. Perhaps the hard way. But I don't want that young man to learn by dying. His father's death was waste enough, even if he did murder that no-good Balantyne, which I happen to believe he did. That night we found Stubby, a handful of hotheaded white men could have wiped out all of Fricatown, and we knew it. What could we have done? Come at their guns with our knives? Thrown rocks and bottles at them?"

Another grimace twisted his face. As the morning brightened the room he seemed to age like Methuselah, making the past seem remote, harmless. "Well, I'll tell you what I would have told that young man. Nothing. There's nothing more to tell. It was a grimmer time then. Grim things happened. But things happen according to their time, don't they? The fact is, from the moment Tom Levity sassed a white man, he didn't stand a chance in hell of surviving."

Thomas was awake, propped against pillows, the hospital bed raised to a near-sitting position. One hand was bandaged, the other taped to an intravenous unit. He sipped orange juice held for him by a pretty black nurse.

"I can do that." Justyn smiled as she replaced the nurse, who eyed her suspiciously. But the reach was more than she anticipated, and she had to lean uncomfortably on tiptoe, causing him to smile lopsidedly. "You look terrible," she said.

"That nurse didn't think so. She said I was a far better sight than an old man's bedpan."

"*Horrible,*" she insisted.

"Inadequate to the way I feel."

"Pear Plumlee was here all night. He just went home. He's not a well man."

"I remember him vaguely. He saved my life, or so the police say."

"Tell me what happened."

He told her his version, or what he remembered of it. Once he fell asleep in the middle of a sentence. A nurse came in and woke him to take a blood sample. When he moved his arm he flinched in pain. "I've been wondering—"

"Yes?"

"Mama, when she made a quilt, would work so hard to make everything perfect—the pieces had to be cut exactly the right size, or she'd discard them. The stitches had to be tiny and precise, or she'd rip them out and redo them. But then, when the quilt was almost complete she'd do something deliberately, outrageously wrong—put a flower petal upside-down or a chimney on the wrong side of a schoolhouse. When I'd point it out she'd tell me to mind my own business. She'd look so strange. Almost frightened. Why? She could have done it all to perfection, she'd come so close."

Justyn smiled. "It's a tradition," she said. Without think-

31

ing, she placed her hand over his on the sheet. "Or perhaps 'tradition' is merely a cultured word for 'superstition.' Quilt-makers believe that only God is capable of perfection, and that the semblance of it in their work might be interpreted as blasphemy. So they go out of their way to show that's not their intention."

Thomas sighed, then blinked, and a noticeable light seemed to reappear in his expression. "Well, I guess I'm following Mama's example. I sure didn't handle this to per-fection!"

Frank opened the door on their laughter, their touching hands. For a moment neither of them saw him.

"I would like to have met you under better circum-stances," he spoke up, coming to stand beside Justyn. "Frank Jones."

"We were talking about quiltmaking," she explained.

"I was worried about you, hon. I didn't get an answer, and then I went home and found your note."

She had forgotten he planned to call for details of a get-together that evening with Ouida and Eddie. "I'm sorry. It happened so suddenly. Pear Plumlee called—"

Frank frowned disapprovingly at the name. "Well, this young man looks as if he'll survive," he said brusquely. "Can you come with me now, Justyn? I need to talk to you. This has already put me behind—" He glanced at this watch ner-vously.

"Yes. Of course." She mouthed a silent "I'll call you" as she followed Frank to the door, then stopped. "What hap-pened to your rings?" she asked, remembering.

"They cut them off in the emergency room. I don't know where they are."

"Pear said he'd give me your belongings. He must have forgotten."

"It would be better if you didn't see Pear Plumlee again," Frank said when they reached the parking lot.

"Do you think he might be behind the beating?"

"Anything is possible, hon, you know that."

"Who *are* the people who might still have an interest in this?" she asked. In the clear air, the sudden eruption of violence still seemed unbelievable to her.

"Well, I guess anyone who's tried to put his life back together. Chub Castille seems to be making this most recent marriage work. You know, you can find him and Monica—I think she's his third—any evening, dancing away the hours at the country club. And Buck Stovall—I suppose he'd be doing the 'Bump' at the Dixie Grill. He's supposed to be quite a womanizer. Judge Mabry avoids publicity of any kind. He has his hands full keeping the reins on his wife—you know Ivey's reputation. Hamp Mills was editor of the *Mountaineer* before he moved up to president of Gargomedia. He's been working for the good of the establishment for as long as I can remember.

"So many are dead—members of the mob, the sheriff and prosecutor, your father, some of the lawyers—frankly, I don't see how that young Levity expects to find out a thing."

Justyn started to protest. Instead, she told him about the significance of Thomas's rings, how they had rung like music to her all the way home. She determined she would get them on her next visit, and have them repaired for him.

5

Could a black man have been involved in the lynching of a black man? Justyn remembered that she had been accused of being a "knee-jerk" liberal more than once, and tried to harden her heart as she considered. When Thomas was better, they would discuss it, but in the meantime she needed to make some assessment of Pear Plumlee. She was afraid she had told him too much. If the attack on Thomas was planned, then certainly it might have been Pear's doing. His wealth and power in the town would make that possible, she supposed, though a voice inside her kept protesting, "How *could* he? It's *not* possible!"

"Jus, honey," Eddie waved his hand in front of her face, "where are you?"

"Not with us, that's for sure," Ouida said.

"Are you all right," Frank asked.

She nodded, smiled, and sipped her wine defensively. It was a typical weeknight at the Green Hills Country Club. Only the small dining room was open. Besides their own party, there were a few regulars—the McFees, who ate dinner there every evening, and the Rices and Browns—as well as a cluster of members entertaining friends or out-of-town guests: a mere handful compared to the weekend's packed house.

Eddie had reserved a table in the center of the room, under one of the magnificent chandeliers that Justyn had, since she was a child, feared might fall at any moment. She sat with her chair pushed back, out from under its crystal tentacles, and leaned toward her food. From the start it seemed that Eddie, Ouida, and Frank were engaged in a race to see who could get drunk the quickest. Justyn couldn't enjoy her meal for the knot in her stomach. *When* were they going to talk about Eddie's and Ouida's "plan"? Or was the object to get everyone so drunk it would be forgotten? And Frank—

damn him!—why was he joining them? He would wake up sick in the morning. Already she dreaded it. She was merely suffering time, listening wearily and warily to their talk, when she saw Chub Castille and his wife enter.

God, he's handsome! she thought. She had always admired his looks, from the time she was a girl and first saw him. That, too, had been here, at the club. Now, as he moved through the tables, in and out of the soft light of the chandeliers, his striking white-gold hair reflected dimensions of light no artist's brush could capture.

"Mother, how well do you know Chub?" she asked, interrupting Eddie's discourse against businesses owning club memberships, which allowed salesmen to entertain their clients on the hallowed premises.

Ouida's dark eyes flashed wickedly, but it was at Justyn's question, not Eddie's snobbery. "How well do I know Chub Castille? Sugar, that's not something to ask a woman, much less your mother," she said throatily. "Do you *really* want to know?"

Justyn blushed to her hairline.

"See? Why don't you try rephrasing the question, Sugar? Or not say anything at all?"

There were stages in her mother's drinking that she had learned to recognize. This one she thought of as *just-starting-to-get-ugly*. She would have to act quickly, for *too-removed-to-think* was next in the sequence. "It's just that I've been wondering about him. What he's like. Was he a friend of Daddy's?"

There were two conversations at the table now: Justyn's with her mother and Frank's with Eddie. Chub and his lovely lithe wife stepped, or floated, onto the dance floor, the only couple responding to the small combo's music. Justyn watched them curiously.

"Beautiful . . . empty. Yes and no."

It took Justyn a moment to realize her mother was answering her questions about Chub Castille. "Empty?"

"He's always been childlike in some ways. Not innocent, mind you—never innocent. But . . . uncomprehending. He's wild when he drinks too much—no, maybe it's when he takes pills and drinks. I don't remember. They've shipped him off several times for shock treatments and such." She mentioned an exclusive mental hospital a couple of hours' drive away, where Zelda Fitzgerald had been a patient. "Each time he comes back he seems *emptier*," she finished.

Justyn nodded, wondering if it was more than drinking and pills that sent Chub away to such an institution. There were certainly local, far less costly ways to treat those problems. She looked back to him and the other scattered guests. Some of them were watching the Balantyne table as discreetly as Justyn was studying the Castilles. But of course, that hadn't changed. She had simply grown accustomed to it. "Balantyne watching" was an established Green Hills sport, always in season; Eddie, with his flagrant spending and mysterious activities in the big house, and the legendary Ouida, with her perplexing beauty and drinking and husband's tragic suicide, rarely let their public down. Though Justyn had tried to leave the family name behind, the Balantyne mystique—or curse—clung to her also. She had her feelings hurt by it frequently, being the butt of gossip. When she rented an apartment in Columbia to finish out her job there, she later learned that Green Hills buzzed with the rumor of her supposed split with Frank. Worse, the talk linked her to her friend and employer, Governor Stan Marston, whose happy family life she would not have besmirched for anything.

Ouida also knew eyes were upon them. But she craved and loved limelight. Swathed in black velvet, she looked particularly stunning and sultry.

"Mother, you're the only person I know who looks truly lovely in black," Justyn told her. Ouida purred. "But, why is he called Chub? It doesn't suit him."

"Because if ever there was an ugly-duckling-to-swan metamorphosis, it was his. He was the fattest, roly-polyist, tubbiest little towheaded boy I ever saw. We're the same age, you know, were in the same grade at St. Andrew's Academy. All he did was sweat and cry and pout. I hated him. All the

36

kids hated him. He was such fair game, Chubby Castille. I don't even know what his real name is. Henry, I think." She drew out a cigarette, which Frank hastened to light for her, and sat watching the handsome man who glided golden and light-footed past their table with his beautiful, swirling wife.

"Then, sometime around puberty he changed," she continued. "I don't mean began to change, I mean *changed*. It couldn't have taken more than six months' time. One moment he was short as I and twenty times as broad, and the next he had grown a foot and more and shed the lard . . . There was a rumor he had some kind of treatments. Hormones? Whatever, all that was left was the nickname. Suddenly the girls were crazy over him and the boys not only envied him, they *liked* him. How could you not like someone so gorgeous? He was Mr. Everything from then on. When we went to public high school he was president of this and that, voted best-looking, along with Ivey Mabrey. Ivey Montgomery, then. Everyone thought they'd marry someday. He went on to Carolina Military Academy and was a top student his freshman year . . ." She sighed and smoked in silence for a moment, drawing deeply. "Funny, I haven't thought of all this in such a long time. You know, there wasn't anything Chub Castille couldn't have done, or been, if only—"

"If only he hadn't gotten mixed up in the lynching?"

"Exactly. Perhaps it sounds dated now, but it's true. It ruined him."

Eddie and Frank were slurredly debating the merits of a local stock. Justyn leapt ahead. "Like it ruined Daddy?"

Suddenly, Ouida trembled. It began in her left hand, which held the cigarette, and moved, like a small earth tremor, violently through her body. Even her lovely dark animal eyes seemed to shudder for an instant in their sockets. When the trembling had passed, she sat quite still and pale for what seemed to Justyn an eternity.

"Yes," she said finally, in a whisper that was not, for once, affected. "Yes!"

Ouida drifted away from them into a mood so melancholy that even Eddie, from his own haze, noticed.

"Sis, want to go home? Sis, are you sick?"

She shook her head at him, smiled vacantly, and remained a world away. Even at the end of the meal, when Eddie signaled the waiter to bring a magnum of champagne, she did not seem to be with them, though she went through the motions of the toast.

Eddie cleverly did not ask Justyn's approval. He simply announced Ouida's impending move as if in celebration. Justyn was too upset at her mother's strange behavior to say anything, and opportunity passed quickly. Frank stared at her reproachfully. The situation was unbearable.

"Mother, let's go to the powder room," she said. Ouida rose obediently. As they passed through the tables, Justyn overheard, "Wonder what the Balantynes are celebrating now? Ed must have made another million!"

Ouida sank into one of the lounge's small, pink-cushioned, deceptively lacy-looking white wrought-iron chairs.

"I'm sorry," Justyn apologized, for the instant towering over her. "It still hurts me to talk about, or even think about, Daddy. I should have realized it hurts you even more."

Ouida reached up and uncharacteristically sought Justyn's hand. "When it happened, people told me time would heal," she said in her worn, natural voice, "but it hasn't. God knows, if I hadn't been afraid of what might happen to you, I would have taken the same way out the day he died. How could I have failed him so? How could I not have known what was going on in his head, when I slept in his arms every night?"

"Mother . . ."

"We had problems. He didn't make much money, and I spent too much, damn it! God knows he had his frustrations, he was so naive and trusting of people. But we had such *good* times, too—or at least, I thought we did. He *loved* me, and he adored you, cared about your future. He didn't seem to mind that I couldn't have more children. He said that you and I were all he wanted on this earth. *On this earth!* I wonder. Sometimes I go back over every word he said that I can remember, looking for double meanings, triple

38

meanings, clues . . ." She shivered. Then, with obvious effort, she straightened her small frame. "Enough of that. Eddie wants to enjoy himself tonight. Eddie *needs* to enjoy himself tonight. Do you understand that, Sugar?"

Justyn nodded, relieved that Ouida seemed to be returning from the far place of her thoughts. As they stood rearranging themselves before the panels of beveled mirrors, Justyn collected her own thoughts. "I want to make a phone call before we go back," she said. "I'll only be a moment."

Walking to the parking lot, Frank stumbled.

"No, I'll drive," Justyn insisted. She had to help him in, and when she got behind the wheel he slumped against his door and watched her moodily. "Is something the matter?" she asked, knowing there was.

"Perhaps it's just that I'm twelve years older than you, and I'm *tired*. I would like to be home in bed."

"I shouldn't have told Thomas that I'd pick up his things tonight, I agree—" She sighed. "But he was worried about his papers, and I have to admit I'm curious to see what other documentation he has."

Once at the Holiday Inn, Frank insisted on going with her, but he groaned as they climbed the ringing metal stairs to Thomas's room.

"Look!" Justyn pointed out across the railing, to the lights of downtown Green Hills. "Isn't it beautiful?" The old section glowed, almost pulsating, Main Street and its intersecting thoroughfares delineated by giant bulbous yellow streetlights, the latest in a long chain of improvements designed to bring business back from suburban shopping malls. She couldn't help but sigh. "The Haley house used to stand just about here, remember? When I spent nights with Jill, I'd stay awake looking out her bedroom window at the lights. The view was so grand . . . my ambition was to have a second-story room like hers, with my own private view of the city. Who could have dreamed that 'downtown' would ever die? It was the hub of everything—not just our business, but our social lives, too. I wonder how this view must seem

39

to Thomas, a stranger to it all." She could not see Frank's expression darken above her. "Imagine thinking of what went on there," she continued, gesturing toward the old courthouse. The square was brightly lit, the grand old marble building, from that vista, a resplendent miniature. It seemed sad that the proud old structure had been abandoned as the county's seat of government for a plain, modern red-brick building two blocks away, and converted into a "mini mall" of crafts and curiosity shops. An ice-cream parlor occupied the spot where the sheriff's office and jail had been. In all probability its proprietors did not know that a man had once been dragged from those quarters to his death.

"Hon, it's late. I've got a nine o'clock appointment in the morning."

"Don't scowl," she whispered, stroking his hand on the railing. That he drew away confused her.

"I don't understand what the hell we're doing here," he said belligerently.

Someone exited a room above them, apparently heard Frank's tone, and changed direction to the back stairs.

"I told you, Thomas has a day or two more in the hospital, and he doesn't want to pay for a motel room he isn't using. Also, he doesn't like leaving all the material he's researched, as well as his manuscripts, unattended. I suppose he feels his belongings will be safer with me than at the mercy of the maid service."

Frank climbed heavily, reluctantly. "What could he possibly have that anyone would want to bother?" he asked more soberly, his back to her as he opened the door with the key the night clerk had given them. Then a whiff—a mere whiff, but recent—told Justyn someone wearing a strong cologne had visited not long before them. No doubt the odor and taste of liquor hid it from Frank.

"I don't know . . . ," she said teasingly, relieved he didn't notice. "Whatever you're looking for in his pockets?" Was it her imagination? If not, whoever had been there—perhaps the person they had just heard—had been careful to leave things as they were.

As she began packing Levity's things she was struck, from her own frequent, solitary stays in motels, at how similar their personal habits were. He had hung clothes carefully but not made use of drawers, leaving other items folded in his luggage. He had placed an alarm clock on the floor, not on the table, by the bed he slept in, and spread papers and clippings he was studying across the other. Like her he seemed to appreciate neatness and efficiency in his travel habits, not leaving much for the maids to clean up after him. She supposed that he also preferred reading to television, except for the evening news—and that, like her, when he came out of the shower he dug his bare toes into the green carpet, dreaming of the green lawn of home. Home. Did he have one, in his heart? On the bedside table where she would have placed the small, framed picture of Frank she always carried in her luggage, Thomas More Levity had propped a glossy, professional study of a quite striking, Nefertiti-esque young woman. Her ebony skin, elongated neck, and sleek head made her seem both classic and modern. "She's *beautiful*," she said aloud.

"Well, I don't think so," Frank said.

"To each his, or her, own tastes," she said as levelly as she could.

"We differ more and more, don't we, hon?" he asked, moving closer. His breath was stale with alcohol. "Since you've been home this time, have we agreed on anything?"

The question caught her off guard. She faced him with puzzled eyes, hurt, chin quivering. The evening had worn heavily. "Not on having children!" she said bitterly.

"Hon, I do want children. It's just that I don't care about being a parent the way you do. I don't want to be tested like a human guinea pig. I *like* it that it's just the two of us."

"If you wanted children, we'd have them," she said lamely. "We *haven't* argued," she protested, sitting down on the bed.

He sat down beside her, groaning as the springs creaked, and put his face in his hands. "It's this," he said, waving at the room. "All those times you've been gone, I've thought it—your restlessness, your dissatisfaction—was something temporary, that you'd work it out. I've always believed that someday you'd come home, *here*," he struck his heart. "But this time you've brought it with you. That damned lynching. Your father."

"Oh, Frank . . ." She put her hand on his knee. But instead of taking her in his arms, as he would have done in the past, she felt that same withdrawing reflex. It struck deep. She had never had to doubt his feelings for her. "But this doesn't have to come between us," she insisted. "The lynching is a connection, a link to help me understand the past, that's all. It doesn't affect what I feel for you—or believe in, for us."

"If only that were true," he answered heavily, rising. "If only it were that simple. But we're man and wife, hon. We're bound together in . . . inexplicable ways. There's no separating us in something like this." He threw up his hands in a gesture of hopelessness. "It's as if we're Siamese twins, and you're taking us somewhere I don't want to go. No, that's not right," he said irritatedly, his voice slurring. "Damn, I wish I could just block all this out and trust you'd come back to me."

"Of course I'll come back to you! I always have. I always will. How can you doubt that?"

His face twisted in a bitter smile. "How, hon? I ask you to leave this alone, and you don't. I tell you that it's dangerous, and you get all the more involved. How can I doubt you? I don't know. I guess I'm starting to doubt everything."

"Including me?"

He nodded.

"Why?"

"Intuition. You're always telling me about your intuition. Well, I have it, too."

Justyn got up in confusion and resumed gathering Thomas's things. She knew that Frank was right, that she was treading on ground that was dangerous in more than one way. She packed suitcases, briefcase, toiletry bag, and rehung the clothes from the closet in their carrier. Thomas More Levity had come for a lengthy stay. She wanted it all to be over as soon as possible. She looked up to see Frank watching her. It made her self-conscious to be handling another man's belongings. "Would you double-check for me?" she asked, attempting a light voice. "Have I missed anything? Shoes under the bed?"

"In a minute. Come here, hon." He moved to the far side of Thomas's bed. "It's been a long time since we were alone together in a motel room," he said huskily, reaching across for her.

▽

6

F<small>RANK</small> <small>INSISTED ON HELPING</small> put Thomas's things in a closet, then went groggily to bed. Justyn put on gown and robe but, when she was certain he was asleep, retrieved Levity's briefcase, took it to the living room, and, tucked comfortably on the sofa, began going through his papers.

Uppermost in the stack were farewell letters from his students. Handprinted in the large lettering of the very young, their message—direct or indirect—was unanimous and simple: *Take care. Come back. We love you.* Illustrated with crude drawings of gaunt children, dogs, cats, squat buildings, the letters inadvertently told her much about the quality of the children's lives. It seemed no coincidence that several had drawn a sun near Thomas's name. Handsome, exuberant "Mr. Levity" must seem like that source of light to them. And she was touched that in the margins Thomas had begun sketching a poem about his students, comparing their faces to dark flowers rich with unrecognized beauty, needing light.

After the letters came a sheaf of his poetry. She undid it nervously. It consisted of two poems, each several pages long. As soon as she started reading the first, "I Walk Along in Ezekiel's Stride," it was as if she were swept headlong into the pages by a blast of desert wind, a sere wind of the mind that billowed and blew, creating marvelous visions of spirits spun out of sand and madness, as much by the prophet's recall as by his foresight.

"God, the man can *write*," she whispered aloud, amazed by the powerful verse. In it there were no restrictions of gender or race, place or time. It sang in a universal voice.

The next, a compilation of several drafts, both moved and perplexed her. Entitled "Coverings," it began with the quietly mimicking description of an effeminate man named Ardemon fussily pulling a nightcap over his head to protect

44

his curls. The scene suddenly shifted, and Ardemon pulled a hood over a falcon's head. Both bloodlust and affection for the highly trained bird were clearly present, though no specific word clearly defined them. She felt a chill as she read on, aware that something horrific was about to happen. The poem, resplendent with raptoring terms and symbolism, was paced, nevertheless, not by the measures of falconry but by Ardemon's personal actions, his slow mincing egotistical movements.

There was a deliberately deceptive tone to the poem, she realized midway. At first it had seemed an ancient scene, but in a flashback Ardemon recalled the particular pleasures of raptoring, and she was jolted to find him a part of our modern world. To obtain fresh food for his falcon, Ardemon—with a daring he considered titillating—snatched sleeping pigeons from their roost beneath an interstate overpass, the darkness cut by light from passing cars below. The warmth of the gentle birds struggling sleepily in his hand as he placed them in a sack, their trill of surprise when they waked in the falcon's cage, only heightened his appetites. His cruel yet calm omnipresence was so subtly and movingly accomplished that she felt breathless. Ardemon seemed real. It was as if she knew him, though she had never known anyone so cruel in her life. Although she suspected that the poem was building toward a powerful climax, she was still unprepared for the knifelike twist when it came.

Ardemon's falcon, a rare and illegally obtained peregrine, shuddered on his trembling wrist, shared anticipation, bloodlust, a keen link between them. But when the moment for unleashing came, Ardemon, daydreaming of the handsome picture they made, grew careless and lost his footing. As the bird exploded into the air with the hood only half off, the hood began its shift forward. Doomed, lifting out of reach, his beloved falcon raced away on powerful wings to certain oblivion.

She sat stunned. What was it that struck so close to home? That Ardemon, hungry and too confident of his own power, sacrificed his ward to vanity? Or that we sometimes kill through love? As Ardemon ran shouting after the vanished falcon, straining up and down the streets of a piedmont town much like Green Hills, he was reduced to a wailing, panting figure berating the sky instead of himself, chasing shadows that flitted like kites, eluding him.

Why should the poem affect her so? She reread it. Apart from the narrative, which was in itself a provocative story, and the imagery, which was brilliant, something ineffable seemed to touch her personally. But what?

Attached to the pages of the poem were other papers. There were notes of Thomas's research on falconry, lists of related words, and one item, a newspaper clipping, that truly puzzled her. It was a wire service story from the Green Hills *Mountaineer*, dated a few months earlier, that detailed a similar incident involving a falconer and young falcon in the nearby Blue Ridge Mountains. Someone had scrawled, "Figure this out, nigger," across the top margin. She reread it and sighed, deeply troubled. Whose message was it? Obviously Thomas referred to it in his writing, but how had it come into his possession? How long had he had it? Justyn felt uneasy. Obviously, there was much she didn't know. About Thomas, as well as about the lynching. Was this what she deserved for searching through his things? How could she ask him the dozen questions this evoked, without confessing she had snooped through his belongings?

For the first time, she felt afraid for herself. Who was she to trust? And this just a moment or two before the phone rang, at three o'clock in the morning. She sprang to answer it before it woke Frank.

"Nigger lover!" a voice, muffled but familiar, hissed venomously.

Her breath stopped as Frank picked up the receiver. "Hello?" he said sleepily.

"Nigger lover!" the voice repeated.

"What?" Frank said groggily. "What?"

The receiver clicked. Justyn waited for Frank to hang up before she did. She sat with her heart in her throat knowing that, as her husband had warned, she had gotten in over her head. But she could see no way to turn back.

46

Frank had let her sleep. She woke too late for morning visiting hours, grateful to delay until afternoon having to face Thomas with a guilty conscience. Instead she cleaned house with fervor, until Tawny's wild barking in the backyard drew her into the redeeming sunlight. A tiny whirlwind had set Frank's carefully raked leaves aswirl, and Tawny chased them, happily nipping and whirling, her blond fur ruffling like a puppy's. Justyn couldn't bring herself to go back inside until lunchtime. Frank had left no note. Did that mean he was angry, or merely running late? After a sandwich and coffee she sat on at the kitchen table, unable to keep her mind on anything but her suspicions. Was Frank right in his instinct? Was she merely a pawn in something she didn't understand? When the phone rang, she hesitated to answer it, but it was only her mother.

"Baby, would you go over to Eddie's with me? I want to show you what we're planning," she said huskily. "I don't want this to come between us."

"Yes. All right. Now?" Anything to get her thoughts in another direction. In anticipation of dusty Balantyne Hall she changed into slacks scarcely less well-worn than the ones in which she cleaned house. In Washington she had bought, for Beesie, a small bust of Lincoln, and she tucked it into her shoulder bag just as she heard her mother's Austin Healey pull into the drive. Tawny barked an alarm that turned quickly to joyful yapping. When Justyn came out Tawny stood happily on her hind legs at the driver's door, getting her ears scratched.

"Oh, Mother, the top down on a day like this? My hair will blow, and it's too cold!"

"I need fresh air," Ouida said stubbornly.

"Then I'll have to get a sweater and scarf. I'll be a moment." When Justyn came back Ouida sat petting the happy dog, aware what a pretty picture she made, a black-haired doll in a white toy car, and offered no apology. Then, before Justyn had quite settled in, Ouida gunned the Healey backward into the street, shifted into forward at much too high a speed, and was almost too late in braking at the corner intersection. As they sped along her route of back streets to the Balantyne mansion, weaving past anything in their path, the powerful little car alternately roared and wheezed at the opposite poles of its limits.

One of Ouida's quirks, as a notoriously poor driver, was that she would tolerate correction or suggestion only once . . . anything after that merely encouraged her. Now Justyn searched frantically for an all-encompassing catchall, considering *Slow down!*, *Watch out!*, and others before settling for *"Mother, for God's sake, be careful!"*

Miraculously, it seemed, Eddie's drive appeared, a gentle arc that Ouida approached as if it were the home stretch of a raceway. They roared past a parked pickup truck with a scant inch to spare. Justyn could have reached up and bobbed the nude kewpie doll that dangled from its side mirror. But then, when they stopped, she saw tears welling from beneath Ouida's dark glasses.

"Why, Mama, what is it? What's the matter?"

"Damn it! I was cutting down on my drinking, I really was, and now," she said, biting her lips, "I'm nervous as a cat." She reached in her small purse, drew out a delicate silver flask, took two ladylike swallows, and made a sour face. "To the past, rearing its ugly snake head again," she said enigmatically, waving the flacon at the house. "Do you know what I ran into this morning, Baby? A rumor that's older than we are. Why is it that some things never die?" she asked bitterly.

"Well, what a nice *surprise*! But, why didn't you *call*?" Eddie shouted down from the front door, a pout in his voice.

"I was going to, but I didn't," Ouida said, her expression lost behind the dark glasses as Eddie hurried to open the car door for her. But he put his arm protectively around her shoulders as she climbed out of the Healey, and kept it there as they walked up the steep steps, Ouida teetering on her high shoes like a child in her mother's heels.

"Jus, aren't you coming?" Eddie called when they reached the top.

She nodded and waved them to go on, but continued to stare at the tall, imposing house that always symbolized turmoil to her. Just then a cloud came between it and the sun, so that it sank into shadow. A cat leapt from a window ledge and ran flat-eared across the wide, unkempt lawn as if its life depended on escape. Something startled a flock of pigeons from the roof. They winged out a half-hundred yards or so before fluttering back to their perch, as if reluctantly. Her mother did not want to come back, Justyn realized suddenly. Ouida knew what she was getting into and was as afraid as Frank or Justyn. Things must be very bad for Eddie, far worse than anyone except Ouida, who knew him best, dreamed.

Justyn sat for a moment more. If her mother moved back, she would have to visit Balantyne Hall more often. Why was it that the house evoked such a mixture of feelings? Awe, affection, and dread among them. When she lived here for a few months following her father's death, nothing had happened to give her such uneasy emotions concerning it.

"Justyn?" Ouida appeared at the top of the steps.

"I'm coming."

"Eddie got a call from his commodities broker. He'll be on the phone for a while," she explained at the front door.

"Well, then, I'll go back and see Beesie. I won't be long, or call me when he's free."

Ouida looked disappointed. "I guess I'll just wander around," she said.

Ouida struggled to clear her head, to avoid the silver flask. She wandered to the third floor, where she seldom ventured. Opening a door to one of the sitting rooms, she was surprised to find it occupied. The man who turned from gazing out the window seemed equally surprised, as well as embarrassed.

"Ma'am?" he said, shifting uneasily.

"Who are you?" She forgot to whisper.

"Oh, Buck Stovall here." He covered the distance between them with large strides. "How do you do, ma'am," he said, holding out his hand.

The handshake startled her, but she found the man's discomfort in her presence amusing. He was not bad-looking. No, he was actually good-looking in a rugged, unpolished way: close to six feet, freckled, with auburn hair fading to ruddy brown; a God-and-country type of man, complete with crew cut and tattoos.

"What are you doing here?" she demanded, though she knew she was too tipsy to be talking to a stranger. She should turn and leave, but he looked so much the part of uncomfortable schoolboy she could not resist baiting him.

"I don't know what I'm doing here," he answered in confusion. "Mr. Balantyne and I were talking, but when he saw you drive up he told me to come up here and wait. I guess he didn't want us to meet."

"Well, screw Eddie," she said lightly. Something flashed in her eyes. "Why, I remember your name! My husband tried to send you to jail, for the lynching of Tom Levity!"

"Yes, ma'am, he sure did."

"I must have seen you during the trial, but I don't remember—"

"Oh, I remember *you*, ma'am. The prettiest woman I ever saw. Still are. White suit, white dress, white every day. Gypsy curls. Couldn't take your eyes off your man."

The idea of exiting left her mind. Fascinated, she sensed the balance of power between them shift. He must be quite a womanizer. Yes, she had heard. But she was nonetheless deeply flattered. She *had* worn white every day of the trial. Zach liked her in it, and she had wanted to encourage him, boost his spirits, in any way possible. How remarkable that anyone remembered!

"Well," she said, smiling, "I might as well wait with you, though Eddie may forget you're here until he sees your truck. That *is* your truck in the drive, isn't it?"

"Yes, ma'am. I'm here to see about doing some remodeling for Mr. Balantyne."

They sat on the sofa. As he stared at her with unsettling directness, his uncommonly pale green eyes seemed uncommonly powerful to her. This was starting to be fun. Looking down to hide her smile, she plucked a cigarette from her purse. Buck Stovall came immediately to his feet and bent over to offer her a light from the small box of wooden matches he took from his jeans pocket.

"Now, that's a first!" she said lightly.

"Ma'am?"

His hands were strong and clean, the fingers well-shaped and covered with fine red down. His scent was a "first" to her also: *unscented*, but clean-smelling. In an instant of deviltry she covered his large hands with her small, quaking ones, as if to help steady the match. His flesh was warm, almost hot, to her touch. When she looked up again those pale eyes, amber flecked, set her on fire.

"The very prettiest?" she asked, softening.

"Yes, ma'am. Oh, yes, ma'am!"

The strangest thought passed through her head, of Shakespeare's Richard III, his power over women. After all these years, this man remembered her in white . . . so what if he had been her husband's enemy? Now her *late* husband. So many years. All the lighters, gold or silver, engraved or inlaid or embossed, that she had resisted . . . a kitchen match? Wouldn't even Zach appreciate the irony?

"Well, what the hell!" she said suddenly, in her best throaty voice. And, crushing out her cigarette, she got up and locked the door.

7

J USTYN FOUND BEESIE, BALANTYNE Hall's housekeeper of several generations, in the cavernous, outdated kitchen, leaning against the high sink, whether daydreaming out the window or dozing she could not tell. She called to her several times before the thin, stooped figure stirred, turned, and waving slight hands excitedly before her, exclaimed, "Jus, honey? It can't be my Justyn! Mercy, these eyes must be fooling me! Come and let me give you a hug, child."

Justyn went gratefully to her. "Oh, Beesie, you're shrinking!" She laughed, kissing the cheek that now hung close to her own, the wrinkled swatch of skin flapping like a wattle against her own still-taut jaw. Beesie was as short as Justyn now, shrunken and bent by osteoporosis.

"You're come to visit me? Have you eaten?" When Justyn assured her that she had, Beesie took off her apron, folded it carefully, and laid it on the side of the sink. "Mercy, it's too cold in here to talk. Come on back to my room."

Justyn followed her up to her sanctuary, aware each step retraced a memory. The night of her father's death, it was Beesie who held her and whispered her to sleep, taking her to her own narrow bed that smelled, as her skin did, like a fernery, dank and old and sweet. In those first days after Zachary's suicide, when Ouida stared straight past her and Eddie's gaze was to the floor, only Beesie did not waver from that terrible but necessary confirmation. She alone voiced to her the hypocrisy of the whole town's showing up for his funeral, who had offered him little business or friendship during his maverick years. Her small, dark, secretive room, hung on the back stairs somewhere between the first and second stories in the oldest section of the house, became sanctuary for a tormented girl, otherwise unconsoled in that seemingly vast place.

Now the short journey up the cluttered back stairs seemed

to take forever, but, once there, Beesie's load appeared to lighten, the pain in her arthritic joints to ease. How well this lair suited her. Here were mingled the confusing scents of musty age and simple cleanliness, of sweet-smelling rose bouquets from Eddie's garden, and the noxious herbal poultices Beesie bought from a local "root doctor" to remedy her various ailments. Here civilization was reduced to solitude: no radio or television, newspapers or books, phone or alarm clock. What Beesie did with her free time was to rock and think, think and rock, or doze. Eddie had mentioned lately that her ninety-some-odd years were catching up with her, that sometimes now when she talked she scarcely seemed to know whether she was awake or dreaming, so intertwined were the names of the living and dead in her mind. No matter, Justyn's visit seemed to rejuvenate her. When she produced the statue from her shoulder bag, Beesie clapped her frail hands joyfully.

"My, Justyn!" she exclaimed, "you always were the truest one! *Mr. Lincoln* . . . now, didn't he do the good Lord, and my mama and papa, proud? He set them free! I wouldn't be here, they never would have gotten together, if it hadn't been for Mr. Lincoln!"

"I wanted to bring you something special from Washington. I'm glad you like it. Should I put it here?" She put it on the bed table beside a china pitcher and basin Beesie still used for sponge baths, the nearest bathroom being half the house away.

"Beesie," she began hesitantly, "you know that Mother is planning to move—"

"Mercy, child, I know! Isn't it wonderful? The good Lord is answering my prayers! If Miss Ouida wasn't coming, I think I'd just lay down and die right now. Mr. Eddie . . . bless his soul, I love the boy, but he worries me to death. He's not himself," she said knowingly, tapping her head. "If only there was something I could do for him . . ."

"What do you mean, 'not himself'?" Justyn sat down on the narrow bed.

"Why, he hollers and screams, has nightmares. Mercy!

53

Sometimes I can hear him all the way down here. But he won't listen. He won't take my potions. And those young people he runs around with!" She threw up her hands and sat down beside her. "Justyn, what am I to do? Your daddy was right to throw them out, I don't care what they say. But your mama's coming to live with us. Things will get better."

The blind leading the blind, Justyn thought woefully. Ouida, with her demons, ridding Eddie of his? Then, "What do you mean, my father threw them out? Who?"

"With your mama living here, you'll come to see me more often, won't you?"

"Of course. Oh, Beesie, don't you remember I've been working in Columbia? That's why I haven't been here more often." This was not entirely true. To visit her she must first brave Balantyne Hall, and Eddie. "But I'm home now. I'll come every few days, I promise. Now, what about my father?"

"What?"

"You said my father did right, when he threw out Eddie's friends. Who? When? Please tell me what you were talking about, Beesie."

"Mercy. I disremember. You remind me of him, you know. Your hair. Your spirit. You always were the truest one, like him. What was I talking about? Who? Mercy, I'll try to recall. I can make memory notes in my mind," she added proudly. It had always shamed her that she had to make an X for her name.

Justyn took both her wizened hands in hers and squeezed gently. "I'll be back soon," she said, "and I'll bring Frank. You know he loves you, too."

"Mercy, child!" she said suddenly, looking at Justyn as if for the first time. "Have you eaten?"

Justyn left her sitting on the bed, nodding toward a nap. As she passed through the kitchen she noticed it was reasonably straight. Somehow Beesie still managed to wage an effective small war there—though one reason there were fewer dirty dishes seemed to be that there were fewer dishes. What had happened to that set of exquisite cobalt blue porcelain that used to grace the dining-room sideboard? And what of great-great-grandmother's silver clawfoot urn? Eddie must have put them away, fearful of Beesie's growing clumsiness.

Outward from the kitchen, order in the rooms deteriorated according to Beesie's waning capabilities. Considering himself an aristocrat, Eddie did little to keep the place clean. The fine Belgian chandeliers, purchased and shipped at great cost by an earlier Edward Valenchat Balantyne, hung almost as heavy with cobwebs and dust as prisms. Bowls of fruit so long rotted it had become green powder rested on tables and mantels. Everywhere there were teetering stacks of old magazines and books. The floor bore tracks, from the past two dozen rains, of shoes and boots and cats. How would her mother fit in here? What would be expected of her?

And where had she gotten to?

A tour of the downstairs rooms produced no one. Justyn climbed the wide front stairs. At the second-floor landing she could hear Eddie talking loudly on the telephone, his agitated voice bouncing toward her like a racquetball. Shivering, she kept climbing on to the third floor that had so fascinated her when she visited as a child.

At one time a ballroom, a grand room for gatherings, had occupied most of this floor, but during the Civil War it had been converted to smaller rooms to house low-country relatives needing refuge from Sherman and malaria, as well as genteel soldiers, many of them injured, who sought a day or two of shelter. Two had died there, and rested in the family cemetery that lay opposite the great expanse of lawn from the river.

The door to the sitting room at the top of the stairs was locked, although Justyn thought she heard voices. Probably cats. And the door to Eddie's darkroom. Poor Eddie, who leaned toward paranoia—did he imagine anyone would want to invade it? She shook the knob to another door, one of the old bedrooms. Her curiosity piqued, she went down the long hall, trying doors. Some opened to incredible disarray. Others were locked, including the one to the old back stairwell, vestigial relic of the original log structure. She was disappointed. She would have liked to open that door and touch the thick log wall again. As a child, only those logs had made the story of the house's origins seem believable.

A door at the far end of the hall opened. The sitting room? Ouida came out but did not see her. Catching her own reflection in the beveled hall mirror, she stood for a moment straightening her sweater and hair, then hurried down the stairs. Justyn followed, intending to call after her, but when she passed the sitting room the unexpected sound of whistling—a lovely, plaintive rendering of "Brown Eyes"—startled her. How pensive and sweet it sounded.

Late in the afternoon Justyn walked down the hospital corridor with something like apprehension. She dreaded telling Thomas More Levity that she had snooped through his papers, but, once it was done, she reminded herself, she would be free to question him about the falconer and perhaps understand why the poem troubled her.

"Well," she said, opening the door to find him sitting up reading, newspapers spread across the bed. "You must be better. You certainly look better."

"As a matter of fact, I feel better than I ever thought I would." He smiled, showing a little of the flash or verve that had seemed so characteristic on the plane. "The only thing wrong is, my visitors are wearing me out. Present company excluded, of course." He grinned roguishly.

"Oh, really? Who?"

"Pear again. Twice yesterday. He asked most of the questions, instead of me. A newspaper reporter, and, this morning—"

Even as he spoke the door opened slowly and a grizzled head appeared.

"Why, Judge Mabry!" Justyn said, more than a little surprised. Very old now and nearly blind, he had become almost a recluse in his retirement.

"I beg your pardon?" He peered in, obviously without seeing. "I must have the wrong room."

56

"No. I'm Justyn, Justyn Jones. I'm visiting Mr. Levity. Are you looking for him?"

"Yes. Yes. Tom Levity's son. But I don't want to interrupt—"

"You're not interrupting. I was just leaving," she said, deciding it on the instant. Whatever brought the ailing judge to Thomas's bedside, it might not be force enough to propel him there again. She motioned furtively to Thomas, who nodded that he understood.

"I'll call you," he said.

The rest of the afternoon, into evening, she expected the phone to ring. She even asked Frank to step outside to feed Tawny for fear she might miss Thomas's call, or that he might simply hang up if Frank answered. But she did not realize her distraction showed until Frank asked, over dinner, in a voice not quite his own, "What's the matter, hon? You look distracted. That Levity fellow again?"

"No," she heard herself hedging. "It's been a dispiriting day. I went with Mother over to Eddie's, talked to Beesie, got overwhelmed. Mother was in the strangest mood. Her and Eddie's plans are so cockamamie. Do you know what they ended up talking about? Not how they're going to make her an apartment in that place, or anything remotely practical— but who's going to pay to have the baby grand piano moved back and serviced! Did you know she pays a small fortune to keep that thing in tune and shining? They got into the silliest argument, both of them near tears, and I told her I felt sick, and to bring me home."

Frank said then that her gray eyes in the candlelight were lovely, that she looked so vulnerable he almost could not bring himself to ask, but he did, "And where else did you go, hon? I was driving by the hospital and I thought I saw your car."

"Yes," she answered, too quickly. "I went to see Thomas, but I didn't get to talk with him, because Judge Mabry came, and I—"

"Judge Mabry? Old Judge Mabry?"

"Yes."

"Why, he hasn't been about in months. He doesn't see anyone. I know—I've tried to contact him about some property, some very important property, and he won't even return my calls. Word is, that nymphomaniac wife of his has finally driven him crazy. The lynching. What did he say about the lynching?"

"I don't know. He arrived just after I did, and looked as if he would leave if I didn't. He's aged terribly."

Frank looked thoughtful. "You know, it seemed he really wanted a conviction in the lynching trial. That was quite a stand to take in those days. It tagged him 'nigger lover' to less than polite society. Although some people attributed his liberal leanings to something other than humanitarian concerns."

She should have asked Frank then what he meant, but she was still thinking about what he had said about Ivey Mabry. "His wife is very beautiful, and still young looking. I wonder how he holds on to her."

"*You're* a beautiful woman, hon. And I'm older. I wonder how I hold on to you?"

Justyn reddened at the implication in his words, waved them away, and changed the subject. "I shouldn't have let myself become upset about Mother's piano," she said. "It's the one healthy pleasure she has. Bless her heart, she does practice."

"I never have understood—did Eddie give it to her, or loan it?" Frank, too, seemed pleased to change the subject.

"I thought it was hers, until today. Something was said about it being part of the estate property, and she said Eddie's friends would spill drinks on it. It was a childish brother-sister argument, and I'm afraid I was a little heavy-handed in breaking it up."

She looked at her watch and sighed. "Well, her day is over by now. She'll be three sheets to the wind, at least, and nothing I could say would make any difference. Tomorrow, she may not remember." Just as Frank apparently did not remember that middle-of-the-night phone call, she thought.

Later, as they cleared the table, Frank said, "If you find

out what Judge Mabry had to say about the lynching, will you tell me?"

His request puzzled her. She took too long in answering, "Of course."

"I mean it, hon. Promise?"

But for Justyn's mother, the beautiful Ouida Balantyne Orms, the day was far from over. Though the curtains were drawn, she lay across her bed as aware of the night, its spell of darkness rising from the forested hills to meet the greenly glowing, cloud-swathed moon, as if she lay out under the stars. She had made such an effort not to drink too much, almost as if expecting Buck Stovall's call, his firm voice. . . . When finally the phone rang, hope sent her heart thudding wildly.

—*Was she as confused as he?*

—*Yes.*

—*Would she meet him? Devil's Rock? In a half hour?*

—*Yes!*

No white in her wardrobe now. Black slacks. A black sweater. Topaz scarf. Trembling fingers, trembling hands. So damned cold. She struggled with the top of the Healey, then cursed the near-empty gas gauge. It took her forty-five minutes to manage the twenty-minute drive away from town and up the abrupt, straggler mountain that seemed to have bounced away from the Blue Ridge escarpment to settle at a peculiar angle jut outside the city. Finally she reached the pull-off where Buck Stovall stood waiting beside his truck.

"Have you been here before?" she asked when he opened the door for her.

"Lots of times."

"I haven't. I always wanted to, but 'nice' girls didn't."

"It's a steep walk to the top. Don't step off the path," he warned her.

"What's off the path?"

"Dog shit. People shit. Condoms. Snakes in summer." He switched on a flashlight and stepped briskly off, Ouida following tentatively on her dangerous heels. In a moment he came back and, steadying her with a strong arm, swept her safely along at his own pace. When finally he stopped, the beam from his light swept over a rock ledge into nothingness. She heard the wind howling up the precipice like a hungry ghost, saw the lights of her distant city as she had never seen them.

Buck took her astonishment for granted. "I've been coming here since I was old enough to drive—fourteen it was then, I think. I'm from south of town, where it's flatter than a pancake. I'd come up here to think or dream or salvage my pride . . ." He stopped and shifted from foot to foot self-consciously. "But I've always come here alone." He squeezed her hand. "Not with a girl or a friend, ever."

She reached up and touched his warm and stubbly cheek. "They say the most awful things about you," she said, her whispering voice almost lost in the vastness. "That you're a skirt-chaser, a cockfighter, a gambler—"

"Yes, ma'am, I am." He lit a cigarette, the match flaring and fading in the darkness. "And 'they' say you're a lush, and loose, and who gives a fuck what the hell else? This is strictly between us, babe. We're lost if we don't believe that."

Lost. She was profoundly touched at the depth of the word he chose. He handed her the cigarette and she drew so deeply she coughed before handing it back. "I'm a lush, but I'm not loose," she said defiantly.

"I know that. Oh, I know that. I know a lady when I see one."

There was scurrying and a hound bayed mere yards away. She was so startled she might have fallen, without Buck's arm to steady her.

"You know, babe, up until this morning I sort of liked my life. Now it seems empty unless I can be with you."

Again she stroked his cheek. She wanted to pull his face down to hers and kiss him, but was afraid. *Lost.* Why had he chosen that word? "Please don't say 'ma'am' to me," she said, the enormity of their differences sweeping over her. "I'm your lover, not your mother. I'm not even as old as you, am I? How old are you?"

"Fifty-five, ma'am."

Her tears came unexpectedly, in a messy explosion. In a moment his large, clean handkerchief was pressed into her face. She blew her nose gratefully.

"You've not once called me by my name," he said quietly.

"I . . . can't," she answered truthfully. "Not yet. In my mind Buck Stovall is that vulgar man who should have gone to jail for his crime, who was my husband's enemy. But *you* are . . . someone quite different."

"Then make up your own name for me."

She was silent. The lights of Green Hills from this distance were more beautiful than she would ever have dreamed. Suddenly she smiled. "May I call you Pet?" she asked.

"Whatever pleases you, ma'am."

"Oh, God!" She blew her nose again loudly, and laughed.

He took off his coat and spread it on the rock. "We can sit and talk for a while. That is, if you're not in a hurry to leave."

"I could stay up here with you forever," she admitted.

When he heard Ouida's car safely down the mountain road, Buck again climbed the steep path to Devil's Rock. There was no doubt of impending dawn. It tinged the edge of blackness with pearlescent pink, a shade as delicate and beautiful to him as Ouida's palms upturned for his help in rising. There was not a detail of her he had missed, and now he went back carefully over each, savoring the memory of her outline as it formed in the diminishing darkness, to that instant of sudden wonder when he turned to find her exquisite profile glowing within his own arm's reach. Slowly he spread his hand over the spot where she had sat, imagining that the warmth and imprint of her small buttocks lingered for his touch.

It had happened so fast he was still reeling. Yet how else could it have happened? A collision it had to be, like that of stars or planets. Twenty-nine years since the trial, yet he remembered how clearly he had lusted. Half a century old now, the girl of his dreams.

He heard himself whistling a song his mother sang as she stood over the dishpan—

Can she bake a cherry pie,
Billy Boy, Billy Boy?

I doubt it, he thought, and laughed.

The wind churned on the rock. He could almost imagine he heard a voice within it. "And would you kill for her?"

He lit a cigarette and smoked slowly, recalling the war, the lynching.

"Yes, I would," he said calmly. "Yes."

$$\nabla$$

8

F RANK BROUGHT IN THE morning paper and, sitting down at the kitchen table, began reading as Justyn put breakfast before him. "Oh, no," he moaned.

"Hm?"

"Come here." He turned the paper so that she could read with him. Half the front page was devoted to lynching-related stories. *"Who killed Stubby Balantyne?"* one headline screamed. *"Decades-old Lynching Re-examined by Son Avenger,"* another said. Her own name leapt out at her from one column of print.

> Justyn Jones, aide to Governor Stan Marston and primary author of the state's Race Relations Study, is involved in bringing Green Hills's most closely guarded skeleton in the closet, the grisly lynching of Thomas More Levity, a black man, for the alleged murder of her cousin, Stubby (T.V.) Balantyne, in 1948, into the limelight.
>
> Mrs. Jones is the daughter of socialite Ouida Balantyne Orms and the late William Zachary Orms, unsuccessful prosecutor at the trial of the mob, who later took his own life. A spokesman for the Governor's office claimed no knowledge of Mrs. Jones's involvement in the unofficial investigation. Mrs. Jones could not be reached for comment on the matter.

"Exactly what we don't need," she said, embarrassed and close to tears. She sat down to read further. One story paralleled what she knew of the lynching; another profiled Thomas, extolling his role as a Vietnam veteran, recipient of a Purple Heart, and featuring a handsome photograph. The most alarming posed the question who really killed Stubby Balantyne? Each article but one bore Junior Mills's byline. The other was signed Poe Williams.

"This will hurt my business," Frank said worriedly.

"I know. I'm sorry. I can't believe this is in the *Mountain-eer*. I'd think Wade Mills would die before he'd let Junior print this."

"Well, hon . . ." Frank rose wearily. He had hardly touched his food. "The bottom line is, you never should have gotten involved in this mess. No good can come of it."

For once she could not bring herself to disagree.

As Frank walked out the door, the phone rang, as if on cue.

"Mother? You don't sound like yourself."

"It's a mucked-up morning."

"Listen, I'm sorry about the newspaper. I—"

"What about the paper? I haven't seen it. Just listen, Baby. There's something I need to tell you."

"I'm listening, Mother."

"I received an anonymous note yesterday. It said, 'Dear Mrs. Orms. The reason your husband was a Negro lover is because you are part Negro.' "

"I don't understand."

"It's gossip about us, dear. Have you never heard it?"

"No."

"I'm glad. I was afraid that might be the reason you and Frank don't have children."

"No!"

"The point is, it's a story with some historical base." She paused. Justyn imagined she had to have a drink in her hand for this. "The story is that my great-grandmother Graybeal, the one from Charleston, was pregnant by a plantation fore-man, a light-skinned black, when my great-great-grandfa-ther—that was the second Valenchat—married her. Well, it makes sense. Why else would somebody that rich marry an up-country farmer?"

"Mother, this is so farfetched—"

"No. Hear me out. I took the tour of the Graybeal home in Charleston. It's on the Ashley River. The guide talked about the Negro foreman, an inventor who built practical devices to help with the raising of rice and indigo. There was a painting of him standing by some contraption he'd built . . . and Justyn, except that it was an old-fashioned painting, it could have been Eddie standing there!" She paused. "Are you sure that isn't why you don't have a baby?"

"Mother," she said quickly, "I want a baby so badly I wouldn't care if were pink or green."

Ouida laughed, the spell broken. "Well," she said lightly, "they say that every third baby is born Chinese. Maybe you'll get lucky and have yellow! Screw the old rumors. As a matter of fact, if you want a baby so much, just *screw*."

Justyn drove to Gargomedia at midmorning. She wanted extra copies of each edition of the day's papers, with Junior's stories, for herself and Thomas. She stood waiting at the information desk when she heard an angry *hmph!*, loud as a bull's snort, behind her. She turned to face Junior Mills, who thrust his girth at her as if in challenge.

"So, I suppose *you* already know where he is," he said.

"No, as a matter of fact, I don't," she replied, not needing to ask who. "—that is, if he's not in his hospital room."

"I checked him out this morning. I told him the shit was hitting the fan, and he wouldn't be safe. For his safety, no one should know where he is."

"For his safety, I suppose, *I don't know* where he is."

The clerk returned with Justyn's newspapers. She paid and turned to go, only to find Junior blocking her path.

"This story is going to make my career," he said, his voice low. "I'm not going to let you or anyone else ruin it for me."

"Why would I want to ruin your story?" she asked, perplexed.

"You'd like to get credit for this. One more feather for you and Stan Marston. Well, you won't. It's mine. It's—"

"Excuse me," she said, trying to brush past him.

"Don't be so high-and-mighty with me. You can tell that black boyfriend of yours—"

"How *dare* you!" she whispered, her face turning red as his. "*How dare you!*" she said more loudly, so that heads of passersby turned. She caught her breath. "If you don't get out of my way I'm going to scream for help. You've got to three, Junior. *One, two . . .*"

Lithely for so grotesque a figure, he turned and strode away. Justyn was close to tears.

"Mrs. Jones?"

A very young, very blond man in jeans and blue sweatshirt approached her. The earnestness of his expression was enforced by sky blue eyes, clear and sparkling.

"I saw that Junior Mills was giving you trouble," he said. "I was going to punch him out if he didn't leave you alone. Please, I need to talk to you, but not here. It might get me fired. May I call you later? My name's Poe Williams. Here—" He thrust a bright blue business card at her. It was as blue as his eyes. Too disoriented to read it, she nodded and dropped it in her shoulder bag. Clutching the newspapers, she almost ran to the elevator. But once in the parking garage, the sight of her mother's Austin Healey parked in the visitor's space next to her car brought her up short. Why on earth . . . ? She thought about leaving, then decided to wait. Ouida's metabolism was too much like a hummingbird's to allow her to light in any one place for long. Within five minutes Justyn heard the familiar clacking of her platform shoes.

"Mother?" Ouida looked distraught.

"Oh, Baby, I'm so glad to see you. I was hoping you'd wait."

"Mother, where have you been? What's the matter?"

"To see Hamp Mills." Ouida took a Kleenex from her purse and dabbed her eyes. "If I cry it will make guck out of my mascara," she sniffed.

"Then don't. You shouldn't wear all that makeup, anyway. You don't need it. Oh, Mother, don't cry! Come on, get in my car. We'll go get some coffee."

Justyn drove around for several blocks, but now that the floodgate had opened, Ouida seemed unable to close it. "Can I take you to my house? Or yours?"

She wiped her eyes and grew thoughtful. "No," she said. "I know a place . . . Have you got a thermos in here? Let's go get some coffee and sandwiches—I'm starving!—and have a picnic!"

She brightened so considerably Justyn felt guilty at her reaction. "A *picnic*? But, it's cold, and—"

66

"Oh, screw the cold! You've got on a jacket, haven't you? Let loose. Don't be so . . . *conservative* about everything."

Justyn bridled, then softened. "I admit, it's a nice idea. I don't have a thermos in the car, but we can get large cups to go." She turned into a fast-food restaurant.

"And cigarettes. I need cigarettes." She handed her a fifty-dollar bill. One of Eddie's, no doubt.

Justyn returned quickly with their lunch. "And now, where to?"

"Devil's Rock."

"Devil's Rock? Mother, are you crazy? It will be cold and windy up there. It's not safe."

"Oh, poo. If anyone tries to rape or murder *me*, I'll push him off the cliff or stab him with the heel of my little shoe. I'll pinch his balls and kick him in the prick, and—"

"Oh, Mother, for God's sake, *all right!*" Justyn could not help laughing, it had been so long since she'd done anything zany. It was not in her nature, or Frank's.

"Park here. Now we walk. You'll have to give me a hand, or I'll break my neck on these shoes."

"I have some tennis shoes." She reached in the backseat. "Here, put these on. And a blanket in the trunk. Are we really going all the way to the top?"

"Sure, Toots. Follow me." Ouida struck off in a shuffling gait, swinging her fanny like a duck's, her pumping arms its wings.

"Mother, my feet are one half-size larger than yours, that's all. Cut it out!"

"Okay, Toots, if it upsets you," she called back, not altering her style. "Don't step off the path," she continued happily. "There's dog shit and people shit, and condoms. Oh, and snakes in the summer!"

"My appetite fades."

"Don't be such a ninny!" Ouida huffed, panting but undaunted by the steepness. When they reached the top she sighed. "Isn't it beautiful?" She spread her arms at the view. "Have you ever been here, Toots?"

"Twice. Once with the Natural History Club, when I was in high school. Don't you remember?" No. Of course not. She would have been drinking. "And again when I was researching a story on Devil McKinner when I was in college. He died here, you know, on this rock. Was scalped by his neighbors, not the Indians. About where you're standing."

"Oh, screw Devil McKinner. Don't get morbid on me, Justyn, just when I'm starting to enjoy myself."

Ouida stood staring into space while Justyn spread the blanket and arranged their food. "Even Styrofoam won't keep the coffee hot much longer. Come on and eat," she said. As she sat down she added, "Ugh, I think it's a sacrilege to use these grinding bowls for ashtrays," noting the round indentations in the rock, cluttered with butts, where the Cherokee had once milled their corn.

"I think you're as stuffy as your father and that's exactly what I'm going to use them for. That's what the Indians would probably do, if they were alive today. Is that Balantyne Hall?" Ouida asked, pointing to a rooftop that towered over others a great blurry distance away.

"Yes, it must be. If we had binoculars, we could tell for sure."

"Strange," Ouida said, as if whispering to herself. "There's a room there, and this place—my two favorite places on earth! I'm fifty years old, Toots." She sighed. "Fifty Novembers, so many of them spent alone."

A gust of wind swept up the rock. They grabbed at the paper wrappers swirling around them. The wind sent a chill through Justyn. She remembered what she wanted to ask. "Mother, tell me about Stubby."

Ouida sighed and lit a cigarette. "He was a dreadful person. Simply dreadful. He would have brought disgrace to the family, one way or another."

"Dreadful? How?"

She blew a smoke ring and watched it dissipate. "Well, first, his name. It's such a vulgar story, I hate to go into it. It seems the surgeon's knife—it was old Dr. Gettys, who should have been retired—slipped during circumcision. He was left with this . . . well, anyway, it apparently didn't hamper his activity. It just made him offensively self-conscious about . . . *proving* himself. He was bragadoccio, strutty, vulgar. I avoided him. He scared me." She smoked in silence for a while. "But men liked him. Eddie saw too much of him. They'd go off together, and Eddie would come back swaggering, talking dirty. Stubby carried dirty pictures and booklets around with him that the boys would snicker over. You know, the sort of behavior that made you ashamed to be a girl. Stubby called me 'P——,' well, never mind. I wasn't very surprised or sorry when someone did him in. Just that it caused so much tragedy."

"Do you think Thomas's father killed him?"

"Tom? Of course not! He was a *Christian*," she said scornfully. "I don't know. I can think of a dozen people who could have cheerfully done Stubby in. Your father always thought that . . ."

"Yes?"

She coughed and ground out her cigarette. "Enough, Baby. This matter is much too serious for old gossip. I'm getting cold. Are you ready to go?"

"What about Eddie? Would he have inherited if—"

"—Stubby hadn't died? No, probably not. I imagine Stubby would have married and had children. There were plenty of 'proper' young women wanting the Balantyne name, that house. That's another reason I was glad to see Stubby go. Eddie wasn't meant for the workaday world." She stood up and straightened her clothes. "Goodbye, beautiful place." She sighed.

On the drive back to town Justyn asked one more question. "Why did you go to see Hamp Mills?"

"Fool's errand. I thought he might . . . stop the stories. About the lynching. Dragging our names into it. Your father's. But he said he's as distressed as I am. He said that Junior did it all behind his back and it's out of control now."

It was not until they were back in the Gargomedia parking garage and Justyn was waiting for her mother to change shoes that a series of images broke loose and came together in her mind: her mother, inexplicably sober and soft and

69

lucid; the dozens of cigarette butts on the mountain, and only two brands, Ouida's one of them; her mention of rock and room, the sitting room, Justyn imagined; and a man's plaintive whistled rendering of "Brown Eyes," a song that might have been written with the beautiful Ouida Balantyne in mind . . .

"Mother," she said suddenly, "are you in love?"

Ouida looked at her with that startled animal look. "What?" she asked, her eyes flaring wildly. Then she quickly collected herself. "Oh, I love *you*, Baby," she purred.

Justyn arrived home feeling cold and stiff and went quickly into the shower. She stood with a stream of the hottest water she could bear soothing the small of her back, when Frank's voice surprised her.

"Hon?" He slid the stall door open. "I made the Timmons's sale! Decided to take the day off and celebrate. Look, champagne! Called . . . Want me to wash your back?"

"Mmmmm. Mother and I went on a picnic."

"A picnic! Is she tanked?"

"No. Suspiciously sober. It was kind of fun."

"*This* is kind of fun." He leaned in and kissed her neck. "Tell you what. Let me get out of these clothes and I'll join you."

The door slid open and Frank stepped in, carrying their giant brandy snifter brimming with champagne. Handing her the glass, he took the cloth and soap and, turning her slowly away from him, pressed against her back. Wrapping his arms about her as she sipped, he began slowly lathering her, his erection firm against her.

"Never enough time with you these days, hon," he said, nibbling the back of her ear. "Either too late or too tired. Now we've the whole afternoon."

Justyn had never been able to find fault with him as a lover. Now the slow strokes of his delighted, delighting hands, the heat, the water, seemed to melt away the worries of the past few days. Yes, and wasn't it perfect, for shouldn't she be ovulating now?

70

* * *

She woke curled against him on their bed, her face on his shoulder. Already his body odors, the rankness of underarm, were returning. How long? Or had they sweated so? Was that the last of the afternoon sun glazing the window?

"Hon, you awake? I let you sleep. You seemed so content. Come on, let's sit up. There's something I need to tell you." He plumped the pillows against the headboard. The tone of his voice brought her wide awake as she sat up and settled beside him.

"It's about Eddie . . . the town . . . It goes back a way," he said hesitantly. "It may have something to do with the panic he seems to be feeling."

"Yes?"

"You know, my parents being middle-aged when I was born, they never told me anything about sex. When I was twelve or so, I guess I was ripe for information."

Justyn nodded, unsure what to expect.

"I started slipping out at night so I could smoke. I'd meet some boys at the Scout hut. We'd talk about girls, you know. Then this older kid, he said there was something better than girls. He showed us pictures of boys, boys and men. It scared me, I tell you. Do you want me to go on, hon?"

"Yes. Go on."

"He got a couple of the boys to say they'd go with him one night, to a 'meeting.' Well, to make a long story short, that night I hid on the hut grounds and followed them when they left." He took her hand and squeezed it. "I followed them for blocks, keeping to the lawns and ducking behind hedges, until finally they started up this long driveway—"

"Balantyne Hall!"

"Yes."

"Who was living there then?"

"Eddie. Eddie had moved in a few months before. After Stubby was murdered the house stood empty except for Beesie and a gardener to keep the place up, until Eddie was old enough to take over."

A sudden chill set her teeth chattering. She pulled the

71

cover up to her chin. "Go on. What happened?"

"I was crazy with curiosity and scared as hell, too. I slipped along that rim of woods and hid in the little graveyard. Then a light went on, on the third floor, and I ran to the hedges near the front porch. I was going to try and scale the house and look in the window, when headlights turned in the drive."

"Who was it?'

"Chub Castille. Eddie came out to the porch and they talked . . . Such filthy talk, hon. He and Eddie were lovers, there was no doubt about it, but it was what they said about the others, about taking pictures . . . You'd know who the other boys were, if I told you. There's no telling *who* in this town they managed to involve . . ."

Frank had taken the hall phone off the hook before he came into the shower. Now it was dark, and he slept. Justyn replaced the receiver in its cradle. Almost immediately, it rang.

"Mrs. Jones? This is Poe Williams. I met you this morning. *I'm* the one who found the lynching story—Junior Mills stole it from me."

"I see. Now I begin to understand."

"I know so much more. My uncle was involved, you see. I've got to talk to Mr. Levity. Do you know how I can get in touch with him?"

"No. But I'm hoping he'll call."

"Would you give him this number, then?"

The next time the phone rang, it was Thomas.

"I'm at some Tobacco Road motel," he explained. "A flea-bag that Junior found. I've been sleeping off the medication. I can't believe what time it is."

She brought him up to date, told him about Junior's anger with her, and gave him Poe Williams's message. She told him about everything, except what Frank had disclosed about Eddie. *"Be careful,"* she said. "You may be getting in over your head."

"We're all in over our heads." He laughed and hung up.

72

"J USTYN? THOMAS AGAIN. Do you have a moment to talk? Have I called you at a bad time?"

"Yes. No. I've been hoping you'd call. Are you feeling better?"

"Much improved. I met with Poe Williams. His uncle, Dillard Beasley, was one of the Lucky Thirteen. Then he got religion. He's a retired evangelist now, not in good health, but Poe has arranged for me to meet him tomorrow at the dirt track where it happened. Dillard helped bury my father. He'll take me to the grave."

She thought of her own father: his grave. "That will mean a lot to you, to know where he's buried?"

"Yes. It will be the first milestone of this trip. I've rented a car, and moved from the motel. I'm camping out at my parents' old house by the railroad tracks. It looks as if it's been abandoned for years. Poe and I will be leaving here about ten tomorrow, if you'd like to join us. But what I'm calling about—I need to pick up my things. I particularly need the photograph of the lynch mob that's with my papers."

Justyn felt her face flame. "There is no photograph," she said. "Only papers. When Frank and I went to your room, I felt that someone had been there, but nothing seemed missing."

"The photograph was right on top. I had been looking at it. There was so much more detail than in the old clippings—"

"But, how did you get it?"

"Someone sent it to me, anonymously. But, why would someone take it? Who would take it?"

"Pear Plumlee knew where you were staying."

"And no telling who else. It would be easy enough to find out."

"I'm sorry it's gone. I would like to have seen it. It must have held some detail . . . Frank will be home soon. Would you like to come over in a little while? Have a cup of coffee with us?"

"Yes. By the way, your friend Junior is mad at me, too."

"He's not *my* friend!"

"He wants me to sign a contract that this is his exclusive story. Of course it isn't. I understand I have Poe Williams to thank instead."

Frank raised his eyes slowly from the paper. "He's coming *here*?"

"To get his things. Don't be difficult, please."

"You're the one being difficult. Why you persist in being involved in this . . . *charade* . . . I don't know."

Stung, Justyn lashed out with what had been on her mind. "Mother called," she said. "She said there's a chance the Balantynes may be part Negro."

"That's been said about everyone with a suntan since there was a South," Frank said lightly.

"She thinks that's why we don't have children."

Frank folded the paper and looked up at her thoughtfully. "Hon, if it's meant to be, it's meant to be. But sit down, let me tell you what my feelings are. You ask, but you really don't want to know, do you?"

She had no choice now but to sit and listen.

"When I first saw you, your father had been dead—how long?—two or three weeks? Your mother called me to find a house for you. I came to Balantyne Hall to talk to her, nervous, knowing bout Eddie. She was so pretty, and a scandal—your father's suicide was still the freshest gossip in town. And then you came into the room, hon, a little doll, your breasts just budding. I knew I'd wait for you. And I did."

"But—"

"No, wait. Hear me out. You needed me. You always have. I'm stability. You're like your parents. Headstrong. Impetuous. Ready to get involved with something like this lynching mess. I would love a child if we had one. But I'm happy without, that's all. We have problems enough as it is. That may not be very sentimental, but it's true."

74

To her relief the doorbell rang. When she ushered Thomas in, Frank was standing, and shook hands cordially. "I'll get coffee," she said.

"I'll get Mr. Levity's things," Frank offered. "Are you going to be staying in Green Hills for long?"

"As long as it takes."

"To do what?"

"I don't know. But I think I'll know when it's done."

Justyn set the tray on the coffee table and they made small talk for a few minutes. Thomas was just rising to leave, when Tawny started a furious barking beneath the window.

Frank went to the side-porch door and called out to her, but she ran across the yard, still barking.

"There was someone there," he said, returning. "A jogger, maybe."

"Cutting across the yard," Justyn said with more assurance than she felt.

"Who else could it be?" Frank's voice was too sharp.

Early the next morning Justyn drove to Balantyne Hall. When she again saw the kewpie-doll pickup truck—this time backed up to a side door—ladder and sawhorses beside it, it all clicked together. A ruggedly handsome man whistled happily while measuring a piece of lumber. *Brown Eyes.*

She crossed the lawn to see what he was doing. He did not see her approach. "Good morning," she said. Surprise, and something else, flickered in his green eyes. So he knew who she was. And she knew for certain, by the brand of cigarettes protruding from the pocket of his flannel shirt, where he had been.

"I'm Justyn Jones. Eddie Balantyne's niece."

"Buck Stovall here." Though he was ruddy from sun, she thought his face colored.

"Are you going to do the remodeling for my mother's apartment?"

"Yes, ma'am."

"I guess it's a go, then."

"Yes, ma'am, I reckon it is."

75

He had sex appeal, she had to admit that. What would Ouida be but a moth drawn to the flame?

"Jus?" Eddie came tentatively out in thin bedroom slippers, looking like a wizened boy in jeans and pajama jacket, his curly hair uncombed. "I saw you from the upstairs window. What a nice surprise! And Beesie's making stickies this morning. We can have stickies and coffee. You've met Mr. Stovall? Good. We can all have stickies and coffee."

The man seemed about to decline, when his eyes met Justyn's, sparking with indignation. His gaze leveled. "That sounds like an offer not to be refused," he said amiably, picking up some tools from the damp lawn and putting them onto the tailgate of his truck. He followed them into the house as Justyn wondered what Eddie's sudden lapse in his social restrictions meant. Did he know about her mother and this man? She doubted it. Eddie had always been as jealous of Ouida as a suitor.

They sat at one end of the large dining-room table. "Confectioneries and pleasant company," Eddie said. "What more can one ask of breakfast?" He swept his arms at the reach of the banquet-size table. "The president of the Confederacy once sat here," he said grandly, "when he was moving south with Confederate gold at the end of the war."

"I know the story," Stovall said. "I've sat here many times myself. But I thought the gold moved in a separate convoy, forty or fifty miles away."

Score one for Buck, Justyn thought. "When?" she asked.

Eddie was distracted. "When, what, Jus?" he asked.

"When was Mr. Stovall at this table?"

"When this was Stubby Balantyne's house," Buck answered cordially.

Suddenly she felt her heart sink. Only at that moment did the name connect in her mind with the lynch mob. One of the Lucky Thirteen, and she was sitting at table with him. Her mother, in her menopausal rut, was . . ."

Beesie intervened, shuffling in with a heavy silver tray of pastries so warm with the aroma of butter, cinnamon, and sugar it seemed the air itself would melt. "Mercy, what a joy," she said, "having our Justyn here. Won't it be a fine day, now?"

Justyn ate under her supervision, licking her fingers in praise of the stickies, deep-fried puffs she had been serving Balantynes for more than three-quarters of a century. With her chicory-blend coffee, it was a gourmet experience.

Justyn could not help wondering if Beesie knew who Buck Stovall was. If she felt some trepidation at serving a member of the lynch mob, it did not show. But then, wasn't that what life must have always been for her, a conflict of loyalties?

Eddie brought her out of her reverie. "What brings you here so early, Jus?"

"I had some questions to ask, about Mother. But I think I've already figured out the answers." This wasn't exactly true, but to her delight the statement caused Buck Stovall to color. His face burned such a bluish beet red she almost felt sorry for him.

It was not until she was driving home that she realized Eddie had outsmarted her, distracting her from her purpose.

She thought of Thomas. It was still early enough, perhaps, to catch him before he left for his meeting with Dillard Beasley. Justyn knew the emotional impact that finding his father's resting place would have. Perhaps he would need some support, even if unspoken. A little uneasily she drove to Fricatown and turned onto the road that followed the railroad track. Quickly it deteriorated from tar and gravel to dirt to hogpath. She was afraid to risk the ruts, and parked. Only a little farther ahead were a bright blue Volkswagen and a low-slung sports model. Poe Williams's and Thomas's, respectively, she supposed.

She had gone only a little farther before she regretted not changing shoes. Dust and grit scuffed through her open-toe pumps, and briers tore at her hose. She passed a small, crude cross—a pet's grave, perhaps? Surely not a person's. She wondered where Stubby's body had been found. The road, little more than a path now, led right beside the railroad tracks. A field rat scurried at her approach. Determinedly, she walked on.

Now she could see the house clearly. A shack, two or three rooms, a scar where a small front stoop had once been attached. Now there were makeshift steps of concrete blocks. Where the path forked to the house, dry waist-high weeds and junk took over. The backyard sloped toward a creek. Beyond, a scraggly patch of scrub pine settled into the distance. Above this line of trees she could just make out the top of the radio tower of a small abandoned local airport.

"It would have looked quite different when my parents lived here." Thomas spoke quietly from the door, watching her approach. "There would have been paint, trim, flowers. Mama was so *clean*."

"Yes. It's good to see you, Thomas. I hope you don't mind my coming."

"I hoped you might. But I didn't want to pressure you. I knew your husband wouldn't approve."

"Hello!" Poe Williams called enthusiastically, coming from the back of the house. He gleamed with such energetic wholesomeness she thought of a phrase to describe him: aggressively gentle. "Mr. Levity is going to let me cover the 'first-person' side of his story. Now I've got to find someone to print it."

"Try your own paper," she suggested. "I have a feeling that Hamp Mills Senior wouldn't mind undercutting Junior's role in this."

"We were just leaving," Thomas said, coming carefully down the makeshift steps. "I can't believe I'm going to see not only where my father died, but also where he's buried."

It seemed impractical to take all three cars, but perhaps unsafe to leave one there. Poe, the only one who knew where the dirt track was, led the caravan. Justyn was glad he drove slowly, for it gave her a chance to study this Devil's Heel section of Green Hills county. It had been annexed a few decades earlier, when it had "seceded" by petition from the adjacent county to join Green Hills. Now, ironically, this redheaded stepchild, mere cut-over and cottoned-out poor land, had become a powerful industrial base, bringing in more revenue than any other district. Even after Poe

Williams's Volkswagen left the main highway for a second-ary road, the vast stretches of flat land continued to be dotted with the great stacks and buildings of new industry.

At last the racetrack arena loomed into view: a red clay field cleared for parking, a slab-fenced circle, bleachers, a rotting grandstand. Forests of scrub pine stretched beyond. A strange tall man waited for them, standing beside an out-dated gray van covered end to end with crudely painted reli-gious slogans. As she drove closer, Justyn saw that someone had irreverently scrawled "Green Stamps" beneath "Jesus Saves."

"Hello, Uncle Dill," Poe greeted him, introducing them. As Justyn shook the man's hand, she hoped she concealed her amazement. He was wild-haired, wild-eyed with a strange evangelical light that reminded her of Thomas's prophet figure, as if his poem had sprung to life. It seemed fitting that a dustdevil churned around him as he led them to the center of the track. When he spoke, his voice was high and whining as the wind that railed round him.

"Here's where we hung him, Good Lord forgive," he said.

"The chainfall. Is it the same? Where did it come from?" Thomas spoke in a level voice.

"It was always here. The boys who raced came here to work on their cars."

"Who took the picture? All thirteen of you were in it, so someone else had to take it."

The question seemed to unnerve him. The fire in the evangelist's eyes faded. He blinked rapidly, but said nothing.

Poe spoke into the strained silence that followed. "Let's get on to the grave. I promised my aunt I wouldn't keep him long. He has a bad heart. He probably shouldn't be out here at all."

They followed the diminished Beasley single file along a little-used brier path into the pine woods adjoining the track.

"We're almost there," Dillard said when they passed an old foundation, the ruins of a chimney still standing. Be-yond, in the shadows of a leaning barn, Justyn thought she saw something move. The place gave her the shivers. "It's

79

here, beside the rock wall." With his nephew's help, Beasley stepped over a low stone wall, the type the early settlers built to keep wild hogs out of their gardens. "No! Well, I never! Son," he said, turning to Thomas, "I'm sorry!"

They all scrambled to his side. Before him yawned a shallow grave.

"Who would dig him up?" Dillard Beasley asked, dumbfounded. "Who but the Lord would take him? An empty grave signifies Christ's triumph!"

Thomas and Justyn looked at each other with the answer in their eyes . . . someone who had something to hide.

"Sam Morrow and I buried that poor Negro with hatred and contempt in our hearts," Dillard said softly, as if to himself. "We pushed the clay in on him and then I stayed to tamp the earth and hide it with leaf mulch. It had turned daylight on us. That terrible blood moon was gone. I saw instead a wonderful white light, and a spirit rose, white as a dove, right out of this grave and past me. It brushed my cheek. It touched me. But the grave was whole. It wasn't disturbed. It wasn't the body that rose, but the spirit."

"Uncle Dill, let's go now," Poe said gently.

"I'm sorry, son," Beasley said again, turning to Thomas, "I don't know what they've done with him. I don't know who took him. Sam Morrow's been gone a long time. This is recent."

"Come on, Uncle Dill."

"No. You children start back. Give me a few minutes alone. I need to say my prayers here."

They left him and walked on, back past the house ruins through the woods until they could see the light from the track clearing. Then they stopped and talked quietly among themselves, wondering who, why.

"I'll go back and get Uncle Dill," Poe said finally. "He's had enough time now."

Thomas and Justyn watched him retrace his steps energetically. Then, they heard his frantic shouting.

"Uncle Dillard's dead! Uncle Dillard's dead!" Poe screamed as they ran toward him.

10

DILLARD BEASLEY LAY FACE up, arms askew, in the grave he had once dug for Tom Levity. He did not look as if he had seen his maker in that last moment, but rather Satan. The one-time evangelist wore the open-eyed horror of one who had been frightened to death.

"How will I tell my aunt?" Poe Williams wailed. "She didn't want me to bring him here. She warned me his heart might give out!"

"Perhaps it wasn't just his heart," Justyn suggested. "Someone might have surprised him. Someone might have pushed him in."

Thomas said nothing. Poe continued as if he hadn't heard. "I've got to call my aunt. I've got to call the police or coroner or whoever one reports a death to. Will you two stay with him? I don't want to leave him here alone. But . . . should we involve you in this, Mrs. Jones? No one really needs to know you were here."

"I'll stay with Thomas for a few minutes, then leave," she offered, relieved to be spared explanations.

They watched Poe hurry away, then stood staring at the body. Justyn was chilled by the dead man's expression. She had never seen a corpse. Thomas, she imagined, must have seen more than his share during the war. Now he looked as if his mind might be far away.

"I may have seen someone in that abandoned shed when we first came," he said, after a moment. "Or it may have been my imagination, or the light. But I thought I saw something move. Could anyone have known we were here?" When he turned to her he was frowning deeply. "Someone could have followed any one of us," he said. "Poe could have mentioned it, or his aunt. We didn't try to make it a secret. But do you really believe someone might have done something to bring this on?"

"If the grave hadn't been empty, no. It probably wouldn't occur to me. But someone obviously has something to lose in this. Something to hide. Too much is happening—the assault on you, the missing photograph, the man outside my house, and now Dillard Beasley's death. He might have told you something, Thomas, something vital. Perhaps that was why he wanted to be alone for a few minutes, to think about what else might be in his conscience or memory that you should know. And I saw something or someone, too. I thought it was my imagination."

"Well, we won't find out now. You had better get going before Poe comes back with the authorities. It *is* better that you not be involved in this, Justyn. Do you need me to walk back out with you?"

"No. Stay with Dillard. If someone was here, they accomplished their purpose. Besides, if I run into any trouble, I'll take my mother's advice . . ." She told him about Ouida's comments as they had hiked up to Devil's Rock, leaving him smiling in his grim vigil.

Frank and Justyn dressed for the party. "I'd rather not go," he said, "but I'll lose business if I don't."

Justyn slipped on a hand-me-down winter-white cocktail dress and matching shoes her mother had grown tired of. Her feet felt pinched. "I don't mind going, as long as we come home early."

"We will. Don't you worry, hon. I want to put my feet up and drink a beer and relax. But this virus that's going through the office has taken its toll. If I don't go, our firm will be woefully outnumbered. Gosh, hon, you look lovely, like an angel," he said, fastening a strand of pearls for her.

The country club sparkled with light. The party, an annual recognition of area realtors sponsored by the Green Hills Chamber of Commerce, brought old and new guard together. Justyn saw that many of the names connected with the lynching were there: Wade Hampton Mills, Sr., and his wife; Junior, bulging in last year's tuxedo, keeping his distance from them; Judge Jonathon Mabry with his notorious wife, Ivey, creating a stir by this rare appearance together at a social function; Chub Castille, the lovely Monica clinging to his arm. But it was her mother, Ouida Balantyne Orms, who turned the most heads when she arrived, radiant in black velvet, on the arm of a crudely handsome man whom the most wide-ranging gossip finally identified as the infamous skirt-chaser Buck Stovall. Eddie followed in their shadow, looking very ill at ease.

"What in the hell is your mother trying to do?" Frank asked.

"Degrade my father's memory. Say 'screw you' to the whole town," Justyn said bitterly. The odd trio made no move to approach them. One of Frank's business partners waved him aside. Justyn took a champagne cocktail from a tray and stood uneasily drinking alone. Her head buzzed.

Frank and his partner returned, both looking sheepish. "I'm asking your husband for a big favor," the man said. "I think I'm coming down with whatever virus is going around the office. I need to go home while I can still drive—but I'm booked for the midnight flight to Atlanta. It's an important meeting. I'm asking Frank to take my place."

Frank looked at her with raised eyebrows. "Do you mind, hon?"

She knew it was petty to mind, though she did. "No, of course not." She managed to smile. Couldn't he realize how agitated she was at the sight of Buck Stovall and her mother? That she needed him?

"Thanks, hon." He leaned down and kissed her cheek. "Would you mind staying a little longer, do some circulating for me? Jack can drive me home to pack, then on to the airport."

Justyn reminded herself that Frank's evening promised to be much more trying than hers, though there were few things she disliked more than small talk. Yet a friendly word and a smile could result in a listing for Frank and, eventually, a sale. Sighing, she moved out into the crowd, deciding to view the evening as a study in human nature. But as she saw

Frank's back disappearing out the door, she felt a moment of panic. She wanted to call him back or, better yet, grab her coat and go with him.

Junior approached tentatively. "Good crowd," he said.

"No blacks. No Jews. Looks like the same old crowd to me," she said sardonically.

He smiled. "Well, your mother brought a token redneck. Too bad you didn't bring your boyfriend. He could be our token—"

She tossed what champagne was left in her glass in his face and walked away. Afraid he might follow, she headed toward his father, aware of the judicious distance they kept between them. But Justyn no sooner sat down on the sofa beside Wade Hampton Mills, Sr., than Ivey Mabry sat down on his other side. Judge Mabry quickly followed to loom over her, jealousy lighting his damaged eyes.

"Ivey, dear, it's time to go home."

"No," she said petulantly.

"Yes. *Now*," he ordered.

Ivey Mabry uttered a shocking obscenity, yawned, then stood up and stretched in a movement pointedly erotic, her silk-swathed buttocks not six inches from Wade Mills's face as she flexed her rippling thighs, arched her back, and lifted her arms so languidly her braless breasts rose and fell within his hands' reach. He pretended not to notice, but Justyn saw his erection before he shifted on the sofa away from her. It almost seemed as if the only thing preventing Ivey from springing onto Wade Mills's crotch was the judge's ravaged arm, somehow strong as a stanchion. Finally, Chub Castille danced up to Ivey and, letting go his own wife, took Ivey from the judge's arm and went swinging her round the room in so mad a polka everyone laughed.

I won't stay here another second. I don't give a damn about Frank's real estate, Justyn decided, when her mother and Buck Stovall next took to the dance floor, embracing as the orchestra slowed the music. But, once outside and in her car, she did not want to go home to an empty house, either. She felt balanced on the edge of depression. What could she do?

She thought of visiting Thomas at the house by the railroad tracks. They still had had no opportunity to talk alone, and she especially wanted to hear his thoughts on Dillard Beasley's death, now that he had had some time for them. If only she weren't afraid of driving through Fricatown at night . . . Then she remembered sighting the old airport tower when she had walked along the tracks that morning. She knew a railroad spur ended there. Couldn't she park there and backtrack to the main line, and the house?

She had only a penlight in the car, but that was enough. The moon was waxing and bright. Though it was a little frightening walking alone, she could imagine no one but Thomas in so isolated a place. She shivered as the cold cut through her thin evening coat, and her feet were pinched in Ouida's evening shoes. She realized she must look a little like a ghost, all white on such a night. Her flesh glowed green. She shivered.

When finally she reached the house she stopped at the edge of the yard and called Thomas's name. A faint light glowed from cracks between blankets stretched across windows. She thought she heard sound from within. "*Thomas?*"

"Justyn? It *is* you! I thought I was imagining your voice." He came to the door and gave her a hand as she teetered on her mother's high heels up the teetering concrete blocks serving as steps. "What time is it?" he asked.

"Close to midnight."

"I must have dozed. I drank a little too much. I swear, after seeing that empty hole, after thinking I could pay my respects at my father's grave . . . and then to have Dillard Beasley . . ." He pressed his eyes as if trying to rub the memories away. A kerosene lamp burned by the door, another inside. "You look pretty," he said when she stepped into the light.

"I've been to a party."

The wick of the second lamp smoked wildly. He adjusted it. "I'm glad you came," he said. "To tell you the truth, I was getting lonely. Could I offer you something to eat? Or drink? I've got sandwiches, moon pies, wine . . ."

"Wine, yes," she said, balancing to remove her uncomfortable shoes. He handed her a paper cup of white wine. "Let's sit on the front stoop in the moonlight," she suggested. "I think it's warmer outside than in here."

They laughed as they sat down—the step was so narrow there was hardly room for both. "It's lovely here at night," she said. "It must have been lovely for them, too."

"Yes. I feel very close to my parents here."

They talked easily for a while, their conversation ranging.

"Thomas," she said hesitantly, "there are some things I don't understand. Where did you get the clipping about the falconer that I saw among your things?"

"It was sent to me. I think by a troubled mind."

"Daring you to find out?"

"Or needing—wanting—me to find out."

She was silent for a moment. "When I first saw you on the plane, you looked as if you recognized me."

"No. There was something familiar. I think it was your expression, a likeness to your father. I had been looking at clippings of the trial when I was in Washington."

"Just what is your relationship with Junior? Did he bring you here?"

"No, he wrote and told me he was interested in updating my father's story, and would I be available for an interview. I had already determined to come to Green Hills. He was the connection I needed."

"One more thing: Judge Mabry. Was there anything in your conversation that I should know about?"

"Nothing substantial. I feel that he knows a lot and is telling little. He wants me to leave this alone as much as anyone. But I believe he feels that my father was wronged."

"Do you know about the Orangeburg Massacre?" Justyn asked.

"The what?"

"Most people don't. Kent State got all the press. But in 1968 three college students were killed and several badly wounded in our downstate town of Orangeburg. By state highway patrolmen. The students were on campus, un-armed."

"And black."

"Of course. There's a book about it, by Jack Nelson and Jack Bass. The point is, I prided myself on how well I re-searched it for the study, never dreaming I'd overlooked a hometown lynching entirely! I should have gone to the Na-tional Archives, not put all my trust in local and state sources."

"Don't be so hard on yourself. Even Junior thinks you did a fine job on the study, considering. Judge Mabry said you take after your father in that respect."

She was touched. "Perhaps I get some of my egalitarianism from the Balantyne side, too," she admitted. "I ran across some puzzling things in my research. In the South Carolin-ian Library I read about a Green Hills house that was part of the Underground Railroad. From the description, I think it had to be Balantyne Hall. And the reason our town was spared Sherman's march was because there were so many Union sympathizers here—and, at one time, a small muni-tions factory. To hear it now, everyone was always pro-slavery and secessionist, but that's not true."

"You should write history."

"I might, someday. I want to write something *pertinent*. You're lucky. You can turn complexities into poetry."

"No. Nothing I've done that's related to this has turned out well. At least, not yet."

"Oh, my God!" Justyn said suddenly. "It never occurred to me—Frank will probably call when he gets to his hotel! I've got to get home."

They bumped into each other as they rose in the narrow door frame, spilling wine and laughing.

"I mustn't forget I brought you a present," she said. "Here."

Thomas opened the small envelope and removed his rings. Immediately they rang like chimes. "You had them repaired for me," he said wonderingly. He tried to put them on, but his hands were still swollen. "Maybe in a day or two." He smiled, slipping them into his pocket. "Justyn, I can't thank you enough. What a nice thing to do for me."

She leaned inside to retrieve her shoes when Thomas grabbed her hand and held his finger to his mouth for silence. She froze. A car was approaching at great speed where none should be, roaring and plowing over ruts and garbage along the railroad tracks.

"Out the back," he hissed, pulling her along through the house, blowing out the lanterns as he ran. Headlights cut across the yard as they bolted across the rough ground, a sound like pelting rain hitting around them.

"My God, Justyn, they're shooting at us!"

When Justyn's tender bare feet hit the ground her knees buckled. Thomas grabbed her by the waist and hoisted her along, stumbling downhill toward the small creek they could hear now. "That dress, they can see you for miles." He set her down and ran back, tearing an army blanket from a back window. With one swift turn he wrapped her in it and propelled her downhill, shot still showering around them. By chance they stumbled into a cavity behind a large tree trunk. "We'll stay here," he whispered close in her ear. "Don't move. Don't breathe. Our lives depend on it!"

They lay surrounded by waist-high broomstraw, heart against racing heart. "I hear voices."

"Shhh." Thomas pressed his hand over her mouth.

They were close. Almost on top of them.

"Where'd that black bastard get to?"

"Should we try the woods?"

"No. If he got that far, he's still running."

"Some kinda luck that nigger has."

"We'll get him next time. Let's go."

Footsteps retreated. Car doors slammed. A car backed up and drove away. Justyn started to get up.

"Shhh!" Thomas clamped his arm around her, his breath against her ear. Five minutes passed before someone moved, mere yards away.

"Damn. I guess he really did get away," a muffled but

somehow familiar voice said. "Let's call it a night." A powerful flashlight cut across the darkness over their heads. The car returned. Doors slammed. They listened until the sound of the engine had completely disappeared.

"They're gone," Thomas said. "We might have been killed, Justyn." He had fallen across her, and they were somehow entangled in the blanket together. She was so cramped she moaned when she tried to move her arms, feeling only a dull tingle. He shifted to help her, his hand inadvertently brushing her breast. For a moment they both lay quite still, trembling. She moved to push away from him, but her body would not obey her command. Instead her legs parted slowly as his knee pressed between them. If he was still attempting restraint, her small bare foot against his ankle, her skin glowing like quicksilver in the moonlight, undid him.

And like quicksilver her tongue moved against his, a liquid heat. His hand found her breast again, the nipple hard as a little acorn beneath her dress. He pulled her skirt up roughly as they rolled a half-turn down the hill. The moon struck her eyes, reflecting their perfect crystalline gray. Then her small hands tangled in his hair and held.

Part II

▽

The Avenger

11

THEY BRUSHED THEMSELVES OFF and shivered. Here they had no choice but to go their separate ways. Thomas watched Justyn's white figure glide across abandoned back fields, waited to hear the sound of her car engine rolling back to him across the now empty night. It was cold, and would grow even colder toward dawn. Where could he go? The riddled house was unsafe, as was his rented car. Sighing, he wrapped the blanket about his shoulders and struck out in the opposite direction, toward Fricatown.

At first he stayed to the lane that ran behind abandoned buildings along the railroad tracks, the ramshackle Pear's Place among them, but when he reached the dark main road it was so deserted he stepped out and walked along it openly. Occasionally a dog ran yapping at his heels or snarled at him from the darkness, but there was no sign of human life. Once, he thought he heard music, but when he stopped to listen it seemed to be merely the wind. Then, as the buildings became scattered, the sound came again, pulsing faintly, a heartbeat, a Billie Holiday old-fashioned torch song. He stopped, licked his finger, held it to the wind, then struck off across the field to his right, toward it. He stumbled once over a strand of barbed wire fence not visible in the moonlight, ripping his pants and gashing his legs, but continued, drawn by the familiar music. At last he plunged through clumps of overgrown shrubbery to the edge of a wide yard. The front porch of the small, unpainted house at its center was brightly lit, and from somewhere within, the sweet, sexy music sounded. No dogs barked at him, but cats seemed to run in every direction. He crouched within the shelter of the hedges, wondering what to do, when he saw headlights bouncing along a winding route from the road. Slipping further back into the shadows, he watched a sagging Oldsmobile pull to within a few feet of the porch. The man who got out and bounded up the steps was big but lithe with a hungry, animal-like spring to his step. In a few minutes he came back out of the house, stopping under the light to zip his pants and rearrange his genitals, his body gone slack as he descended into the darkness. Somewhere within the house a baby cried, then another. Thomas waited until the headlights disappeared. He was about to rise when he heard something approaching through the hedges. Two young children stepped into the moonlight not yards from where he squatted, from a path he had not seen. They ran up the porch and knocked on the door, shouting to make themselves heard. Someone turned off the music. When the children spoke now, he could hear their sharp, crisp voices distinctly.

"Miz Bones, our papa real sick in the stomach again. You got something for him?"

They stood patiently waiting under the light. In a few minutes a tall thin woman stepped out the door and bent down to them. She glowed like a great bird in a red caftan, the flowing sleeves her wings.

"You give these powder to him, you hear?" she said. Her voice, musical but restrained, suited her frame. "You tell him eat nothin' but mush-n-milk until these powder be gone. One dolla, please."

Following the exchange, the children ran down the steps, across the yard and past him, giggling.

"Did you see her earrings?"

"Yes! Little Jesuses, weren't they?"

Thomas's legs ached terribly, but he dared not move. The woman stood, her tall head cocked to one side like a listening bird. A sudden breeze stirred a dozen sets of wind chimes clattering around her. "Who's out there?" she called. "I know you're there! Who are you?" She no longer spoke in patois.

"You don't know me," Thomas shouted, groaning as he stood. "I'm Thomas More Levity. My parents used to live over by the railroad tracks. I was there a while ago when someone shot at me. I guess I'm looking for a place to hide."

"I heard the shooting. Everyone in Fricatown heard the

shooting. That's why the place is closed up tight. And I've heard of you. Well, I'm glad they didn't get you. Come on up here under the light, where I can look at you."

Thomas walked slowly across the yard and up the steps. A curious odor grew stronger as he approached her. Chicken? Yes, she reeked of stale fried chicken. At close range he saw grease stains on her hands and her red caftan. She was tall as he, an imposing figure. But he could not help shuddering when he saw how her features were marred by knife scars that ran across her face like irregular molehills. "Miz Bones," he said, "I—"

"*You* call me Paralee," she said. "I wanted to meet you. Maybe I willed you here. You can stay here." She stepped back into the house, beckoning him to follow. A lamp burned in the tiny front room. The ceiling hung so low it barely cleared their heads. Children, from wailing twins not more than a month or two old, to toddlers and school age, lay sleeping on the sagging overstuffed sofa and chairs, pillows propped against them to keep them from rolling off. Thomas was distracted from trying to count heads by dodging the wind chimes and mobiles that hung everywhere around him.

"Don't worry, these babies ain't all mine," Paralee said, looking back at him. "Just those two on the sofa, they are," she said proudly. "My boy's asleep in the other room, and I got grown ones. These others I take in."

They passed into the kitchen, a slightly more spacious room. Here not an inch was undefiled by grease. Walls, ceiling, floor, furniture . . . the odor was overwhelming. A barrel of chicken scraps waited to be stripped into buckets of meat and buckets of bones. A wood cookstove in the corner added to the oppressive heat and smell. Trays of bones dried on the oven and warmer-oven doors.

"It's a living," she said, noting his revulsion. "It keeps us away from Detroit."

"You're from Detroit?"

"Jesus, no! I was born on Dafuskie Island. You read books? White fella write a book about us."

"Of course. *The Water Is Wide.*"

95

"We didn't know it was Dafuskie then. Home didn't need a name. You wouldn't know. You not down-home fella, for sure," she said, smiling as if mocking her own occasional low-country patois.

"No," Thomas admitted. "I was raised in a mostly white neighborhood in California. I didn't see much of *my* people."

"I never even see white fella until I four year old," Paralee countered softly. "We be island folk. My papa fish. Then one day Papa boat float home, capsize. After a while Mama load us up, all our things in two sacks. Five boys and me, we help. Hitch ride on boat to Charleston. Mama hear of Detroit, we got cousins there. White fella offer us ride in back of truck. We get to Detroit I don't know how, him stopping and taking Mama off into woods. He leave us at Detroit. Mama sit down on corner and cry, she forget our cousins' name." Paralee sighed—a long, mournful sound—and then laughed, dropping all remnants of her island speech. "You know, I don't remember another thing until I started school. I started out good in school, until I got so tall they laughed at me." Her eyes flashed. "They sent me to a head doctor. He said I did mean things because I was several people—the island child, the street child, the wild child, the too-tall child . . . I told *him* my papa was a blue-gum nigger and that *his* granny taught me juju. I said I was casting a spell on him, and I made a little doll and wore it to our meetings and stuck pins in it. He had a heart attack and died, me sitting there in his office. I quit school and set up a juju stand. I been doing juju, hoodoo, voodoo ever since."

"Why did you come back?"

"Back? I'm on my way back. I want to go back to the island. Hear that water plashing. Die an old woman there, salt in my hair, like my grannies. But, now . . . my children, I couldn't feed them there. My man, Monk, he wouldn't leave here. You see him? He come once a week, maybe. He got drunk, cut me and our boy up, now he don't stay here."

Her shifting speech confused Thomas. A rooster crowed in the yard. "I'm very tired," he said.

"You can have my bed."

He thought of the reek of grease. "No. Let me have a mat and a corner somewhere. I don't want to inconvenience you."

She looked thoughtful. "There's an old rolled-up rug. You could sleep out there, on the back porch. None of my visitors goes out back." Absentmindedly she picked up a ragged wishbone and began stripping it. Catching herself, she explained, "My children go through the garbage at the fried-chicken restaurants. On a good Sunday they get enough to keep me in bones for a week. I use the bones in my crafts and sell the meat to the neighbors for dog food."

Thomas could not stifle a yawn. "The rug?" he asked.

She wiped her hands on the caftan and disappeared into the only other room. In a moment she returned, carrying a roll of carpet on her broad shoulder, her muscles bulging like a man's. "I hope it isn't filled with fleas," she said. When she stepped onto the back porch she pulled a string and light swept incredible clutter. She pushed some aside with her foot until there was sleeping-sized space for the folded rug.

Thomas took the blanket from his shoulders and spread it while Paralee went in search of more bedding. In a moment she returned with ragged quilts and a pillow. Mercifully they did not smell of chicken. He lay down and was already drifting into sleep as she kneeled and tucked the covers more solidly around him.

"There's an outhouse out there," she said, pointing toward the eastern edge of the yard, which was just beginning to lighten, "or just pee off the porch."

He dreamed of his mother's hands, her lovely quilts, Naja. He had not slept so deeply or long since leaving California. But when he awoke it was to a white woman's voice drifting out to him through the cracked kitchen window.

"Oh, Mrs. Bones, these will do beautifully! You've outdone yourself!"

Thomas raised up and peered in. A well-dressed woman held a bone necklace to her blazered front. The jewelry was made Egyptian-style in honor of the current Tutankhamen craze.

"Let's see, now . . . at five dollars each, for a dozen, I owe you sixty dollars? All right, then, I've seventy in our budget—how much are the chimes? Good, let me have two chimes also—they'll make such *lovely* door prizes."

Thomas lay back, smiling. What an entrepreneur, this Miz Bones! He suspected the large pockets of her caftan were as full of incredible ware as a Fuller Brush man's kit or a tinker's wagon. Then he grimaced. His bladder was long overdue release. If only the woman would take her purchases and leave! Trying not to make any noise, he slipped out of his makeshift bed and padded barefoot across the afternoon yard to the outhouse. From there he heard the woman's good-byes, her car leaving. When he went back to the house Paralee again sat at the kitchen table, stripping bones. A mug of coffee and a cigarette were beside her.

"Don't you ever sleep?" he asked.

"A little, in the evenings," she said quietly, then called, "Children! You can make noise now. He's awake!" Immediate babble started up from the rooms and yard. "I don't trust sleep," she went on quietly. "You know, when you have the gift, as I do, sleep is when the others can get back at you. When I go to sleep I hear them trying to get in."

Thomas's stomach growled loudly.

"There's bacon and eggs, if you want to cook. I haven't got time. Or you can walk down to the road, turn left, and go to the cafe a half block down."

The idea of fresh air, of getting away from the pervasive reek of stale chicken, won. "I could use the exercise," he said. "Can I bring you something?"

"No. No, I'll cook again in a little while. The children will be needing supper."

By day the cleanly swept yard appeared bright and wide. It must have seemed a vast enough playground to the dozen or so children who played on the shinily painted swings and jungle gym. Thomas watched them with enjoyment as he walked in tire tracks and weeds toward the distant road. When he saw an automobile approaching in the lane he thought of changing course, then realized that would attract attention. Instead, he kept his eyes on the ground as he had seen other black people do. The car, a long, low-slung gray limousine, crept past as he stepped aside. He breathed more easily until it backed up to him in a choking swirl of dust.

"Thomas! Thomas! Is that you?" The voice from the backseat was muffled. Thomas strained to see, through the tinted glass, who it was being chauffeured to Paralee's. To his surprise, he recognized Pear Plumlee. The man opened the window the rest of the way and reached out to shake Thomas's hand. "But, what on earth are you doing here?" he asked, laughing abruptly. "No, don't tell me. Paralee never turns away a stray."

Though Pear smiled charmingly, it was as if a skeletal finger tapped Thomas on the shoulder warningly. What meant the metamorphosis, poor man to rich? "I might ask the same of you," Thomas said quietly.

"I beg your pardon?"

"What you're doing here."

Pear's laughter increased decibels. "Didn't she tell you?" he asked. "No, she wouldn't. Paralee is my sister. My *half* sister," he corrected himself, his staccato fox laugh ricocheting out the window as he waved the driver on.

$\triangledown$

12

So LITTLE SEEMED NEW in Fricatown, Thomas wondered
if his parents might have walked the same dusty shoulders
that served as sidewalks, past the peeling White Rose service
station and cluster of roadside shacks to the Liberia Cafe,
the sign promising "Home-Cooked Food" seeming as old as
the building. Behind the greasy glass were a few booths with
sagging, rump-sprung seats, unmatched tables and chairs,
and a counter with a half-dozen wobbly stools. A large
honey-colored man with a dish towel tucked into his pants
appeared from the kitchen.

"What for you?"

"Could I get breakfast at this hour?"

"If you don't mind potluck," the man said affably, busying
himself at the grill behind the counter. Ten minutes later he
placed a platter of fat-back, sawmill gravy, fried eggs, and
biscuits before him. Thomas ate with relish, enjoying especially the strong, chicory-flavored coffee. He had regretfully
declined second helpings when Pear Plumlee appeared.

"I thought I'd join you," he said, sitting down opposite
and placing his expensive gray hat on the next chair. "Fran-
cis," he called. "Coffee. And what's the cobbler *du jour?*
Peach? Fine. A good-sized bowl." He nodded. "My business
with Paralee didn't take long. You still look surprised. Yes,
we're quite different, but in some ways much the same.
Despite what you may think of her, Paralee is nobody's fool.
Our fathers may have been a world apart, but we sure had
the same mother. My daddy was white, Paralee's was black,
from the island, and tall."

"She's a tall lady, all right."

"I'm glad you said lady." Pear smiled. "It's not that I think
you'd take advantage of her. It's that I need your help to
protect her."

"How's that?"

"There's a man hanging around, someone who brings her grief. She keeps an itch for him. But she doesn't need any more grief or any more scars, and he'll give her both. Sooner or later, he'll kill her. But as long as he thinks you're keeping an eye on her for me, he'll stay away."

Monk. The man he had seen last night. "What makes you think he won't kill *me*?"

"I'm all that stands between him and jail." Pear smiled, finishing the cobbler and waving for more coffee. Through the dim window his chauffeured limousine gleamed incongruously. "Well, you've been wanting to talk with me, Thomas."

"Yes." He wished he could feel at ease. "You and my father were friends?"

"Yes, I considered Tom my friend."

"Do you have any idea what really happened?"

"Yes."

Thomas's heart seemed to skip a beat. He waited.

Pear did not look him in the eye. "There's more than a generation between your time and mine, son, just as there's more than a generation between my time and slavery. Don't be misled by your father's calling himself a preacher. He wasn't holier-than-thou or fire-and-brimstone. He was just a prophet, ahead of his time in his dreams for us. He never attracted much of a congregation. He was always scrabbling. Only a few blacks thought he wasn't crazy, and even fewer whites. Zach Orms thought things could be changed. And there was a self-declared Communist, I forget his name. The others—the first time I saw your daddy flare up, I knew that sooner or later they'd kill him. He wouldn't accept his 'place.' I was surprised he lasted as long as he did."

Little spasms of pain had been crossing Pear's face, but now he grimaced. "Your mother," he continued with effort, "was a very comely woman. Stubby Balantyne liked our honey, our molasses, our brown sugar . . . especially *light* brown sugar, like your mother. A lot of us believe she killed him."

Thomas stared.

"It made sense, son. The blood in the house. It probably happened while your father was out making rounds in the cab. Stubby got him to let him out at my place, then walked on to Tom's. She grabbed a butcher knife, and more power to her. Tom came home, got her to go somewhere safe, fixed Stubby so it would look like the train cut off his head instead. Might have worked, but for some kids out where and when they shouldn't have been. I'm sorry, son, but you asked."

Thomas nodded.

"I've got to go. I'm running late. Is there anything else?"

"Dillard Beasley, the man who buried my father, died yesterday. Can you think of any reason someone might want him dead?"

Pear's eyes widened, flared. "Now, why would anyone want that?" he asked, meeting Thomas's gaze solidly.

Thomas shrugged. He smiled, remembering his mother's voice, how easily she assumed the dialect when once she read the stories of Br'er Rabbit to him. How wily and convincing the clever fox had been.

Thomas stepped out into the twilight air and breathed deeply. How nostalgic was the autumn. Maude. Mama. The woman in California with her neat, middle-class bungalow and pristine uniform was once the dusky, sensuous Maude who lived with volatile Tom Levity. "Lived with." He was aware that no one who spoke of Maude and Tom had referred to them as married. Perhaps that was to be expected, in the context of the times, but it hurt him to think it might be so. Perhaps *that* was why there was no "Junior" after his name. He knew so little about his parents. Did not even know his mother's maiden name—had not thought to ask until it was too late, when he was confronted with filling out her death certificate.

Slowly, dejectedly he followed the darkening route back to Paralee's. His mother had brought him up with evening readings from the powerful King James Bible. He knew intimately those tales of tangible sin, guilt, and treachery, and something of their weight had stayed with him as other aspects of his religion drifted away. Now he felt that weight dragging at him, ball and chain. What was his errand, but a fool's? He had left the woman he loved and a good job, taken his modest inheritance to come to a place where no one wanted him, had set tranquil lives adrift, merely to find out a "truth" that might be more painfully shameful than anything he had encountered in his unassuming life. Memories, thoughts overwhelmed him. Down the road he saw a general store. There was no need to return to Paralee's so soon. Instead he determined to purchase pad and pen, find a quiet place, and collect his unsettling thoughts on paper.

When Paralee saw the look on his face she left him alone, with the merest nod as greeting. He sat darkly away from her, watching her strip meat from bone. Finally he rose, sighing so heavily it sounded like a moan, and went out and lay down on his mat. Though the moon had not yet risen, its light was already cast from beyond the horizon. He rested on his elbow, watching shadows move across the yard. Some dogs wandered through and for a moment sniffed hungrily at the screen. When they were gone, a cat jumped down from its hiding place in a chinaberry tree by the back door. A line of children skipped to the outhouse, giggling, holding hands. It would seat three of them at a time. He smiled. His students had no such space to wander in, no safety in moonlight. For most, it was down a dark hall to a stinking urinal, danger lurking beyond the burned-out, busted bulbs. Perhaps he should simply go home to them, to Naja, now, while something could still be salvaged of his illusions . . .

And yet, already the word *home* did not conjure the house in California, but something of this essence, of Green Hills: of the reek of chicken, the spicy fields, the night-rich air, rural in nature, primitive in promise . . .

If Naja knew, she might come on the next plane and fetch him bodily back to her world, their world . . .

"Did you know"—Paralee's singsong voice floated out to him—"that during slavery, sympathetic whites tied bits of string near their doors, as a sign of sanctuary?"

"Are you talking to me?" he asked quietly.

"Yes."

"No, I didn't know that," he answered from the darkness.

"Little signs, small signs, can be important. They are designed to be missed, you see. I learned that from the Gypsies. A family of them came through a few years ago. The law was after them, they had to move fast. But one of them was sick, and they left him here with me. When he got well and ready to move on, I asked him how he would find them. By the rag-signs they left, he said—small strips of cloth tied onto road signs or tree limbs, up high if they could stand on the bumpers or hoods of their cars, out of the reach or notice of passersby. Just as they did in old times, by standing on the tops of wagons or their horses' backs. Leaving messages that were just for the Gypsy's eye."

"Paralee, what are you trying to tell me?"

The children's voices drifted in from the yard like echoes. When finally Paralee spoke, her voice was very close to the screen between them. "Listen to me," she said. "What you're trying to unravel is not tied together in one long piece. It's bits of string, hanks of cloth. You keep charging around looking for people to come to you, telling you how it was, and you'll end up fooled or dead for sure. *Bits of string*," she said forcefully.

He dreamed of red string and woke with the nucleus of a poem forming in his mind. Red string, Gypsy traces, a bloody hank pulled through the assenting flesh of blood brothers, or bride and groom of an Apache wedding. Words tumbled through his thoughts like rocks in the polishing—though again it was voices from the kitchen that wakened him.

"Oh, but she is the prettiest little thing I've ever seen!" a woman said joyfully. Thomas sat up and peered through the window. A middle-aged black couple sat facing Paralee under the light. Paralee bounced one of the toddlers, freshly dressed, on her lap. The little girl looked resplendent with shining pink ribbons tied in her hair.

"Yes. Yes. She is the one all right, are we agreed?" the man asked breathlessly, turning to his wife. "Are we agreed? Is this the one?"

The woman reached out her arms in affirmation. Paralee handed the child to her.

"Lord! Lord!" the woman cried. Turning to her husband, she tried to say something, but her lips worked soundlessly.

Paralee clapped her hands. "Ain't nothing prettier than a new mother and her baby," she crooned.

"We can't thank you enough," the man said huskily. "We've waited so long."

"Seeing that baby with a good home . . ." Paralee clapped her hands in joy again.

"Here's the money," the woman said, reaching deep into her cleavage.

Paralee counted the warm, moist bills carefully. Her smile appeared askew in the light, distorted as it was by scars. "That child has seen a few bad times, despite she so young," she said. "You treat her right, you hear?"

"She'll be treated like a princess," the man said, leaning over to bury his lips in his wife's hair, and then in his new daughter's.

"Are you a one-woman adoption agency?" Thomas asked from the doorway, when the couple was gone.

Paralee smiled at him. "Yes, Miz Bones sells babies, which is legal in this state," she answered. "Nevertheless, if you report me I'll cut out your gizzard."

"But, where did you get that child?"

"That one, from a thirteen-year-old. Do you know, she's pregnant again? A regular baby factory. If I can, I'll convince her to have her tubes tied. If," she said, her eyes, flashing, "she liked babies, it would be different. She just likes making them. I paid her twenty dollars for that child, brought her home and she cried for days, she was in such neglected shape. So I put her in that rocker and worked it with my foot night and day until the rhythm finally got her to trust, to relax. Then she slept until I thought she wouldn't wake up." She took a step toward him, her head almost scraping the light bulb. "You want to help? I got orders for necklaces tomorrow. Can you string these for me? Use this one for a pattern. The bones have been cleaned and baked. You don't have to worry about getting your hands dirty."

They worked and talked through the night. Paralee was a talented listener, whose empathy encouraged confidence. Thomas found himself telling her his story. He told her about his Naja, and the growing guilt he felt about leaving her behind. Finally, he told her about Justyn.

Paralee rose. "Love trouble is the worst trouble," she said. "We pay for our little sins. We pay on the installment plan." Then, solemnly as a high priestess, she moved across the room and knelt before a small cabinet. As she opened the door a flood of odors, acrid and sweet, strong and subtle, escaped. She withdrew a small amulet and, rising, returned to him with the same stately step. "Sleep with this under your pillow."

"What is it?"

"Something to help you in matters of the heart."

"Thank you," he said, accepting it without interest.

"There's something I want you to do for me, but you may not want to."

"What could I refuse you, Paralee?"

"Tomorrow some people are going to bring a very sick child here. I want you to spit in its mouth."

"*What?*"

"I only practice what has been practiced for as long as people remember," she said quietly. "A child born after its father's death has certain healing powers."

"Yes. Justyn told me about that superstition. And, I think I remember someone else . . . When I was a boy, a confusing knot of kin came to visit us. I'm not sure who they were. Cousins, my mother's great aunt, I think. The old woman asked me to touch a sore on her face, to cure it." Strange the memory should now give him pleasure, when at the time the act had horrified him. He could see it now, how he reached out with a small and violently trembling hand, almost gagging: on the old woman's wrinkled cheek was an infected mole that oozed sickeningly. He had shut his eyes.

The cry of a baby in the next room startled him. *Family.* Children, his and Naja's. Generation upon generation. He gripped the amulet so tightly that sweat from his palm activated the odors of herb and spice, drenching the air around him.

"You will, then?"

"Yes. And will you tell me what you know about the lynching?"

"It was before my time here."

"But, you must know something. Pear was here. Pear was a player in it."

"And Pear is dying, and I can't help him, and your coming has upset him much more than you realize. I won't involve him in anything."

"Do you think I'm foolish for pursuing this?"

"Foolhardy, not foolish. I wouldn't. I'd put a curse on them and let it take it's course. You're liable to get that white girl killed, not to mention yourself. I'd put a curse on whoever did what they shouldn't, and let it be. I can do it for you, if you want."

13

SLEEPLESS FOR THE SECOND night, Justyn stalked the house, rummaging as if expecting to find a salve or solution in every drawer or closet. Instead, each folded shirt, each rediscovered piece of costume jewelry, reminded her of Frank, their relationship. Too neat by habit not to rearrange as she explored, in the lonely hours following his call she alternately disrupted and restored to order her surroundings, while her mind—restless as her body but with no such simple task to occupy it—bounced guiltily back and forth to that one subject, her transgression. That Frank had sounded so trusting only added to her guilt.

At the first sign of daylight she knew she had to escape the house, but where could she go at that hour? Devil's Rock! She warmed to the improbable idea of that desolate place. Thinking with some enthusiasm of how that grand view must look in the early hours, she made a thermos of coffee, stocking a backpack with it and jelly and bread. She wished she had thought of going there sooner—it would have been beautiful to watch Green Hills brighten from that spot. She dressed quickly in jeans and hiking boots, warm sweater, jacket, and scarf. When Tawny met her sleepily in the yard she whistled her into the car. It might be dangerous to climb up the rock alone, but Tawny would at least let her know if someone else approached.

It *was* a grand view, well worth the effort. To the south and east stretched Green Hills. To the north and west the Blue Ridge escarpment rose, Devil's Rock a mere impediment compared to that great wall of ridges. Justyn sat soaking up their quietude as another would the sun.

Green Hills spread before her like the whistle-stop town of an electric train set. She could trace her history there as if years or distance did not exist. There was the subdivision where her first twelve years had been contentedly spent. And there, across from the old courthouse, was the red-brick building, soon to be razed for a municipal parking lot, where her father had his law office. A miniature town. Miniature problems. Tombstones too small to be seen. She ate breakfast slowly, remembering.

Remarkably, the sun struck beveled panes at Balantyne Hall, a sudden pulsating magnification of silver light that resembled nothing so much as a pointing finger. Poor Eddie, he was probably paranoid enough to think it was. No wonder Ouida felt so strong a need to protect him. It wasn't that he lacked friends—his social position guaranteed him welcome in any Green Hills home—but that he seemed so lonely in the circle he had made. The light Justyn thought she saw flare occasionally in his eyes seemed almost one of terror. Before, her heart had always gone out to him. But now, with what Frank had told her, she felt confused.

Beside her the Cherokee grinding bowl was still desecrated by cigarette butts. She knew for certain whose. Angrily, she scooped them clean with napkins. She rubbed her hands against the cold. Camels and Parliaments. What would Buck Stovall and Ouida Balantyne Orms be able to tell Thomas about the lynching, if only they would? Was there any way she could entice or incite them? She shivered and drew her jacket closer.

At least the cold meant there were no snakes out. The rock would be an excellent place for rattlesnakes to sun. The image set something flickering in her mind, a memory dangerous and slumbering, camouflaged from her as cleverly as the native timber rattler in its lovely "velvet" phase . . . but what?

With effort she tried to tether her ranging thoughts. The lynching. Oddly, she had researched the word and found that it dated from Revolutionary times, when a band of renegade patriots led by a man named Lynch disposed of Tories just as Devil McKinner's neighbors had disposed of him. Violently, without benefit of the law. Ironically, according to regional lore Lynch and some of his followers later came from Virginia to South Carolina to settle at the foot of Table Rock

Mountain, now in view, with its spectacular "chair," not a dozen miles from where she sat. But here, as at Balantyne Hall, history and myth grew obtuse. Green Hills seemed such a civilized place. Yet the murder of a cousin, the lynching of a black man, the suicide of a father . . .

There was a legend among the Cherokee that on the anniversary of a snakebite the pain returned. It was that way with her father's death. The ache returned each year even before she realized the date, the reason.

She could not stop shivering now, and sat hugging her knees. Tawny, upset by her disquietude, moved closer. The blinding light emanated for an instant more from Balantyne Hall, then faded as the sun moved on. Beyond the quiet village that was old Green Hills a clustering of clouds shadowed the new industrial parks that stretched southward, clouds and buildings melding in gray sameness. Sixteen years. The town had changed greatly since her father's death. Zachary Orms's unorthodox views regarding civil rights were now law. But back then people had considered him a traitor, like Devil McKinner. How difficult had things been made for him?

She could feel the cold settle almost to her bones. It must be what lingered here of Devil McKinner's savagely displaced spirit that caused a premonition of evil to coil its way in her thoughts, to slant and shade, scales glistening—

"*My God!*" she said aloud so suddenly Tawny lunged barking from her sleep and might have bounded blindly off the rock, if Justyn had not grabbed her collar. "My God!" she said again, more quietly, the thought no less alarming. For a moment she felt as if her whole life quivered on its axis. . . . Such a thought had to be wrong, impossible, misguided. . . . And yet, there it sat in the open now, rattling its warning, an incessant whir that might have been with her always, it seemed so familiar. . . . *What if Zach had not killed himself? What if . . .*

"I'm being ridiculous," she said aloud.

But a moaning wind swept suddenly up the rock face, disputing her. Tawny lifted her muzzle to it, listening, and howled as if Devil McKinner's ghost had come to argue. *Of course* ordinary people were capable of murder: neighbors, friends, family—didn't his own indelible blood on the rock prove it?

"I'm being ridiculous!" she said more firmly.

But people were capable of anything. Their image was still vivid in her mind, two of the lynch mob—*murderers*—dancing contentedly at the country club with their beautiful women. If Chub Castille and Buck Stovall could get away with a heinous crime, could someone else not do the same, in secret, while pursuing a "civilized" life?

She shivered with a clattering of teeth. *Ridiculous*, and yet, couldn't someone have shot her father knowing the town would *want* to think it suicide?

It did not seem so unlikely, the more she considered it. "Flaubert's picnic," she reminded herself—if it could be imagined, it most likely had or would happen. Certainly someone *could* have shot her father and placed the gun in his hand. She doubted the police had searched for signs of murder.

Tawny sat down in front of her, whimpered, and plaintively offered her paw.

"You're right, it's time to go home," Justyn agreed.

It was a quick walk down the mountain, but she was dispirited that she had resolved nothing. When she pulled into the driveway she thought she heard the phone ringing. She had not been inside but a few minutes before it rang again.

It was Thomas. He talked quickly and poetically about his new friend, this Miz Bones Justyn had known only as an eccentric figure, a town character. Thomas assured her the woman's heart was full of largesse.

"But, if she's Pear's half sister, can you trust her?"

"Who else can I trust? I've got to stay somewhere." He was silent for a moment. "I wanted to apologize. I didn't mean—"

"No, nothing to say, ever! I'm all right. Just not proud of myself."

111

"It was my fault. It isn't your guilt."

"I wasn't raped, Thomas."

He was silent.

"What are you going to do next?" Justyn said.

"Look up Poe Williams. I've been thinking about what you said, about Dillard's death. I want to know everything Dillard Beasley ever told his wife or his nephew about the lynching. Maybe he mentioned someone, something. And you?"

"I'm going to take a 'sentimental journey.' I've been thinking about my father. I saw his old office building today, that's going to be torn down. I want to visit it one more time."

Justyn changed clothes, choosing an outfit casual but appropriate to the old downtown. That is, for the old downtown as it had been sixteen years before. She knew that her father's surviving law partner, though a maverick, was nostalgic for the old days and preferred to think of her as "little Justyn."

Once inside the building, a part of the original courthouse square, she found that most of the offices she passed were already empty. A dentist-group was in the process of moving. She had to step around crates and chairs in the halls. Dentistry! What would Zachary Orms have thought of that in a building once exclusively reserved for law practices?

The door to Orms, Ashley, and Levin was locked. She started to walk away when she thought she saw a shadow behind the glass. She tapped lightly. The door opened only slightly, but she recognized the tall, matronly woman within.

"Carol?"

"Justyn? Why, dear, come in!" She swung the door wide and hugged Justyn to her overlarge bosom. "I apologize for having the door locked," she said as she ushered her in, "but we've had so many strange people wandering in lately. Workmen looking for a bathroom, scavengers looking for something to steal . . . But welcome, welcome! Why, you don't age at all. Mr. Ashley saves all the clippings about you. He's so proud. Coffee? What brings you here? A last look at the old place? Business? Cream or sugar? Why, your hand is cold as ice!"

Carol had grown older, but her mannerisms hadn't changed. Justyn took her coffee and sat down on a sofa that was as cluttered with magazines and books as if it sat in a much-used den. Carol scooped the clutter up in her arms and deposited it in a chair. "Voluble and voluminous." Justyn remembered her father's apt description of his secretary, and smiled. "Uncle Ron isn't here, then?"

"No, dear, he's in court. All day, I'm afraid. He'll be so sorry he missed you. Is there something I can help you with?"

"Well—" she began, and faltered. Why *had* she come here? What was it she wanted of this place? "Are there any of Daddy's papers left? I guess I'm feeling sentimental, but I was wondering about his records, old court cases. I'm particularly interested in the lynching trial he prosecuted."

"Yes, I'd read in the paper that you were. But there's nothing, I'm afraid. I don't know what Zach did with that material. That young newspaperman, Poe Williams, has already been here asking about it. I looked everywhere. I think of your father often," she said, sitting down at her desk. "I wonder how he would have mellowed. *If* he would have mellowed." She laughed. "He always took the stairs two at a time, never slowed down," she said fondly.

Justyn sipped her coffee, disappointed.

"I'm glad to see you take an interest in him," she continued more somberly. "I know it's been difficult, the suicide and all. It's easier to forget. There may be records still packed away and stored. I know your mother didn't want them at the time, and I don't blame her. But there is something Mr. Ashley found in cleaning up. It's a sort of journal Zach kept, in his own shorthand in that terrible writing of his. It's unreadable to us. Maybe you can figure it out."

Justyn emerged into the sunlight with the dusty, heavy ledger clutched close to her chest. Her father's journal! She'd get it read if she had to hire a decoder. It would be like him to keep it at work, where he would not have to explain to Ouida.

As she lay it on the car seat she thought again of a rattlesnake, coiled and waiting. Perhaps she shouldn't try to read it. Suppose that terrible childish worry, that in some way *she* might have done something to cause . . . "But, I *must* read it," she said aloud.

It had warmed considerably. Sunlight gleamed on the wide bright street. The lovely old white marble courthouse gleamed in stately indifference to the ice-cream parlor and trendy shops within. She could not imagine all that had happened there on such a day. It was too pretty to wrestle with the psychological pressure the journal promised. It was a day for adventure.

Instead of driving home Justyn drove to Balantyne Hall. Buck Stovall's truck was parked on the grass by the right wing, and Eddie's El Dorado was pulled close to the front steps. She drove through the back gate to the kitchen door, hoping neither man would notice. It was Beesie she wanted to see.

"You told me that my father argued with Eddie's friends and threw them out of this house, but you didn't tell me who they were or when it happened."

"Mercy, I disremember," Beesie said enigmatically, and went on slowly peeling potatoes, her arthritic fingers painfully pushing a dull knife.

Justyn noticed the stubborn tightening of Beesie's wattled chin. "Well, perhaps it doesn't matter," she said pleasantly. "Eddie has so many friends, I don't see how you could keep them all straight, anyway."

The old woman suddenly glowed. She was as proud of Eddie's social position as if it were her own. "Mercy, don't he now? They come and go, come and go. Invite him 'round to everything."

"But, 'old' friends are still the 'best' friends," Justyn said, quoting a favorite saying of the governor's, "and I guess Uncle Eddie has a few who have stayed loyal over the years."

Beesie nodded agreement, her lashless eyes watering. "Mr. Chub and Miss Ivey, they might as well be Mr. Eddie's brother and sister. Miss Ivey, ain't she pretty? Pretty as a girl. How old she be now?"

"Mother says she's her age, about fifty. And who else? Who are Eddie's other old friends?"

But Beesie was growing suspicious. "I disremember," she said stiffly, concentrating on a potato. Then, after a long moment, she looked up and straight into Justyn's eyes. "You leave Mr. Eddie and his troubles alone!" she said almost threateningly. "He suffers enough. Mercy, he suffers enough!"

Buck Stovall stepped into the second-floor hall from the rooms he was remodeling for Ouida's apartment. He needed to go downstairs to check a fuse box. But the sound of Eddie's agitated voice arrested him. He stopped and listened.

If the dollar was up, and gold down, or vice-versa—either way, Eddie probably could not remember—it affected him morosely, for his entangled borrowings were now so scattered in futures and commodities he could not keep straight whether his intended fortunes rose or fell with each day's ineffable market. This Buck learned from what he overhead. Eddie was involved in a particularly volatile conversation with his commodities broker in Boston. He was being asked to invest more money.

"Good *afternoon*, brothers and sisters!" a voice shouted.

"Turn down that damned radio!" Eddie shouted down to Beesie. "I'm on the phone!"

The doorbell sounded.

"Mr. Eddie?" Beesie called back, ringing the little handbell she used to get his attention, now that her voice had grown so faint. "Young man at the front door to see you."

"In God's name, *who*? If it's a delivery, you take it."

The handbell tinkled again.

"What, Beesie, *what*?"

"He say it personal. He won't go 'way, Mr. Eddie."

"He'll have to wait. I'm on the *phone*," Eddie screamed, sounding close to tears. Then footsteps ascended the stairs. A pimply-faced youth passed on the landing. "What on earth are *you* doing here? I'm afraid I don't remember your name. But I remember *you* . . ."

"Of course you do, Mr. Balantyne. The point is, I remember *you*. I remember where you live, this big house with the interesting room upstairs. Now, I'm in a bit of a jam, Mr. Balantyne. I've wrecked my car, and I've got to get it fixed, and I've got a payment due . . . you know—"

"No, I don't know," Eddie said rudely. "What's this got to do with me?"

"I thought you might let me have—"

"Blackmail? Is this *blackmail*?"

"Yes, sir, I suppose you might put it that way. Why not?"

"That's a laugh. I'm flat broke."

" 'Broke' to you is probably not the same thing it is to me. I need a few hundred, Mr. B. I really do."

"I just told you I don't have any. Can't you hear?"

"Well, if that's what you say. Gee, I hate that. But, I understand your sister has money. Maybe if I went to her—"

Eddie must have sprung at him. To Buck's amazement, the two men toppled down the steps. He started to go after them, saw Beesie, and retreated. Below, Eddie offered a compromise. "I have three fifties," he said. "That's all. Will that do?"

"Gee, Mr. Balantyne, I guess it will have to, for now. Thanks, I really appreciate—"

Buck felt a rush of air from the front door's closing. "I'm not the only Edward Valenchat Balantyne to take risks," he heard Eddie say. "The first Val risked his life every day, didn't he? Trading with savages, taking those overloaded rafts on the river. Bloodpelt for wampum. Bloodpelt for firewater. Bloodpelt for gunpowder. If he were alive today, he'd be playing the market, wouldn't he? Beesie, would you clean out that Chippendale sideboard? I'll have someone out to look at it tomorrow. And that old guillotine in the third-floor room? I should have gotten rid of the damned thing long ago. No, don't you go near it. It's dangerous. I'll take care of it. What was the name of the museum that wanted it?"

14

THOMAS FELT HE HAD to be alone. He walked down to the pay phone on Fricatown's main street to call Justyn. She greeted him hesitantly. "Are you still looking for a new place to hide out?" she asked.

"Yes. I'm uneasy at Paralee's, with Pear perhaps knowing everything I do."

"Then, I think I've thought of the perfect place. Close to town, but secluded. Safe, I think, unless you're followed."

"I can handle that. I'm going to get a different rented car. I'll be careful. What is this place? Give me directions."

"It's where I left my car the other night, an old hangar. There used to be a small airport, but it's been abandoned for years. A concrete building sits at the edge of a forest, on an old runway. You could drive your car inside. I didn't see any sign that anyone had been there for years. It's not a quarter mile from Paralee's through the woods, but the road exits a good deal farther from the highway, behind a billboard, over an abandoned railroad spur. It's closed, barricaded, but you can drive around. There's a bright orange feed-and-seed billboard sign that marks it."

"Thank you, Justyn." He brought her up to date, then added quietly, again, "Are you all right?"

"I think so," she said tentatively. "A little afraid, a little angry, but puzzled, more than anything. I seem to be thinking the worst of every situation."

"Perhaps it's best to be suspicious, until we know what's going on."

"Yes. I just wish Frank were here, much as he might disapprove, but he called to say he'll be gone a few days more. Thomas, when you go to retrieve your car, would you do me a favor?"

"Of course."

"I left my shoes—Mother's shoes—at your parents'

house. Please get them. They probably have her initials in the sole. I don't want someone finding them."

"Certainly. No problem."

A deputy's car cruised by the phone booth. Thomas's voice grew tight. "I'm not sure I even trust the law here," he said. "I'd better cut this short. You know where I'll be," he said.

Paralee sat on the porch steps, holding a bottle for the baby in her lap.

"Can you really do it?" Thomas asked her curiously.

"Do what?"

"Put a child up for adoption and not be found out. I assume that was someone else's child you gave away."

"Yes."

"Doesn't someone—a social worker?—wonder?"

"Almost never." She smiled. "If you're poor—or better, poor and black—life is a shell game. You see, we really do look alike to most of them. They come here and they remember *me*, but the children run in and out, and they say, 'How many young'uns you got?' and I call in however many I need them to see. The others run to the woods or hide in the outhouse, and I say they belong to neighbors or family. It's like trying to count chickens. I tell the children, 'Don't say nothin' less I tell you to.' The white folks come back, I show them a different bunch, call them the same names, who cares? They don't.

"Here in Fricatown we move around, change names. Those people stay across the way"—she pointed to the next house, barely visible through the trees—"they get power bill in their baby's name. If they move, can't pay the bill, they get power in somebody else's name. Don't matter. Sometimes it's not so bad, being considered ignorant." She rocked the baby in her lap and laughed. "Now he's peed on me!" She wiped the baby's diaperless bottom with her skirt and wrung it out. "We keep the shells moving, get by, as long as we don't make waves, draw attention.

"When my man cut Joey and me, now, that made waves!

118

We were in the hospital, and I had to loan the children out. Pear helped me get settled again. He's a good man sometimes, even if he did—" She caught herself, and looked away. "If not for him, I never would have gotten the children back, and Monk would still be in jail."

She gathered a handful of dry skirt and bunched it under the baby, displaying dark, long, firmly muscular legs, not unlike Naja's. "I shouldn't begrudge Pear, but I do," she said guiltily. "Inside, he thinks he's white as a judge. I mean, inside, people shouldn't be *either*, should they? Pear don't know what it's like to be strapping and black, like Monk, or strapped and black, like me. He ain't got no sympathy. Loyalty, yes. I'm his sister, but there's the difference. Sometimes Monk gets so resentful he don't want to be reminded of *nothing* black. And there me and Joey are, black as coal, like the dark side of the moon. That's when he goes crazy. It ain't me or the boy he wants to kill, it's *blackness*." She shuddered and put her hand to her cheek, stroking the jagged molehill of a scar that bisected it. "When Monk cut him, I knocked Joey out with a frying pan, to put him out of his misery, he was crying so. I thought I'd killed him. Poor Joey. A child with a scarred-up face is like . . . who are those people in India?"

"The untouchables?"

"Yes. No nice girl is ever going to look twice at our Joey. Her folks wouldn't allow it. His chances to ever make something of hisself went that night his daddy cut him up, the same as mine. These scars brand us as niggers to everyone. Even those knives I use to cut chicken, I dream about. You heard that story a knife don't hurt? Shit! Knives and blood, blood and knives I dream about. If I had some other work to do, I'd do it and not have a knife in the house! I'd buy my food already pared and peeled and skinned. Oh, my!" she shivered so violently her crucifix earrings rattled like snakes' tails. "Tomorrow, next year . . . Monk will kill us someday, I know."

"Let me hold the child. You get into something dry," Thomas suggested.

"Yes! Then I'll bathe him." She handed the baby to him and stood, shaking out her damp skirt front. Then, with a sudden gesture, she raised the caftan over her head like a bird spreading its wings, and in an instant stood before him splendidly naked. "Tuck this dry part under her," she said unashamedly, bunching the garment carefully. Her breasts swung tightly at him as she leaned to the child. When she stood erect her dark pubic hair and nipples seemed as exaggerated as if painted on a statue.

He remembered Pear's concern, and pulled his eyes away from her to the child. When he crooked a finger the baby clutched it with tiny fingers and sucked eagerly. Paralee lifted the child from him and went into the house. Joey galloped by, whooping, carrying a bouncing toddler on his back. A pretty little girl with hair braided neatly into cornrows wandered by, studiously collecting sticks.

"And, don't it beat all, I still love him?" Paralee called from the window, and began crooning softly.

He knew Paralee objected to his going, so, later in the afternoon, he simply slipped away, stopping in at the cafe for coffee and change for newspapers and telephone calls.

"I see you talking to Pear Plumlee, I worry," the proprietor said, pulling up a chair to join him on an otherwise empty afternoon. "He lay something heavy on your shoulders?"

"I'm afraid so," Thomas said, thinking of his mother.

"I wouldn't set much store by it, if I were you. I've known him for some time. Used to work for him, as a matter of fact. Truth is not necessarily the gospel for him." He sipped and sighed, winking. "As a further matter of fact, I used to work the chain gang with him. Or was supposed to. Pear was too small and couldn't or wouldn't work to amount to nothing, so right off they put him on the county farm, milking cows and slopping hogs and pulling collards. Compared to the rest of us, busting rocks and digging ditches, he was on easy street. But it was still nigger work and he hated doing it. Pear ain't never had no truck for being a nigger.

"Then, *whoop*, he got out. Heard someone high up got him out. Someone white, of course. Story was, they either had to have Pear dead or out, he knew so much."

"About what?"

A customer came in.

"I'll talk to you again," Thomas said.

"No. That's all I know. But you might do well to smoke on it."

It took the rest of the day to prepare for his move. But when finally he began settling in at the abandoned hangar, he found it to be, as Justyn had said, an excellent hiding place. He scouted the grounds approvingly, with a veteran's careful eye. There were no recent cigarette butts or beer cans or condoms scattered at the road's end. The small tower was as brier-encrusted as a princess's bier. The hangar door, web-enshrouded, took considerable force to pry, it had been swollen shut so long. But in the office he found a dusty, serviceable desk and an army cot, welcome remains of someone's long-ago habitation.

It was late when Justyn made a sandwich for her supper, sitting down to eat at the kitchen table with her father's journal, still unopened, before her. Finished eating, she was still sitting, lost in thought, when Tawny's frantic barking roused her and sent her to the window. Was that a flash of white, a ghostly figure spying at the far edge of the yard, or her imagination? She felt her face redden and shook her head angrily. Who would be spying on her? Later, in the shower, she gave in to troubled thoughts. What right had she to pry into her father's past? If he had wanted to end his life, to obliterate whatever he had become, who was she to pry these many years later, and especially on behalf of a stranger's cause? She thought of destroying the journal, of taking it back.

But it seemed to beckon. She could not resist its call. Drying quickly, she stepped into a warm robe and retrieved the ledger from the kitchen. She settled on the living-room sofa, only to get back up three times—first to pour a glass of wine, next to find a dustcloth for the sooty cover, and finally to draw the drapes against spying eyes.

Could her father ever have dreamed his daughter would someday be holding this book, she wondered as she began a random reading, slowed by Zachary Orms's peculiar handwriting. He had relied on his competent secretary and dictation for most communication. But once Justyn's eyes began to adjust to his left-handed, backward-slanting scrawl, she thought uneasily for a few minutes that he had written in some kind of code, and she knew she was no cipher. Eventually, however, she could see that he had merely abbreviated in logical fashion, capital initials for names, "&" for "and," etc. She labored through a rather dry if somewhat sardonic description of encounters with a well-known client who would not pay his bill, and was beginning to read more rapidly when a puzzling entry stumped her:

Wd frm clk tdy tht IM & CC fckg stndg n clkrm n dbt hpng JG fnd thm. A cdnt blve, chd, sd tr!

She sighed, rose again for paper and pen, and began slowly transcribing: "Word from chalk (no) clock (no) *clerk* today that IM *Ivey Mabry* and CC *Chub Castille* . . ."

"Oh, my God!" she said aloud as her father's cryptic sentence suddenly sprang to life before her:

"Word from clerk today that Ivey Mabry and Chub Castille fucking standing up in cloakroom no doubt hoping Judge Mabry find them. Ashley couldn't believe, checked, said true!"

$\triangledown$

15

By the time Thomas finished setting up camp at the abandoned hangar it was quite late and he fell asleep almost immediately. He woke late: the morning had almost slipped away from him. Shivering in the cold building, he made coffee and fried toast over a camp stove. But when he carried his frugal breakfast out into the sunlight he found that the old runway was already warm enough for malingering blue-tailed skinks to be sunning themselves on the cracked pavement. A red-tailed hawk circled overhead. He sat down cross-legged, warming his hands on the coffee mug, and stared at a skink intently. What did the small lizard eat? Was it completely mute? His students would be plying him with a dozen such questions, or shouting back at the hawk who now punctured the morning air with lingering *scree-ing* sounds. The thought of his schoolchildren warmed him more than the sun. Deprived as they had first seemed to him, they had the capacity to make him happy . . . with their curiosity, their dreams, their joy. *Happy.* Once, toward the end, he had asked his mother why she wouldn't talk to him about the past:

"Because I want you to be happy."

Her ghost was with him today as he drove again to the dirt track. Accused murderess, perhaps, but mother, she clung, disconnected memories of her flashing into his thoughts like strobe lights. He remembered her joy when the small maid service she had started became prosperous enough for her to assume administrative duties only. She glowed as she packed her uniforms away. When she knew that she was dying, her obituary became her favorite pastime—she wanted it recorded how she founded and owned the business; became an officer of the community's once all-white businesswomen's club. Driving along roads he knew must have been familiar to her, he almost felt that she was in the backseat, instructing him, "Son, turn here." Nor did he feel alone when he followed the footpath to the empty grave that Dillard Beasley had said once held his father's body. He could almost hear the beating of her heart as he knelt and stared wonderingly at the void.

What had been the point of removing his father's body? What secret could those moldering bones have told? And why had Dillard Beasley died there? The woods around him stretched unfamiliar and sinister. Now he made his way there slowly. It was dark within, but he had brought a flashlight. He shone it on the ground, the long-trammeled earth, the fresh outline of footprints. Someone had been there. But who? And when? The memory of his mother faded in the cold light of his father's death. Tears stung his eyes. Yet he lingered, hunkering and rocking meditatively as he stared at the telltale earth. Outside, newly fallen leaves rustled and came to life as a small whirlwind formed. He looked out as it lifted and grew, shrieking faintly, the ghost of a ghost. From here, the intruder could have watched until Dillard Beasley was alone. And only the squirrels chattering now in the trees would have witnessed what happened next.

A couple of miles from the dirt track Thomas found a pay phone at a country store. "Mrs. Orms," he said, identifying himself, when Ouida answered. "You mentioned that we might talk about my father?"

"Yes, but call me Ouida." Her voice was husky but alert.

"I wonder if I might visit you?"

"I'd like that. Yes, tomorrow is hectic. Bridge and—but today, well, here I sit, all alone, thinking about the past, when who should call? I live in Haddon Place Condominiums, second floor on the corner right."

"Is two o'clock too soon?"

"The sooner the better. Come thirsty."

Ouida greeted Thomas in a plunging white hostess gown that complemented her sultry dark hair and eyes, her small perfect figure. She looked beautiful, and Thomas found himself telling her so. She laughed with husky pleasure.

"And you are almost, but not quite, as handsome as your

father," she countered. "White women weren't supposed to think a black man handsome in those days, but I'll bet I wasn't the only one who did."

"It pleased me, that day at the Nullifier, when you said I resembled him. No one had ever said that to me before."

"Have you no pictures of him?"

"No. Mama said there weren't any."

"Perhaps not. Poor Maude. She left here in such a hurry. I hope she didn't become as bitter as me. You know, I'll ask Eddie about pictures. As a boy, photography was his life. I think he must have taken pictures of everyone in Green Hills, Fricatown included. Would you like a drink?"

"Thank you. Yes, I would. I don't think I've relaxed with a drink since I came to Green Hills. But, here"—his wave encompassed the room around him, a carpeted, luxuriant white space—"I don't feel as if the Ku Klux Klan is going to come bursting down the door for me."

Ouida laughed, but reddened.

Thomas heard her in the kitchen performing her ritual. The muted opening and closing of the refrigerator door, a clinking of tongs and ice, the pfizz of liquid, the rattle of swizzle stick against crystal. It was a pity she drank so much, he thought. Because of her husband? Of the eternal wear of time on beauty? Of boredom?

Ouida returned with their drinks. As if she could read his thoughts, she said, "Justyn's sun rose and set with her father. She blames me. She'd like me to do penance forever!"

"That doesn't sound like Justyn," he said loyally.

"Well, what do you know? I made sandwiches and forgot to bring them out. I don't like to eat alone, so I waited for you." For a moment she seemed annoyed, but returned composed, with a prettily garnished platter.

"Very good," Thomas said with enthusiasm, between bites. "Especially the chicken salad, my favorite."

"Yes, it's a Ladies League recipe. The League . . . yes, perhaps I am unfair to Justyn. She wouldn't join the League, and told them why: except for a token Yankee or two, there are no outsiders, no blacks or Jews . . ."

"You were going to talk about my father."

"Oh, yes, keep bringing me back when I stray. I always stray, no pun intended. Tom was the first black I got to know as a friend, through Zach. I remember asking him if blacks got chigger bites, if they sunburned. He laughed at everything." She reached for a cigarette from a mother-of-pearl box on the glass-topped coffee table, asked Thomas for the lighter. When he leaned toward her, he was suddenly aware of the power of her liquid eyes at so close a range. No cliché to call them agate pools, dark, mysterious, and beckoning.

"Zach represented your father for some minor-but-serious racial infraction—drinking at a 'white' water fountain, I think. They lost, but it brought them close. They were both simply ahead of their time." Her voice became gravelly as she forgot to whisper. "It was as if they had been looking for each other. I don't think either of them had many other, if any, close friends. It was enlightening. Your mother and I came to know one another, to share confidences, especially about the men who made passes at us. We had that in common!" She inhaled deeply, then snuffed out her half-finished cigarette. "Justyn calls these 'cancer sticks.' " She laughed. "She's such a purist."

"Justyn's a fine person."

"And I suppose I'm not?" Ouida's mood changed swiftly. "No, I'm the first to admit I'm not. Justyn had her father to learn her values from. My parents weren't moralists. But, if only Zach hadn't . . . I was coming round, I really was." She drained her glass, then drew another cigarette. This time, when Thomas leaned close to light it, she held his eyes almost as if by force. He tried to pull his gaze away, but her dark irises, black almost as the large and ink-dark pupils, transfixed him. "Just testing," she said softly. "It would upset me to think I couldn't seduce you. But, don't worry. I'm not going to."

"You're quite a woman, Mrs. Orms."

"You're supposed to call me Ouida."

"Ouida."

"I don't know what else I can tell you about your father.

126

Zach spent a lot of time with him. I think they were looking for laws to test, the more absurd or obscene ones. The ones that anyone but a genuine racist would have to think a little ridiculous. Look like him you do. I know that must be very disturbing to some people. You could be his ghost."

"Sometimes I think I am."

"I believe in ghosts. Zach's comes to me sometimes. At least, it used to. Always agitated, as if there were something he wanted me to know."

Thomas smiled. "My mother's has been with me today. There's so much about her that I don't know. Her maiden name, for instance. Do you happen to know it?"

Ouida sat pensively for a moment. "No, I don't. I'm sorry. But I believe she came from the Devil's Heel section. It used to be a poor area, poor whites and blacks. Now it's all been razed. If you're not going to drink that, I will," she added without pause, reaching thirstily for his drink.

"Pear Plumlee thinks that my mother killed Stubby, that my father died to protect her . . . and me."

"No. Yes. I don't know. Anything's possible," she said confusedly, a little drunkenly. "Stubby was a gross man, vulgar, always trying to pull people down to his level. He called me 'Pussy' before I knew what it meant. When I was a little girl he fondled me and whispered dirty things. I hated him! There's a joke reminds me of him. A little girl answers the telephone and the caller asks to speak to her mother. 'She's not here,' the child says. 'Well, then, you'll have to do,' the caller says, then whispers, *'Pee-pee doo-doo!'* " She laughed, then smoked in silence for a moment. "I was always terrified at Balantyne Hall, because of him. Yet he put on such a show of good manners around my parents, they would never have believed me. They adored him. He was rich. The heir. I suppose they entertained thoughts of my someday marrying him, despite we were close kin. They chided me for not rushing into his arms and returning his hugs and kisses, the bastard! Once, when I was eight or so, he pulled me into a closet and stuck his finger up me. I used to plan ways to kill him. I've never told that to anyone!"

127

The door knocker sounded.

"The police, come to arrest me!" She laughed, but sat on. "I felt such relief when he died. What he did to your mother was much worse." The knocker sounded again. "I'm not expecting anyone. I don't know who that could be. Excuse me," she said, putting out her cigarette, and rising slowly.

Thomas stared unseeing at the room around him. "Buck!" he heard her say in a surprised, gravelly voice, from the foyer.

"I was in the neighborhood. I wanted to see you. God, babe, you look beautiful. What's the occasion?"

"I wish you'd called. Tom Levity's son is here. Do you think you should come in?" she whispered, too loudly.

For a moment, there was silence. Thomas rose. He could see Buck Stovall framed in the doorway. Then the man spoke. "Hell!" he said, turning abruptly. Ouida's face flamed. Thomas could hear the angry sound of his steps departing.

"Oh," Ouida said. "Oh." When she came back into the room she was as nervous as a teenage girl who had offended her beau. She mixed two more strong drinks, though Thomas had declined; brought tea cake but forgot forks; made coffee but misplaced the cream and sugar, consuming both of the drinks in the process of hunting for them. The slight tremor in her hands increased.

Thomas listened to her rambling conversation, then gently brought her back to the subject of the lynching. "About your husband . . . Is there anything you can tell me that he might have mentioned? Who did he think killed Stubby, if not my father?"

Ouida's head jerked slightly, but her dark eyes did not waver from his. "I think Zach blamed himself for letting the lynching happen. It wasn't his fault, of course—he had asked the sheriff to look out for something to happen. But Zach was sick with flu, too weak to get out of bed. I don't know more because I wouldn't let him talk about it. It upset me so. It still does. But wait, I had forgotten, there *was* something . . . I never knew what, but something came to light, not long before Zach died. We argued. I didn't want him dredging up the lynching again. It had hurt his business, cost us friends. I think he told Eddie, whatever it was. I overheard them arguing."

"Don't you remember any details? Anything at all?"

Ouida did not answer. "I wonder why he left?" she said finally, vaguely. She sounded so wistful he did not know whether she referred to Buck Stovall's recent hasty exit, or her husband's long-ago suicide. "Zach received death threats during the trial," she added. "Did you know that?"

"No, I didn't."

"It made me so nervous, I developed an ulcer. Couldn't drink or smoke or eat hardly anything. And there were other problems, from the stress. I almost had to have a hysterectomy. After Justyn's birth, I couldn't conceive again. No more children for me." She stared at him, her mood swinging.

"Is there any other detail you might remember?"

"Would you like another drink?"

"No, thank you."

"I can't remember anything. After all these years of trying to forget . . ." Her eyes teared, seeping mascara.

"I'm sorry I've upset you," Thomas said. "I'll go now."

Ouida looked at him hopelessly.

"I wish your husband and my parents were still alive. We might all have been friends," he added thoughtfully.

She brightened. "Oh, wouldn't that have been nice?" Smiling, she added, "Can you see yourself out? I'm so tired . . ." She kicked off her slippers and lay back on the plush sofa pillows. Thomas caught a tempting glimpse of thigh through the long slit in her skirt. "I wonder why he left?" she repeated softly. "You must ask Beesie. She's old as Methuselah and remembers the oddest things."

"Ask her what?"

"Your mother's name. Your mother's *maiden* name. They must have jumped over a broomstick." She giggled, her meaning lost on Thomas. "Zach must have thought someone *important* killed Stubby," she added ruefully. "*That* would have set Eddie off. He's always afraid of scandal."

As he descended the stairs, Thomas heard piano music start up from Ouida's apartment—blues played so slowly and mournfully it sounded like a dirge.

After a frustrating search in the courthouse that turned up no new information, Thomas went to the Nullifier for an early dinner. A bit of graffiti on the men's room stall gave him more insight than he anticipated. In a small, pinched hand someone had written, *New people are N.O.C.D.—"Not our class, dearie."* Underneath, someone with a wide and confident sweep had countered, *Poorbucker, sharecropper, dirt farmer, black—"Not our class, dearie?" WHO SAYS?*

As he was leaving, he asked one of the black waiters, "Do you know Eddie Balantyne?"

"Know? No, I serve him, if that's what you mean."

"That's what I mean."

"Nice man, Mr. Balantyne," he said, perhaps sardonically. "Is that all?"

"I'm sure it's not, but it's all I'll say."

Of the pretty black cashier, with whom he had chatted earlier while he waited for a table, he asked, "Is Mr. Eddie Balantyne a nice man?"

She smiled sweetly. "I wouldn't know. He don't like girls."

"Colored girls?"

"Female girls. And you?"

"I like what I see." He grinned truthfully. She looked like a luscious confection in her starched and frilly low-cut uniform. "But my woman is jealous as Jezebel. I can only look."

"You ditch her, come back to me. I can do more than just *look* good."

Thomas smiled and turned to leave.

"Wait!"

"Yes?"

She looked about to be certain they were alone. "A little buzz going round—"

"Yes?"

"Mr. Balantyne way behind in his bill. He may lose his privileges."

* * *

Back at the hangar Thomas lay in the dark, hands folded behind his head, wondering how and if he should tell Justyn what he'd heard about Eddie. He was troubled, and his mind drifted again to the empty grave, and there it lingered as he fell asleep and sank into a nightmare.

Somehow he had gotten into a hedgerow maze. There were people after him with guns and syringes. As he ran deeper into the center he heard them calling to each other: "Buck!" "Ivey!" "Chub!" "Hamp!" "Over here!" "This way!" "Quickly, or the hawk might carry him away!"

The path grew narrower, its twists and turns closer together. Now he saw that the greenery was not a nurseryman's hedge, but saw brier and thistle of ominous density. He knew in his heart there was no way out. His mother had warned him not to enter, but he ran on with foolish hope, straight into the center, where yawned an empty grave.

"No, no!" he shouted, refusing to leap into the hole, but someone pushed him and he fell. Lying helpless on his back, he saw them gathering at the rim, their weapons glistening in a sun that almost blinded him.

"Are you hurt, son?" a sonorous voice called. His pursuers parted to make way for Judge Mabry, who now was Father Time, a gleaming sickle clutched to his chest.

"Yes, I am, grievously," Thomas answered in stilted tones.

"He's hurt! He's hurt!" the chorus swelled, filing through the maze to gaze at him: Justyn and Frank, Ouida and Eddie, Junior and Poe, Dillard Beasley, his eyes frozen in the wide-eyed glare of the dead. "He's dying! He's dying! Tom's son Thomas is dying!" they began to sing, clasping arms. "Clap hands and pray! Clap hands and pray!" they swayed in unison like a Georgia choir, parting yet again for Paralee and Pear to enter.

"I'm not dying!" Thomas laughed, and leapt up, doing a buckdance step or two into the grave, to show them.

"Oh, yes, you are! Fooled us! Fooled you!" the chorus countered. To Thomas's astonishment, the judge began swinging the sickle at him. Its terrible blade sliced through the air, an arc of silver light trailing droplets of blood as Thomas shielded himself with his arms.

"No!" he screamed. "No, I don't want to die!"

He woke, heart racing. The vaulted building beyond the small office still rang with his screams. He lay shivering as much from fear as from cold, shaking so he was barely able to reach down and pull the blankets up about him. How long he lay he did not know before warmth finally came back to his body. Groaning, he got up, lit the kerosene lamp, and made a pot of strong coffee. Perhaps he might go back to sleep if he tried, but the thought of returning to the nightmare dissuaded him.

Stifling a yawn, he put on his jacket and stepped outside. The night was so beautiful he went back and brought the pot of coffee and mug outside. The moon and stars had a calming effect, bringing to his mind Old World astrologers who had read the riddles of the universe in that wondrous spectacle. What an enchanted life, to chart moon and stars—

A ball of white fire streaked low across the sky, trailing a greenish-white plume so close he thought he could hear and smell its sizzle. A stunning meteor! He stood amazed. Phenomena. Nature was full of them. And so was mankind. Quantum leaps and surges happened. He had seen it with his students, if he persevered . . .

He *would* get at the truth. If he persevered, despite attack or deception or nightmare, charting the moon and stars of his small history . . . He drank the coffee, drank in the moon that had regained its reign of the night sky. Then he went back in, lit the lamp, and began writing: a description of the nightmare, the meteor, his thoughts, his fears.

16

JUSTYN STOOD IN A scattering of leaves in the gray yard, her mind leaping decades, backward and forward. So much time had passed, and yet the long-ago events surrounding her father's death cut with the pain of fresh loss. This morning the house seemed so filled with anguish, she had to escape it. Now she looked about at the ordered lines of lawn and shrub, tree and pavement, and saw reflected her life of the last few years. If Thomas More Levity had not come to Green Hills, she might still be as limited, as secure, her dissatisfaction a vague and unnameable thing.

But he had.

And this morning, pitting instinct against reason, she had made an imprudent, perhaps threatening phone call. Her normally cautious heart still pounded fearfully. No turning back; no turning back. As if to accentuate the irrevocable, a car suddenly shimmered to the curb before her in an emerging ray of sunlight. Monica Castille unfolded, stepping like a disdaining princess to the sidewalk.

"You insisted you be given information my husband might have, about the lynching?"

"Yes." Justyn blushed, ashamed.

"Then I hope you'll be satisfied with what I've brought," Monica said, offering her something large and bulky: a scrapbook. "Chub can't take anymore pressure just now. Anything he has is in here," she added curtly. "I'll need it back as soon as possible. He values it. He doesn't know I've taken it, and I don't want him to. Please, will you look at it, and then leave us alone?"

Justyn nodded, trying to hide her disappointment. A scrapbook. She had hoped for revelation, a startling confession. *A scrapbook?* She watched Monica drive away. She made an elegant study in beige: beige hair, beige skin, beige clothes . . . Sighing, Justyn carried the heavy book to the front steps.

It was filled with newspaper clippings, most of them from the society columns, and photographs, most of them of Chub. She wondered if a mature thought had ever crossed his mind. She leafed quickly, dispiritedly. Concerning the lynching, the trial, there was nothing she had not already seen. Chub's collection was not nearly so complete as her quickly assembled one. Instead, his painstakingly documented role in Green Hills society filled most of the pages, except for an occasional short notice that Henry Clarence Castille III had been arrested for this or that charge, later dropped—vandalism, malicious mischief, drunk driving, leaving the scene of an accident, even "mooning" in youth and "streaking" in middle age. The irresponsible-at-heart never seem to change, she thought, recalling Eddie's constant escapades.

Was Chub's participation in the lynching simply one of those misadventures that got out of hand? Too serious and public an offense for the charges to be conveniently dropped? Certainly, not all of Eddie's pranks had been harmless. What about Chub's? When Justyn was a child the phone had often rung in the middle of the night, Eddie needing Ouida to come rescue him, or Zachary to come to his legal aid. Justyn remembered their whispered arguments, her father's disgust. A woman had been burned by firecrackers Eddie threw; a stray dog had been blinded when Eddie fired a target pistol "by accident"—to name but a couple of instances.

The sun came out in force now. Gray tones vanished. The yard bloomed a mellow ocher. Birds scratched under the nandina bushes. Tawny barked and feinted grandly at the mailman, who was her friend.

"She's a good dog." He smiled, handing her a swatch of letters.

"Not last night, she wasn't. She barked until I had to bring her in."

"If she barked, I'll bet there was something there."

"I suspected the same thing. But I looked. I even came out with the flashlight."

"Maybe a cat. Another dog. But, I'd be careful," he cautioned. "You eat 'em up, he added to Tawny, scratching her ears for her.

Justyn sat on the steps, the big book balanced on her lap, and returned to it after sifting through the mail. Ivey and Eddie were often included in the accounts Chub kept. They seemed to have formed a triumvirate early on in their lives.

Beesie had said that Zachary ran Eddie's friends from Balantyne Hall . . . her good, fair, mannerly father . . . for what? What in their behavior could have angered him so?

Monica Castille had been sincere in thinking the book important. To her, it was the key to Chub's life. "Look at this and you won't even need to talk to him. He's here, in these pages, all of him," she had seemed to say.

What was she missing?

She resettled more comfortably on the step. The sun was balm. Carefully and intently she began a page-by-page study. The first item on the first page concerned Chub's fourteenth birthday party, a country club dinner dance with several young couples in attendance. Stubby Balantyne served as one of the chaperones.

Despite the warmth of the sun, she shivered, as if suddenly in deep water.

Thomas took an indirect route to Paralee's, walking slowly, approaching cautiously from the rear of her yard. The way seemed clear. He could hear children playing out front, but there was no sign of anyone else about. He quickly crossed the exposed expanse and was about to step up on the back porch when he heard raised voices from within.

"Do you think I don't know what you and them white boys did?" Paralee yelled.

"Shut your mouth!"

Thomas stooped instinctively and ducked under the floor. From here the voices were muffled, yet the words still audible. He recognized the man's voice as Pear's.

"I'm sorry," Paralee said more calmly. "I'm in a corner."

"*You're* in a corner! I'm *dying*!"

Thomas heard movement; someone getting up from a chair.

"We both want the same thing, for them not to kill him?" Pear said.

"Yes."

"Then tell me where he is, so I can warn him."

"Brother, I don't know."

There was a sound of a car approaching. Thomas backed a little farther into the dark cavity under the porch.

"My driver's back," Pear said. "Are you going to give me that medicine I asked for?"

"No. Not yet. But I made a new poultice for you, to ease you. You get your wife to wrap it up in a hot towel, at bedtime, and put it over the hurting."

Thomas waited for a few minutes after he heard the car drive away, then crawled out. He wanted to escape unnoticed, to think about the strange and upsetting words he had heard, but he was only halfway across the yard before the children spotted him and came running, joyfully shouting his name. Paralee called to him from the back door. He almost expected that, with her gift of second sight, she must have known he had hidden under the floor.

"I came to see how you are, and to apologize for leaving so abruptly."

She came down the steps. "I'm on my way out to the plant shed," she said, pointing to a long building at the end of the yard, beyond the privy. "Come with me. I want to talk with you."

Thomas accompanied her, questions gathering. But, when she turned, the look on her face cleared his thoughts, her expression was so distraught. "Paralee, what is it? What's the matter?" he asked.

"Shoo! Go away! Go play!" she said to the children, who scattered reluctantly. "Come inside," she said to Thomas as they reached the shed. "I've got to gather some things."

The building's pleasant pungency reached halfway across the yard, and Thomas approached it curiously. He saw that it served as an herbarium. The high side, standing eight or nine feet from the ground, was open, supported by poles, while the low end lay close to the earth, against the edge of the woods. Leaves and pine needles dislodged by a sudden wind clattered against its tin roof and slid screeching down the tin slope, as if they had voices. Hundreds of bunches of dried things—roots, stalks, flower heads, whole plants— hung under the eaves in neat rows. Beyond, in the dark and aromatic interior, board shelves held innumerable glass and crockery jars, neatly arranged and labeled.

"I've got to prepare more yellowroot for Mr. Morrow," she said, reaching into the eaves. "It helps his kidneys and blood."

"What is yellowroot?"

"A plant grows along the creekbanks. Takes an awful lot to get a dram of juice. And this is ginseng—'sang' "— she picked up a jar of powdery root—"an aphrodisiac . . . I'll bet you don't need this!" A smile barely pierced her somber face.

"Paralee, what is it? What's the matter?"

"When good and evil look and sound alike, how do we tell them apart?" She leaned against the shelves. "Pear want me to make him a medicine, in case the pain gets too bad. It's already too bad for him, I know. He'll take it as soon as he gets it."

"You mean . . . something that will *kill* him?"

"Yes."

"What a terrible thing to ask of you!"

"Pear's in a terrible way."

"Is it possible? The medicine, I mean."

"Oh, yes!" She laughed bitterly and swept her arm in a wide gesture that took in the whole shed. "Here are almost as many ways to die as to live. Oh, there are the obvious— deadly nightshade, the highly toxic ones—but every medicine is a small poison. That's how they work, destroying whatever is destroying you. Pear wants something special— quick, natural-seeming. Oh, yes, I can do it."

"Will you?"

"Do I have a choice? I owe him. What's in the stars is in the stars." She shrugged, then straightened resolutely. "Pear want you to go away. To run away. But you're doing the right thing in trying to clear your father's name. A spirit without a proper send-off has to linger. A ghost with something on its mind can't rest."

"Paralee, why are you telling me this?"

She looked away from him. "Where are you staying? I need to know," she asked, instead of answering.

"Why?"

"In case I need to warn you."

"Warn me of what?"

"Of whatever. I need to know."

"Justyn is the only one who knows. She can get in touch with me if you need me."

Paralee seemed not to hear, already absorbed in her science. But when he turned to leave, she reached toward him, her eyes wide.

"Don't go. Please. Something terrible is going to happen. I feel it!"

Thomas shrugged and smiled. "Something terrible *has* happened, Paralee. *Is* happening. I have to go. You know that. You just said so yourself. *I'm doing the right thing.*"

Thomas entered the Nullifier as its doors opened for the early lunch crowd. He was standing at the bar with a token Bloody Mary when Chub Castille entered. At close range he was as handsome as his legend, only beginning to show the tarnishments of age. Thomas waited for him to settle at the bar, then took his drink and joined him.

"I'd like to speak with you," he said, confident he was recognized. With something less than a shrug, Chub acknowledged him. "I don't believe my father killed your friend Stubby Balantyne," Thomas said. The disconcerting eyes he stared into were heavily lidded, platinum fringed, ice blue, and totally disinterested. At length a look of annoyance flickered in them.

"Of course the damned nig—of course he killed him."

"But suppose he didn't. How do you *know* he did?"

Something hot and threatening seemed to flare in the cool

blue depths of Castille's eyes. "I can have you thrown out of here. You annoy me."

"And I can talk to the media. You know, the press isn't on your side anymore."

"I'm sorry I'm late," a strained voice interrupted. Monica Castille stepped between them and took her husband's arm possessively. She stared at Thomas with a strangely pleading look.

"Some other time?" Chub said to him, not attempting to hide the sarcasm in his voice.

Thomas was about to sit down to lunch alone when he saw a familiar bulk plowing angrily toward him through the crowd. "Hello, Junior," he said good-naturedly.

"I thought you disappeared."

"Only for the moment. Are you having lunch? Would you like to sit with me?"

"I've been having to bluff my way through stories, while you've been giving that hick Poe Williams—"

"I haven't 'given' Poe anything. He's worked hard for what he's learned. And," he added, an edge coming into his voice, "as far as I know, he hasn't 'stolen' anyone else's story."

"Look, if it's money you want . . . "

Thomas sat down and motioned Junior to join him. The waiter brought menus. "We aren't speaking the same language," Thomas said quietly. "My story isn't for sale. I told you that. When I agreed to come here it was for my own reasons, not to enact some preconceived drama whose scenario you had already written. You don't know the outcome any more than I do. Now I find it wasn't 'your' story to begin with. Even so, I don't see why there isn't enough here for both you and Poe. You're different, you see things differently—it isn't as if you're competing."

"But of course we're competing! Let him write features if he wants to. *My* story is the news! I see a Pulitzer in this. I see a way to make my shit-headed old man eat crow. *I* contacted you. *I* made all this possible!"

"That's not quite true," Thomas insisted. "You did contact me, though, and share your information, and for that

139

I'm grateful. I'll be glad to share what I learn with you, though not on an exclusive basis."

"Then, where in the hell are you?"

"Do you mean, where am I staying, or where am I in this?"

"Both."

"To answer the latter, I suspect that Pear Plumlee knows more than he's telling about this whole thing, and he wants to keep me from finding out."

"Pear's crud."

"And it seems that Eddie Balantyne may know something. Aside from the fact that I make him so nervous, he *is* Stubby's heir."

"Interesting you should mention him," Junior said more amiably. "He came in a moment ago, saw you, and passed up his center-stage table for one in the other room."

"Did Chub Castille join him?"

"Yes. And wife, Monica. Do you have eyes in the back of your head?"

Something thrilling as the hunter's horn sounded in Thomas's heart. Somehow, it was all going to come together, if only he could trust his instincts, sort them.

"It really was foolish of you to run off," Junior continued, less ominously now that their food had come. But Thomas did not hear, his mind leaping to a sudden possibility. He ate quickly. When the waiter came to refill their glasses, he asked instead for his check. "No, this is on me," Junior broke in. "I'll charge it to the paper. Do you have to rush? There are a number of things we need to talk about."

"I'll give you a call."

"Truce, then?" Junior asked hopefully.

"Truce or stalemate, it isn't broken," Thomas said, standing up to leave.

17

Thomas thought he had reason for hurrying. It had occurred to him at the Nullifier: what better time to visit the legendary Beesie than when the master of the house was away, enjoying a leisurely lunch?

A pickup truck was parked to the right of Balantyne Hall. Thomas drove to the left, out of sight of the road, and parked near the kitchen door. Within he saw a wispy dark woman who turned when he called her name. When he introduced himself she opened the door and motioned him in.

"Mercy! My Justyn told me you might be coming to see me"—she smiled toothlessly—"but I thought I might have dreamed it. Is she with you?"

"No, ma'am."

"Well, let's see . . ." She looked about the spacious, cluttered kitchen. "Have you eaten?"

"Yes, ma'am."

"Then I'll fix us coffee and pie. Do you like peach pie?"

"Yes, ma'am."

"I put up my own peaches, you know. Mr. Eddie and his friends can eat a dishpan pie in an evening," she said proudly.

While she made coffee and spooned pie into dishes, he began his questions. Did she remember his parents? Their families? His mother's last name? Beesie hummed, nodding affirmatively at times, but it was not until he had eaten and drunk to her satisfaction that she found her voice again.

"Your mother was Maude Barrett from out Barrett's way. Used to be a big plantation farm. My grandmother belonged to them before the Balantynes bought her off them. Had brothers, sisters, her great-grandaddy belonged to Barretts. Your mother was light from Barretts. The white ones are your kin, from way back. From slavery times."

"Wait," Thomas said, "I've got to write this down. I—"

But there was no slowing Beesie once her memory started to flow. "Never could have done much with that land. No water. No good bottoms. Just poor dirt . . ."

Thomas had grabbed a small pad from his pocket and began scribbling. Was she talking about black Barretts, or white? "My mother, Maude—her parents?"

"Come to town like everybody else. Fricatown. Your grandmother worked for the Rainses, your grandfather for the Smythes. Good folk. But your mama a baby when they died. Miz Sunflower Townes took her back to the country, raised her. How come she so good with a garden." She wound down as suddenly as she had begun.

"Beesie, who killed Stubby Balantyne?"

Beesie blinked her lashless lids emphatically, then leaned forward to stare at him intently. "Tom, I'm so glad you're back," she said.

Thomas felt he could not breathe. "Beesie, who killed Stubby?" Getting no response, he forced himself to rephrase the question. "Beesie, please tell me, so that I can rest."

In the moment before she answered, he thought that truth was within his grasp. She seemed to know. But when her words came, they were without meaning.

"Son, they all did. Don't you know?"

"I don't mean the lynching, Beesie."

"Don't you know?"

"Know what, Beesie. Tell me!"

"I miss my nap," she said tiredly, looking toward a grease-stained clock that seemed to have stopped years ago. "Are you one of Mr. Eddie's friends? Mercy, have you eaten? There's plenty in the icebox. Will you help me to bed? I think I'm too tired for the steps. These old legs give out sometimes. Up there"—she pointed—"up there's where I stay."

Thomas escorted her up the back stairs, supporting her in the narrow passageway, waiting until she was settled safely in her bed. Outside her door, on the close dark landing, he stood listening. Hammering came from the next floor, but otherwise all seemed quiet. Did he dare? His heart drowned out the hammering. He started upward. A few steps, and he wondered where in that vast house he was? He wished he had studied it more closely from outside, but all that he remembered were the massive columns. Slowly he followed the narrow stairs, testing each with his foot, occasionally wiping a sooty cobweb from his face. A flashlight, a flashlight, his kingdom for a flashlight! He approached the sound of hammering, felt a doorknob with his fingertips. The second floor. He continued past and upward. At last the steps ended at another door. The knob turned rustily in his hand, opening into a hall so wide and bright that for a moment the light blinded him.

He closed his eyes to the light. Panicked, he expected to open them to a gun, Eddie's outrage, but found himself quite alone. The rhythm of the hammer below had not broken. It must be his heart that pounded like ominous footsteps. He clenched his fists and breathed deeply, willing himself to calm. Here was opportunity he might never have again!

The house astounded him. He had never been in such a place. From where he stood, looking down the wide door-lined hall accentuated with mirrors, fine old furniture, paintings, and jardinieres, it seemed as if he had stepped across time. Ladies in hoop-skirted dresses, black servants with hair tightly bound, might step into this hall from any door. He was at once charmed and shamed. One owned the other. It was unconscionable.

Resolutely he started forward. Then, remembering the back-stairs door yawning behind him, forced it shut. The noise it made, the effort it took, had a sobering effect. Watchfully he moved toward the other end of the hall to the wide, chandeliered, brightly windowed front stairs. Its view was of the empty expanse of front lawn, an empty arc of driveway. He had time, he reassured himself, but he must hurry!

He stepped into the nearest unlocked room and closed the door. It was a sitting room. Dust, ashtrays brimming with cigarette butts, old magazines, as well as more costly clutter rested atop priceless furniture. Though he saw nothing of significance to his purpose, he sensed, like a man divining water, some current in the house responding to his presence. Here had lived the man whose life Tom Levity had been accused of taking. What secrets lay within?

When he returned to the hall, he found the next room locked. Why? Remembering an adjoining door in the sitting room, he hurried back. It was sealed by old paint, but he managed to pry it open, stepping finally into a room crammed with packing crates and valuables. It took him a few minutes to realize their significance, until he found receipts for sales of Limoge, Fabergé, and other irreplaceable items. Eddie must be making a habit of selling the family treasures. Did Justyn know?

Next was what appeared to be a guest bedroom, neatly kept. Hurriedly he looked around, then passed through to an adjacent room. Here curtains draped the windows darkly. He saw the outline of a bed, paintings. A faint smell hung in the air, reminding him of Vietnam. Curious, he stepped to the windows and pulled the cords. When he turned it seemed for a moment he must be dreaming . . . a large round waterbed, red satin sheets, mirrored ceilings, erotic paintings of satyrs, youths, and an occasional nymph in orgy. Cocaine spoons and a mirror lay on the small bedside table. Now he recognized the familiar odor as that of marijuana mingled with incense. Fascinated, he started toward the bureau, then froze. A sound in the hall? He slipped quickly into the next room, the last on that side of the hall, stepping from strange dream into nightmare.

In a dusty, spider-webbed corner someone's motheaten big game trophies were stacked, deep in dust. The rest of the room housed ancient battle gear and various antique devices designed to inflict pain and death. A dismantled hangman's scaffold stood next to a guillotine. He shivered at actual sight of Dr. Guillotin's macabre legacy. Not a room for children to explore, he thought grimly, moving quickly through.

He heard a sound again, but more clearly. It was a power saw from the floor below. Good. The more noise the carpenter made to cover him, the better.

He crossed swiftly to the other side of the hall, trying doors until he found one that wasn't locked, a long out-of-date bedroom being used for storage. Fearful now of time, he passed through to the next room, locked from the hall. It was a small gymnasium housing expensive exercise equipment. An adjoining door opened easily into the final locked room at the rear of the house.

Thomas stepped into total blackness. For a moment it was disorienting, until he found a light switch. He found himself in a well-equipped, though cluttered, darkroom. Negatives hung drying; file cabinets lined one wall. His pulse quickened. He was midstride across the room when the sound of a key in the door paralyzed him. It seemed an eternity before he could leap backward, hitting lightswitch and doorknob as the other turned. He slipped gasping into the gym room, swallowing a sudden but strong need to cough.

"Well, what do you think, Boots?" he heard Eddie Balantyne say. A cat meowed in answer. "Should we get to work, or take our nap first?" There was the sound of a file drawer opening and closing. "Oh, let's take our nap. There's too much work here. Get off the counter. Bad cat!"

A door opened and closed. Thomas felt he waited five minutes, though it could not have been so long, before stepping back into the room. When he first switched on the light, he saw nothing changed. Then he noticed a file folder resting newly on a cabinet.

As stealthily as he could, his own breath sounding to him like a bellows, he crossed to it. He could not open the clasp, look at the contents, quickly enough . . . *Paydirt! Had he not felt it all along! From the instant Justyn showed him that snapshot on the plane, had he not suspected that the same person also took the photograph of the lynching! Now he* held proof that, no matter his age or reason, Eddie Balantyne had been present at the lynching!"

His hands shook. He must take this and leave. But would such opportunity ever fall his way again? What else was in the folder? Aside from the familiar print, there were others. Eddie must have shot several rolls that night. In some the lynchers were milling, indistinguishable. In one Buck Stovall loomed clearly, in another Dillard Beasley. Chub Castille appeared in all, either clearly, his expression animated and excited, or blurred, given away by his fine fair hair.

He put a copy in his coat pocket, then turned the key in the cabinet and selected another folder at random. Junior Mills *in medias res* with another male? No, wait, it was not Junior. Perhaps his father, taken years ago. The resemblance was striking. And here, a lewd nude study of Ivey Mabry, looking deliciously young and agreeable. The muffled sound of a door startled him. He replaced the files as he had found them and bolted to the gym-room door.

18

J USTYN DROVE TO THE hangar door and waited in the darkness. Tawny, asleep in the backseat, woke suddenly, barking, when Thomas stepped out of the woods.

"I was visiting Paralee—Miz Bones," he explained. He opened the car door and shone his flashlight to guide her inside. "I would have stayed here if I'd known you were coming."

"Why didn't you call?"

"It's a long story. I had a bit of a scare. Your husband is still away?"

"Yes. For a few more days. I *miss* him."

"That's why I went to Paralee's, to talk to someone. It's a strange time to be alone, isn't it?" He lit the kerosene lamp, his face glowing suddenly in the mellow light. She saw that he was sweating.

"Eddie called, with a wild story about someone breaking into Balantyne Hall and stealing a photograph of the lynching. So I called Mother, to find out what she might know about Eddie's having such a photograph. She told me that he and Chub and Ivey had seen Stubby's body the night he was murdered. That would account for his nervous behavior, don't you think? And Chub's?"

Thomas sighed. "Have a seat on the cot," he said, sinking onto an old desk chair. "I don't know what I think. But the photograph *was* stolen, I know that. I'm the one who took it." He told her about his trip to Balantyne Hall, his visit with Beesie, about the series of photographs he saw.

"I suppose Mother was telling the truth then," she said, still disbelievingly. "But, I know that if she thought a lie would help Eddie, or Buck Stovall . . . oh, I think *he's* up to his neck in this. What can she see in that vulgar man, except sex?"

"Sex is not an 'except,' " Thomas said irritably. "Do you want to see the photograph? It's a copy of the one I was sent."

Justyn studied it with a sick feeling.

"Eddie took this, I can tell. There was a whole folder of different shots. I wish I had taken it."

"I don't understand."

"Eddie was there, that's what there is to understand. You said he was there the night Stubby's body was found?"

"Ambulance chasing, Mother said."

"Well, there you are. Maybe he was ambulance-chasing after the lynch mob." Thomas began sweating profusely. He groaned and rubbed his shoulder. "I think I took the binding off too soon," he said with effort, rubbing his collarbone. "Jesus, I know I did! Whoever mugged me did a good job."

Tawny's sudden barking sent him bounding to turn off the lamp, but the trespasser was merely another dog. After some ominous growling outside the window, it went on its way with a hearty jingling of tags.

"I'll tell you what I'm most afraid of at this moment," Justyn said into the darkness that closed around them. Thomas fumbled to relight the wick. "I've had this funny fluttering in my stomach, unlike anything before . . . I think I'm pregnant. After all these years, I think I'm pregnant, and I'm not ready for it. All this uncertainty . . . If I am, I'll have to have an abortion. I don't know that I can bear it."

Thomas succeeded in lighting the lamp and sat down beside her. Taking her hand, he said reassuringly. "There's no reason for you to be involved any further. It's going to be worked out. I'll work it out."

Tawny barked again.

"I've got to go," Justyn said, rising. "This is too risky. I shouldn't have come."

"No, no. I'm glad you did."

It was the perfect moment to tell him about Eddie, all that Frank had told her, but she was too ashamed. The moment passed.

When they stepped outside the rounding moon was rising. A lovely and surprising brightness preceded it over the runway. Tawny's fur glowed. She wagged her tail joyfully as Thomas saw Justyn into the car.

"I'm going to follow you home," he said. "I want to make sure you get there safely."

After watching Justyn safely inside, Thomas drove purposefully to Judge Jonathon Mabry's house. He had decided to watch the Mabry's, wondering what would worry the judge even yet. He parked discreetly across the street, just out of reach of the streetlight. One of a section of deep yards and spacious houses, the Mabry's English Tudor was dark within, though an ornamental gaslight illuminated the area near the front door. He slouched low in the seat, hoping the police would not select this hour to pass by.

It was still dark when he noticed a figure approaching, a runner, a white man dressed in white. He came pounding down the sidewalk with what must have been considerable speed, though he moved so gracefully he might have been drifting in slow motion. Something about the lithe figure seemed familiar, but it was not until the runner reached the Mabry's yard and veered inward, his hair flashing under the street lamp, that Thomas recognized him as Chub Castille. Chub stopped and, bending as if to tie his shoe, looked long and carefully Thomas's way. After a moment, apparently satisfied, he broke into a slow lope across the Mabry's yard and into the shadowed trees that edged one dark wing. Was it Thomas's imagination, or did he see another white figure, this one seeming to glide ethereally, pass into the trees at a point where they should meet? He was considering following, when approaching headlights sent him hunching further down into the car seat. A low beige sportscar pulled to the curb opposite him. Its top was down, revealing Monica Castille, a bathrobe wrapped high about her throat, her uncombed hair tangled by the cold wind. She must have waked from sleep to find her husband gone. Her intuition as to his whereabouts was apparently correct, Thomas noted wryly, settling in to watch the melodrama.

For a few minutes Monica, beautiful even in dishevelment, sat nervously watching the house, lighting and half-smoking several cigarettes. Suddenly she leapt out of the car and hurried unevenly on slippered feet up the drive to the front door. She clapped the knocker and pounded with her fists. From his vantage point Thomas saw, without doubt this time, the ethereal figure glide back into the dark wing of the house. Chub broke from the woods farther down the street, disappearing quickly in the direction from which he had come. Two or three minutes later the light above the front stoop of the Mabry house snapped on, the door opened, and the gauzy figure stepped out into view. Even at that distance Thomas could see that Ivey was a good actress. Her body language—stifled yawns, a diaphanous stretching—was that of a woman disturbed from deep sleep. The two women talked for only a moment. When Monica Castille returned to her car her expression beneath the streetlight had changed from one of wild anger to relief.

But, after Monica had driven away, it was Ivey whose mood changed . . . to one of fury and tears. Thomas saw her wipe her eyes and storm into the house, slamming the door so hard he could hear it and almost feel its percussion. He imagined her sitting down on the cold tile foyer floor, face pressed in her hands, bemoaning the fact that always, always they spoiled her good times, Jonathon or Monica, or now this accursed Negro spying across the street as if he were a private detective . . . for he felt certain she had seen him.

Justyn was also awake, her thoughts vividly at work as she finished Chub's scrapbook and went back to her father's journal, imagining what he could not say, filling in blanks, a text he dared do no more than suggest. Apparently he, too, had been investigating the lynching. Going backward in time he had found that Eddie had been part of a foursome that included his older cousin Stubby. From his suggestive notes Justyn fantasized scenes in which the four friends gathered in Balantyne Hall: Ivey Montgomery, dressed in something sheer and lovely; Chub, still unmarried, shining—hair, eyes, and skin glittering; Stubby, bearlike and hirsute, delightedly licking his whiskers over Eddie, the youngest among them, sweet as a pot of fresh honey . . . and so eager to please. Wicked, witty dialogue filled the spaces:

"I'm a voyeuress," Ivey sang delightedly, waving a dildo like a wand at them, "the Marquise de Sade."

"Spoiled little rich girl," Chub taunted her, but with affection.

"Not rich enough," she said. "Daddy says I've got to find a rich husband."

"What about me?" Stubby said. "Then we could keep it all in the family."

"Not rich enough. Daddy says there are only two or three in town who are, and they're all old."

"I'm going to be rich," Chub said quietly.

"Going to be doesn't count." She giggled. "Daddy's getting restless. He doesn't trust me."

"We're going upstairs," Stubby interrupted, taking Eddie by the hand.

"Me, too," Ivey said.

Chub rose and followed. On the way up, he stopped to look in the beveled mirror, bending to smooth his hair. Above him Ivey made a face, blew him a kiss, gave him the high sign.

Eddie was unaware he was the center of anyone's thoughts. He lay too deeply asleep, sedated, dreaming that the fires of a biblical hell licked at his feet, his shanks, rising, rising. The devil, in the guise of Thomas More Levity, a huge woolly Afro barely hiding his horns, danced round him, peeing into the fire, his urine a combustible that only excited the flames, making them leap. Now and again, with a flick of his sharp tined tail, he slashed him. The sight of his own blood oozing made Eddie scream louder than the flames that crackled and snapped and roared.

"Help me! Help me!" he pleaded to the men who stood around, but they only turned familiar faces from him. "Aieee!" he yelled, as a flame seared his quivering penis.

"Wake up! Wake up!" the devil hissed, prodding him with a red hot pitchfork, branding him.

"Aieee!" he screamed.

"Wake up! Wake up!"

The light of flames faded into one small burning ember. It was Beesie who stood over him, feebly shaking him, a fading flashlight glowing faintly in her hand. "Are you all right, Mr. Eddie?"

He wanted to turn on the light, to flood the room with assurance, but dared not. It was a long moment more before he could overcome his fear. "I told you never to come up here," he said weakly.

Beesie ignored him. "Is something the matter?"

"Yes, I had the bed turned up too high," he said, reaching to adjust the control. His feet and legs, his naked genitals, did tingle from the heat. "I'm fine. I really am. You go on back to bed." The light turned away from him. Beesie's slippered feet made shushing sounds as she furrowed through the thick carpet. "Wait!" Eddie sat up, rocking from the waves his sudden movement made, and pulled satin sheets around his bare chest. "When you see that root doctor again, I need some poison."

"Poison?"

"For that tomcat that's been skulking around. He's a renegade. Two toms dead, and tonight he ate Jennie-Fur's kittens. That's what I was having nightmares about," he lied with sudden inspiration. "Can you do that? Can you get me some poison?"

"Will that make you happy? Well then, mercy, I'll see. I surely will. Now you go back to sleep, Mr. Eddie."

His bed grew too cold. He felt the clammy November darkness in his veins. He did not want to think of Levity, but a face (the father? the son?) seemed to hang like a pulpy moon from the ceiling, confusing him. He floated, suspended on cold memories. Insidiously, that other long-ago November night pressed in on him.

It was autumn and the night air was spicy, filled with nostalgia and . . .

His bed was too cold. The terrible November darkness was in his veins. He did not want to think of Levity, did not want to dream of Levity, not father or son. Yet that face still seemed to hang.

. . . the subtle death of leaves: a season. A full moon added splendor and light . . .

"Come up! Come up! Come up!" the ancient cuckoo squawked from the hall. An ornately carved Black Forest, it had chimed annoyingly at Balantynes for at least a hundred years. Eddie woke quickly, cheered. The clock could easily be sold to a collector. He had not thought of that.

Thomas ate breakfast in an all-night cafe a few blocks from Balantyne Hall, lingering over coffee and pondering his next action. A meeting with Pear? But worsening health must be crippling the man. His wife said he was not even able to talk on the phone.

"More coffee?"

"Yes, thank you. Excuse me. Have you lived in Green Hills long?"

"Been running this place twenty years."

"Do you know anything about the lynching thirty years ago?"

"No, I lived out in the country then. Never knew it happened until I read about it in the paper a week or so back. Man's son is in town. You him?"

Thomas nodded.

"Black fellow in the kitchen knows something about it. He'll be taking a break in about five minutes, if you'd like to step out back and talk to him."

Thomas was surprised to find that the man who waited for him was Paralee's knife-wielding lover, Monk. But if Monk likewise recognized Thomas, he did not acknowledge it.

"Thank you for talking to me," Thomas floundered, stalled by the habitual look of anger in the man's badly disfigured face. A taut knife scar pulled the right eye downward, a similar furrow above the left brow lifted it quizzically. The fury that glared from within seemed directed impersonally at Thomas, the fine November morning, the increasing traffic visible between a gap in the buildings, and perhaps the extent of the universe beyond. Paralee was probably right: this man would someday murder her and perhaps the chil-

153

dren. "I understand you might know something about—"

"I know who you are. What I have to say is, I was there the day they dragged your father out of jail. I was the only colored there. You would have thought I was the only colored in town." He stopped and spat, then added bitterly, "I was going to do something, I don't know what. But I couldn't let them take him without nobody trying to do nothing."

A team of tanker trucks sped by, close to the building, their roar making the ground tremble.

"What did you do?"

"Nothing. He was already dead."

"*What?*

"Your father was already dead when they hauled him out of jail. I know a dead man when I see one. The drunks thought he was passed out, but he was *dead*. Wasn't nothing I could do for him."

"Who else knew this?"

"Whoever killed him, I guess. Kidney punch, 'nigger knocker'—" Monk spat and rubbed the phlegm into the pavement with his shoe. "Dead no more than a few minutes, I'd say, before they brought him out."

"I don't understand."

"Dead is dead. What's to understand? It's all a crock of shit, anyway, this fucking life."

Part III
▽

The Falconer

19

Tears were something Justyn seldom allowed herself, but when she found a large rock freshly landed on newly fallen leaves near the front door, she could pretend no longer. Someone *was* spying on her. During the night Tawny had barked and then yelped loudly. She could have been blinded or even killed if the trespasser's aim had been truer. Was this connected to Thomas? Of course—wasn't everything?

She stood for a moment at the living-room door, staring at Frank's empty chair. She felt guilt, a faint rage at life. Aside from a child, what was it she wanted?

That was simple. What she wanted was to see this story through to its end. She wanted to know what had really happened to Thomas's father, and to her own. She wanted to know what role members of her family had played in the lynching and its aftermath. She wanted to understand a little better the race relations in the town she had purported to study: *her* town. She wanted to know why Dillard Beasley died at that time in that place. She wanted to see the shape of the pieces of this broad puzzle and to put them together. Even if she had known how painful it was going to be, she still would not have avoided that fateful meeting with Thomas. She wanted the truth that badly. Its promise seemed worth the price.

But she did not know the truth yet because the pieces were so scattered. She *couldn't* tell Thomas everything she knew or suspected—partly out of family loyalty, and because she was uncertain what it meant. She suspected that Thomas, too, held back his suspicions.

Thomas sat in his car at the restaurant, stunned by what he had been told by Monk, trying to put into perspective the knowledge that someone had killed his father before he could be lynched. He might have sat there all morning, confusion unnerving him, if a familiar figure had not slowly crossed the cafe parking lot, from a wooded corner to the sidewalk. With a shock he recognized Beesie. Moving with the slow shuffle of the very old, she seemed much too frail a contender for brutal traffic there. He leapt out of the car and ran to her, calling her name, but when she turned her squinting inscrutable stare on him, he could not tell if she recognized him.

"I have a car. I can drive you wherever you're going," he said amiably, trying not to frighten her. "Where are you going?"

She cupped her hand over her eyes against the sun, careening to look up at him. "Go 'way! Go 'way," she said, "or I don't know where I been!"

"If you'll tell me where you're going, I'll be glad to drive you there."

"I'm going to get Mr. Eddie some medicine," she said slowly, as if talking to a child. "I be all day if you stand in my way. Go way!"

The wind from a rush of traffic made her totter, but she started determinedly across the busy street amid the scream of screeching brakes and frantic horns. Thomas followed, shielding her, widespread arms holding the amazed drivers at bay. He accompanied her for several blocks until Balantyne Hall loomed into view. Sighing, he stopped and made his way dejectedly back to his car.

"I'm glad you called," Justyn said, her mood lifting at the sound of Thomas's voice. "I was going to drive out to the hangar to try and catch you. Poe Williams called. He wants to do a feature on Balantyne Hall. He talked to Eddie, cleared it with him. Eddie suggested *I* take him on a tour of the house. Would you like to come?"

"Has this to do with the fact that it was Stubby's home?"

"I'm sure it does. Poe is apparently no one's fool. I think he shares our view of what happened to his uncle."

"I'd like very much to go."

"Then meet us at two. I'll give you the grand tour that I sometimes do for National Historic Register Visitors."

"With family secrets, a few skeletons thrown in?"

"Certainly!" She laughed.

"You look perfect for a picture," Poe Williams said when he saw Justyn. She wore a peach sweater and skirt, a color that seemed to make her fair skin glow. "Wait, I want to get a picture of you, too, Thomas." The two stood obligingly on the steps and smiled at the camera before entering the house.

"What a place!" Poe said. "I've always wanted to see inside. I used to imagine that I knew the people who lived here. I'd pretend I came to visit."

Be thankful you didn't, Justyn thought, but said aloud, "Well, some of it is off limits, but I'll do my best.

"Before we tour the house, let me tell you a little about the structure," Justyn continued. "The columned brick face you see outside actually represents the third house structure, completed in 1859, shortly before the outbreak of the Civil War." Her soft voice took on an informed tour guide authority. "Vestiges of the original house, a two-story log cabin built around 1770 by my four-greats-grandfather Valenchat (spelled c-h-a-t, but pronounced s-h-o-t) Balantyne, are visible only in a log wall left standing in the back stairwell. The log house faced opposite this one, toward the river."

"The river was used then?" Poe asked.

"Yes, by Indians and traders and settlers. The traffic of canoes and rafts must have been quite heavy at times. From the back you can still see traces of the drive that led down to the water and Valenchat's trading station. The Indians brought furs and pelts. This was Cherokee territory then. Valenchat literally carved this place out of wilderness—the 'incredible tangle,' as early explorers called it."

"Did he have a land grant?" Poe asked. "Valenchat, I mean?"

"No, he traded and bought his land from the Indians. He selected a wife from them, as most of the early traders did. She died in childbirth, with her baby. When he remarried a few years later it was to a white woman, my four-greats-grandmother. They're all buried in the family cemetery." She waved downhill toward the group of gray tombstones at the far edge of the deep yard. "The Indians' graves aren't marked, although some of the slaves' are."

"Valenchat's background sounds much like Devil McKinner's," Poe said.

"Yes. McKinner settled only a year or so earlier. He and *his* Indian wife had eight children, seven of them sons. But he sided with the Tories and was killed."

"Who killed him?" Thomas asked.

"His neighbors. I've wondered if Valenchat had anything to do with it, but I doubt it. Val was badly wounded in an early Revolutionary skirmish—a festering leg wound that later proved fatal. I can't imagine him climbing the mountain to Devil's Rock and helping to hack poor McKinner to death, much less scalping him." She shivered.

"It sounds as if Green Hills's history has always been violent," Thomas observed.

"Yes." She could not help smiling ruefully. "But, to continue, Valenchat's grandson, Valenchat II, built the second stage of the house, a frame structure, in 1820—a massive three-story rectangle with a recessed Greek Revival portico, an attempt at a proper home for his bride, a woman of the planter class from Charleston. She must have been horrified! But it was her money that kept the family affluent until the war. The Civil War," she explained to Thomas, "although around here we don't need to say which war." She waved her arms at the house around her. "The current house was built over that structure, the face away from the river, no longer used for commerce, toward the road that had developed with the times. The house as you see it survived the war in reasonable shape, as did most of the town, probably because Green Hills had strong Unionist leanings. Do you have any questions before we go in?"

"As long as we're here, I'd like to see Valenchat's grave, maybe get a picture of you by one of the headstones," Poe said.

"Can we wait until we come back out?"

"Sure, the light should be all right then."

As they climbed the front steps, Justyn pointed to features of the architecture. "The bricks are made from clay dug here on the grounds," she explained, touching them lightly before pushing the doorchime reluctantly.

Eddie answered the ring, welcoming them with a flourish. But after brief hellos, avoiding Thomas's eyes, he announced he had to be off to a meet with his broker. "Enjoy the tour, Jus," he said, hugging her to his thin frame. "Lock up when you leave. I think Beesie's asleep."

As they moved through the ornate rooms of the first floor, Thomas and Poe shared aloud their amazement at the wealth of antiques and art that graced the spacious rooms. They seemed to take no notice of the dust and disarray. "Well, I'm merely a poor cousin—or, in this case, niece," she explained. "I've certainly never felt that any of this affected me." She could not explain the sense of family, of family history, that waited there among the belongings that were not hers.

As the two men followed her up the stairs to the second floor, Poe said matter-of-factly, "I asked Uncle Dillard's doctor about the heart attack. He said yes, a surprise, a shock, even a sudden noise could have brought it on."

The spell of beveled glass and glittering prisms on the landing seemed to deny the ugly possibility Poe suggested. Then the annoying whine of a power saw starting up abruptly as a scream broke the protective spell of beautiful light.

"We might as well see Mother's new apartment," Justyn said. "I'm curious." She led them into a suite of rooms on the right side of the wide hall. They came upon Buck Stovall and a helper installing a kitchenette sink. Stovall reddened, glared at Thomas, grunted a gruff, disapproving hello to Justyn, and went quickly back to work, his muscles bulging.

"Eddie asked that we not go on the third floor, but we'll go to the head of the stairs. The whole floor used to be a ballroom, a 'play party' room," Justyn continued, noticing how uneasily Thomas stared above him, "but during the war it was divided into smaller rooms for relatives escaping low-country heat, malaria, and General Sherman. Soldiers on the way home, the more genteel ones, sometimes spent a night or two. One, a one-armed captain named Ned, said he had no home left to go to, and stayed fifty years. He's buried out there with the family. Beesie remembers him well."

As they went back downstairs Poe rushed ahead. "I want to get a few pictures," he said excitedly, disappearing toward the living room. Thomas waited for Justyn at the foot of the stairs. He smiled.

"Damn you, Rhett Butler!" She laughed, shaking her fist at him.

He grinned toothily, crinkling his eyes and twirling an imaginary mustache, "Et tu, Scarlett!" he said huskily, spreading his arms for her.

Suddenly an embarrassed, angry Buck Stovall cleared his throat loudly to warn them of his presence.

A flock of resident pigeons lifted from the roof as they made their way down the front steps. Eddie appeared from the side yard, without explanation, to accompany them, chatting amiably with Poe about a set of dueling pistols the young man had noticed in the library.

A few dozen headstones, eight generations of ancestors, were the most notable monuments. "Slaves," Justyn affirmed to Thomas, nodding toward rows of mounds at the back marked only by fieldstones. Their graves served as buffer between the cemetery proper and forest. Beyond, the distant river soughed.

"Jus, don't leave out the dear departed Cherokee 'first family,' " Eddie said mockingly. "She was supposed to be an Indian princess."

"Eddie, when did you have the gravel put on?" Justyn asked of the freshly covered slave graves. "It looks good."

"When I got tired of paying someone to pull briers. I decided it would be cheaper in the long run."

"That was nice of you," she said sincerely.

Thomas walked to the mounds. "Is it true that the Cherokee owned black slaves?" he asked.

"Yes. They were considered spoils of war. It's a complicated culture we come from, Thomas. Everyone a little bad, some a lot."

"It's beautiful here," he said. "I love the sound of the river."

"I'm glad you like it," Eddie smiled. "I could arrange for you to be buried here, if you'd like."

"I'll want to be buried in California, with my wife and children," Thomas said.

"One never knows," Eddie said, smiling sadly, as if the bell tolled. "The offer stands." Stubby's tombstone rose above the rest. Eddie touched it fondly, his eyes clouding.

"I've got all the pictures I need. I'd better be going," Poe said.

Thomas and Justyn made apologies also, and took their leave.

Justyn looked back when Eddie did not accompany them. He still lingered among the tombstones. A calico cat had wandered from the house to join him. For a moment Eddie looked so forlorn she hated to leave him. She knew that he wanted to be buried there, and that he and Ouida had argued because she preferred to be with Zach across town. Would he alone represent this generation of Balantynes in the family plot? She shivered and chided herself for her maudlin thoughts as she drove away. Death seemed a long time in the future for Eddie, and anything might happen in the years between: perhaps even a wife for him; children.

Yet, the moment, the glance backward, her perceptions seemed to etch themselves in her mind, as if already she were wondering what might have changed if she had followed her instinct, gone back to her uncle in this moment of obvious loneliness.

When Justyn had gone Eddie stood on alone while the wind and ancient river soughed. "I remember it as if it were yesterday," he said to the cat that now rubbed and purred against his legs, "the night Stubby died. I wish I could forget it, just remember him."

The cat cocked its head, listening, and then bounded away, toward the river. Eddie looked up. A dark figure wafted toward him from the edge of the woods. For a moment he was frightened. Then he recognized Beesie. "Did you get it?" he asked.

Beesie reached in her frail bosom and thrust a small package at him. She was so tired the gesture almost threw her off balance. She stood with thin chest heaving, blinking her lashless eyes.

He took her arm guiltily and walked with her toward the house. She had been gone so long he had almost despaired of her.

Through the back door, the kitchen, up the back stairs, he felt only gratitude and affection. But when she was settled in her dark bed and he had stepped again into the narrow well outside her room, the past once again overwhelmed him. It was down these very stairs, all the way from the third floor . . . blood. Sometimes it seemed to drip from everything.

He found himself on the second floor without remembering how he got there.

Buck Stovall faced him with raised eyebrows, a hammer in his hand. "Yes. What do you want?"

Eddie's hand went to his head. "Too much on my mind. I forget. How's it going?"

"A little ahead of schedule. She wants to move in right away. I'm bringing in a crew tomorrow to tape the Sheetrock."

"That nigger is upsetting her. I'll be glad when he's gone." Eddie thought of it as testing the waters. He was more than a little pleased at the lean look of anger that settled slowly over Stovall's face before he turned back to his work.

20

EDDIE AWOKE IN HIS third-floor bedroom aware there was something of the night he did not want to remember.

The bathroom door opened and Chub stepped out, toweling himself. "Halloo!" he said cheerfully. "I didn't want to wake you. I felt like a shower. Mind?"

"Of course not."

"Couldn't sleep. Did two miles in the dark. Dogs barking everywhere. Thought Monica wouldn't look for me here. Used my key." He sniffed in exaggerated fashion. "What's that?"

"Something new. Something old. I smoked a joint soaked in cinnamon oil and I think I'm allergic to the damned oil," Eddie said, remembering. "Duke had to hold my head half the night. Now the light hurts my eyes. I must be dehydrated."

Chub made a consolatory sound and came to sit naked on the bed. "Massage?" he offered.

Eddie groaned gratefully and, pushing back the covers, turned onto his stomach and spread his arms wide. He lay rocking on the bed's waves as if floating. When Chub's powerful hands went to work on his neck and shoulders he sighed so heavily it sent a shudder through the waterbed.

"We're getting old," Chub said in rhythm to his kneading, "when this brings more pleasure than you-know-what. And you the baby of us all!"

"Don't mention age," Eddie moaned ecstatically. "There! That's the place. Rub there."

"How's the new 'Duke,' aside from pimply-faced and a supplier of bad stuff?"

Eddie sighed, weighing his answer, aware it would be measured seriously, despite Chub's bantering tone. Duke was a name they had used indiscriminately over the years for the succession of boys, a wicked idea that occurred to Eddie because his grandmother had used the same name for all her German shepherds. "A dog!" the answer came to him whimsically. "A mistake. Cinnamon oil—artificial, at that—you're right, I must be getting old."

Chub stopped his therapeutic pummeling, stretched his fingers, and grinned. "Got to get dressed and trot home," he said, but not emphatically. Eddie caught the question mark in his voice and lay still. "Say, kid, how do you feel now? You feel like it?"

Eddie dozed and woke, winced. Chub had opened the drapes and stood dressing in the sunlight. He watched him enviously. The Greeks would have had the sense to make a god of him, he thought, remembering Greece and its ancient, consoling light. Sense without shame. The happiest time of his life, their summer there, when Chub was between marriages. One statue might have been Chub himself, even to the damp curls, a little of the golden yellow still remaining. Had he told him? He did so, haltingly, trying to find the right words.

Chub sat to tie his running shoes and let the flattery wash over him without acknowledgment. But, after a moment, he spoke quietly. "What are you planning to do about our problem?"

"Which problem?"

"The nigger."

"Oh!" Eddie said. His squeaking voice made him feel silly. "I'm hoping Buck Stovall will take care of that for us."

"And if he doesn't?"

"Well, then, I have a plan. I'm working on it."

"Perhaps you should fuel the fire."

"Which fire?"

"Stovall."

"Yes." Eddie rolled over and sat up, tightening his brow in concentration. "Any suggestions?"

"The nigger and your niece. The nigger and your sister. You'll think of something."

Eddie, shivering at Chub's intuitiveness, pulled the covers

up about his neck and tried to organize his thoughts. What day was it? Was Stovall due today? What else could he say to him? Intrigue. Once he had thought it sport.

"Don't be paranoid," Chub said good-naturedly, as if reading his thoughts.

"What?"

"You're cringing. You know how I hate cringing. Like a damned dog. Like Duke."

"Oh, *you!*" Eddie laughed, throwing a pillow at him.

It was the right thing to do. Chub caught it and feinted toward the door, passing it back like a football. Suddenly he stopped midstride, his eye on the window. "Damn! It's your sister," he said, "turning in the drive."

"At this hour? What time is it? Why didn't she call?" Eddie leapt to his feet and began throwing on clothes. "Quick. Hand me my shoes. I'll get her out of the way, then you go out."

"Well," Chub said, frowning as he watched Eddie dress, "what I want to know is, how are we going to handle things when she's *living* here?"

"Don't worry. Didn't I tell you not to worry? No sweat. No sweat at all. Don't you trust me?"

Chub's expression changed. "Everything's A-okay, huh?" he said with sudden cruelty—adding, with satisfaction, "Watch it, kid, you're cringing again."

Ouida, sober and nervous, looked haunted with her glistening eyes sunk in dark circles.

"What's wrong?" Eddie asked, forgetting his irritation. He took her by the arm and led her into the dining room, then seated her at the table facing away from the door.

"I didn't plan to come," she apologized breathlessly. "I was out driving around, and I thought, I've either got to talk to someone, or have a drink, and who else could I talk to? Justyn? She's keeping her distance," she added bitterly.

Eddie sat down across from her. "I suppose it's about Stovall?"

"Yes."

167

A wave of jealousy swept over him when she blushed deeply—over that man, and at her age! "You can't blame her for disapproving of your suitor," he said evenly. "After all, he's screwed every whore in Green Hills."

"But that's past."

Chub crept across the doorway and out without making a sound.

"Besides, he's not our class," Eddie added.

"You didn't think Zach was, either."

"That was different. He wasn't hardscrabble."

"The point is, Buck's asked me to marry him."

"*What?*"

"And . . . Well, you see, I know I'm supposed to move in here with you. I don't know if you'd want us both, or . . ."

He waved his hands in front of his face to hide his outrage. "Wait. This is all too sudden. You know I can't think before I've had my coffee. Let me tell Beesie to start us some breakfast." He rose on legs that wanted to buckle and forced himself to walk stiffly back to the kitchen. Beesie stood leaning against the sink, dozing. He gulped deeply for air, his head swimming. Stovall, here! It was inconceivable. All that had kept him going was the knowledge that Ouida was moving in, that it would be like old times, brother and sister against the world . . . He managed a quivering smile when Beesie started awake; gave her instructions. She poured coffee and fixed cream and sugar, a bottle of brandy on a tray.

"Now, where were we?" he asked, returning, his mind racing. What time was it? It couldn't be more than seven. His head ached terribly. When would Stovall come? A half hour? He musn't waste a moment of his time alone with Ouida. "Do you really intend to marry him?"

His sister sipped at her coffee and sighed. She looked touchingly forlorn, wrapped in a bulky sweater as if it were a cocoon she might hide in. She was trembling. He had to remind himself that what he plotted was for her own good.

"It's what I want," she said tiredly. "I've been alone a long time," she reminded him with uncharacteristic shyness.

Eddie steeled himself and fixed his eyes on a spot on the

yellowing wallpaper behind her. "Did *he* tell you that he's not seeing other women?" he asked in a careful voice.

"Yes. Of course," she said, startled. "Well, I think he did. Maybe I just assumed . . . Eddie, what do you know? Do you know something? Don't tease me about something like this," she said miserably.

"It's probably nothing. A few phone calls. I've heard him talking—"

"Uh!" The light went out of her eyes as if he'd struck her.

Again he steeled himself. One lie could destroy a thousand truths. Who said that? Chub? Stubby? "I don't want him making a fool of you, Sis. That's all," he said consolingly. "Just be sure your leopard has changed his spots."

Ouida turned to the brandy without realizing it, lifted her cheek for Beesie's feeble peck when the old woman appeared with a tray of toast and jam. She chewed a few bites perfunctorily. "I guess I'd better leave, if I don't want him to find me here," she said sadly, shivering.

"Take Balantyne Road," Eddie advised her as he saw her out. "Stovall comes in the other way."

Justyn marveled at the splendor of the early sunset, the blazing, changing light signaling the earth's movement toward winter solstice. Any other year she would be thinking ahead to the holidays, not mystery. What she had thought of this morning did not seem as feasible now, yet she could not talk herself out of the idea: if Frank, as a child, could spy on Balantyne Hall in the darkness, why couldn't she, an adult? What might she learn? Of course, times had changed. It was no longer safe for child or woman or man to wander the streets of Green Hills alone at night, but she knew the neighborhood, knew a place on the river where she could leave her car adjacent to the grounds. She would circle through the woods to the cemetery. It was too risky to take Tawny, as she would have liked, but Balantyne Hall was no Devil's Rock she reminded herself as she cut the headlights and followed an old trail, merely a light swath now, a few hundred yards off the road.

The moon was almost full. With merely a penlight she could see well enough to avoid fallen branches on the forest floor as she threaded through underbrush to the woods' rim. Before her the sudden space of vast lawn and sky yawned like a universe, tombstones glowing eerily as green cheese. Frank had said he hid behind hedges near the front door.

Like a thief Justyn had dressed in black for the occasion, and like a thief she crept within shadow of the trees until she reached the place where the dark back side of the house almost reached the darker line of trees. Swiftly she ran along the wall of the house, hugging it until she reached a long rectangle of light from the living-room window. Eddie's voice swelled from within, high and shrill with anger.

"*You* bungled it this time," he said, "but you want to blame me!"

The window was open, despite the cold November night. Then the odor of marijuana drifted out, and she understood why. A thin fire trailed thinner smoke, and all remaining traces, out the sluggish chimney.

"I'm not blaming you," Chub said, joining him at the window, pale hair backlit, forming a sort of halo. But his voice was hard.

"I did the best I could." Eddie's voice went nasal, became a whine.

"If you had done the best you could, we wouldn't have a problem, now would we?" Chub leaned forward to flick a butt through screen the cats had shred. Could he see her? Surely not. Yet she felt exposed, and sank more deeply into the rustling nandina. "Ah, it smells good out here," Chub said, leaning even farther over the low sill toward her. "Like autumn, which it is, thank God. And late. I've got to get going, kid."

"I wish you'd stay. I don't want to be alone tonight."

"Then don't be. Go out and find yourself a new Duke. You're good at that."

"No! I mean, I want to be with *you*." Eddie's voice filled again, but with fear. "At this time of year, when I think about *that* night, when Stubby—"

170

Chub's hand closed over Eddie's mouth. *"Don't say it!"* he said warningly. But, in an instant, his mood softened. "I want to go home to bed and not have bad dreams. I suggest you do the same."

Justyn watched Chub's car drive away, saw the last light on the third floor go out. When she moved stiffly, the dry nandina leaves rattled like bones. But the old house, stations drawn for the night, seemed to take no notice. Its slumbering noises, low creaks and groans like those of an old ship, followed her across the yard to the green-glowing tombstones. Nothing discovered, nothing gained. And yet . . . what had Eddie bungled? What might he have said about the night of Stubby's death, if Chub had not stopped him?

Her car shone in the small clearing ahead. She stumbled, and switched on the penlight reluctantly. It only made the remaining stretch of forest seem more dense. What was that noise? She tried to hurry, tripped, and fell sharply, flinging the light yards away. She crawled toward it when hands closed over her, muffling her scream.

"You might as well stop struggling," a familiar man's voice hissed close to her ear. A tongue slathered her cheek. Arms hard and unyielding as steal locked around her. Chub! "Here I was, planning to go home to a boring wife, when what does luck put in my way, but Little Red Ridinghood. You sneaking bitch, I could almost see your eyes glowing in the dark."

Justyn struggled for air, his hand hard on her mouth.

"You *are* a witch, aren't you? Well, no one's coming to save you. Not your sissy uncle or husband or nigger boyfriend—"

His free hand moved inside her sweater to her bra, which snapped with a flick of his thumb. She thought of her baby that just might be beginning, and jabbed desperately with her knees, but his rough hand went into her panties, groping, forcing her legs apart. "Good and wet," he purred as she writhed. "I always thought you'd be hot inside all that cool," he moaned huskily, grabbing, thrusting. "Does it hurt? You like it, don't you. Well, I'm going to do you every way there is. By the time I'm finished with you, you'll know what it is to be fucked, you fucking, spying little bitch!"

171

21

J USTYN LAY ON THE cold ground, fighting the one sensation she would never have anticipated: sleep. Wearily she curled into a fetal position, hands pressed between her breasts for warmth. Her cares, her life before, seemed worlds away. She would sleep, perhaps she was already asleep, and then she would wake.

An insect crawled up her leg. She kicked and the dry leaves rattled. She reached out and scraped an armful of leaves to her, over her. Soon she lay in a half-cocoon of leaves, their small bit of warmth the sedative she needed. Night noises faded. Her breath slowed.

When she woke, moonlight almost as bright as day altered the forest. Screech owls were calling above her, their shy whinnying sounds pleasant to the ear. She sat up slowly, amazed at the leaves spilling from her, remembering slowly, in sequence. Chub!

She ached. She hurt. She felt dirty, furious, and ashamed. How long had she lain here? How could she bear this sensation of being slathered in spittle and sperm? She grabbed a handful of leaves and rubbed her face and arms, but the feeling of sticky filth persisted. Moaning, she got up. Her clothes were twisted and torn, as ruined, she felt, as her body. She stood groggily, trying to get her bearings. The screech owls went silent. Beyond the trees she heard the river soughing—moaning, it seemed to her—and she stumbled toward it gratefully.

Thomas thought to visit Paralee, whose somber face had been with him throughout the day, but he no sooner padlocked the hangar door and stepped into the adjoining woods than he heard the sound of footsteps approaching on the runway. Remembering Vietnam, he froze among the trees, a shadow among shadows. Buck Stovall passed not yards from him, so close that in the revealing moonlight Thomas could see the revolver in his hand. Choking, he held his breath with effort as Stovall pounded on the hangar door and then broke a window with his fist. The sound of shattering glass and Buck's curses filled the night. When the crunch of tires and a bright sweep of headlights interrupted him, he turned and faced them stolidly.

"Levity, you bastard!" he bellowed.

There was a whirring noise and someone waved a hand-kerchief out the partially lowered window. "Wait!" a frantic voice called. "It's the judge, Judge Mabry. I'm his driver. Who are you?"

Buck shook his head and lowered the pistol, walking slowly to the car. Thomas couldn't hear what was being said in low voices, but in a moment Stovall helped the judge from the car and led him close.

"But, where's my wife?" the judge asked in panic. "I was told she was here. Are you certain?"

"As far as I can tell, there's no one inside. The place is locked up from the outside, tighter than a drum," Stovall reassured him. "But I just broke open a window. I've got a flashlight. Let me go in and check."

Thomas listened to the judge's close, stentorious breathing for what seemed an unbearably long time before Stovall reappeared, his bleeding right hand wrapped in a stained handkerchief. "No, there's no one there. Levity's been staying here, all right, but there's no sign of a woman."

"But, where can she be?"

"Not here. Who told you she would be here?"

"I don't know who he was. A voice on the telephone. The call woke me."

"Did he say she was with another man?"

"Yes," the judge admitted wearily. "And I believed him. She wasn't home. She hadn't told me she was going out. It took me a while to find someone to drive me. But, what are *you* doing here?"

Buck sighed heavily and lit a cigarette. "The same ruse," he admitted ruefully, his hand suddenly shaking. "God, I would have killed him, thinking he'd had his hands on Ouida!" He sighed again. "And then you would have found me. I came here hotter than hell, ready to kill them both."

The two men stood silently for a moment sharing, unknowingly with Thomas, awe at the twists of fate.

"But, who would do such a thing?" the judge asked dispiritedly, leaning heavily on the cane he carried.

"I don't know, but I think I have a pretty good idea. I know more than one reason a particular person would like me out of the way. And I was fool enough to fall for it. I left my car out on the highway. Would you give me a lift back out, Judge? I'd rather not have to explain to Levity what I'm doing here."

Thomas found Paralee sitting in the kitchen, legs parted, red caftan gathered about her sinewy thighs, stripping chicken that she sorted into tubs before her. She motioned toward a chair with a nod of her turbaned head, but Thomas declined. He poured himself a cup of coffee and stood restlessly by the stove, expecting her to notice his shaken state. But her thoughts were not with him.

"Pear's dying," she said quietly. "They say it won't be long now." Everything about her seemed elongated, like an El Greco painting, her pupils almost elliptical in the light of the bare overhead bulb. "I expect I be sending 'round that medicine any minute now," she added softly. Chicken plopped methodically into the bucket. "He gave me a letter to give you when he's gone. You'll have it soon. In the meantime, he say for you to be careful."

Thomas's heart quickened. "Do you know what's in it? Bits of string?"

"Perhaps a whole ball of twine. Who knows? No, I don't know."

"Is there anything you can tell me now? People are wanting to *kill* me, Paralee."

"No, this is Pear's business," she said firmly.

Thomas mulled her words impatiently. The moonstruck November darkness seemed suddenly to deepen in expanded shadows outside the window. He was no longer safe. He would have to find another place to sleep tonight, but not here. "I love you, Paralee," he said quietly.

The ruins of an old pier jutted into the river. Justyn remembered it well from childhood swims. She stripped, and then slowly descended the gently sloping bank, holding on to it.

The water was muddy and cold; her feet sank in sludge. For a moment she doubled with cramps, but they passed. Carefully she washed herself, relishing somehow the cold, the discomfort, as if it were a hairshirt helping her toward salvation.

Then the shattering cry of a waterbird in distress brought her out of her trance. Reality closed in, and she doubted she was going to be able to bear it.

It was after two A.M. before Thomas settled into the Ritzcroft Hotel, Green Hills's newest and largest convention center. Paralee had argued that such a public place, with all rooms centered around a common and brightly lit roofed garden, might be safest for him now.

A shower and heavy meal from room service made him drowsy. When he woke, it was ten A.M. He lay languidly for a while, dozing and stretching, thinking about Naja and her warm, sinewy dancer's body. But when he woke fully it was Justyn he telephoned.

"I wanted you to know I moved again," he said. "I'm at the Ritzcroft. I slept like the dead. How about you?"

"Not so well. In fact, I didn't sleep at all. I fell off the front porch last night, straight into the pyracantha," she lied. "I'm a little the worse for wear. Oh, Thomas, I'm so glad you called."

"I can't hear you very well, Justyn. You'll have to speak up."

"I said I fell. I'm all scratched up."

"Then shouldn't you see a doctor? In your possible condition . . ."

"Later," she said tiredly. "Right now, hot baths and coffee are the remedies. Thomas, what do we know? Do we know enough now to do *anything*?"

"Can you come here for lunch, around noon? I thought I'd ask Poe and Junior, so that we can all compare notes. It's time to let the papers unfold the story a little further, don't you think?"

Justyn merely nodded, but Thomas didn't seem to need an answer. Then, "Yes, I'll be there," she said firmly, and hung up.

Thomas held a table for four. "You look like you tangled with a cat," he said, rising and pulling out a chair for her.

"You should have seen me before makeup." She managed a smile.

"I feel better than I have in days. Oddly, I like it here. A large desk and good light in my room. Think I'll be able to get some writing done. I'm anxious to get back to my poems. I haven't done anything except work on my journal and a few quick letters."

"Here come Poe and Junior."

"My good friend, her royal highness Justyn Jones," Junior said, bowing grandly. "My dear, you look *terrible*."

"Thank you. You do, too," Justyn said, and was immediately ashamed for matching his insult.

Poe's hair was tousled, his cheeks red. He threw a smile like a barrier between them. "I've been to a fire," he said excitedly. "A warehouse. Suspected arson."

"Now, *that's* more your style," Junior said.

"What to drink?" Thomas asked. "This lunch is on me, by the way."

With a glass of wine, Justyn began to relax. Thomas ordered a second for her before the meal arrived. As they ate, he explained his plans.

"Let's see what we can put together," he said, "to keep the pressure on."

"My old man will shit," Junior said happily.

Justyn told her story first, omitting what Frank had told her, but giving her impressions of Chub's scrapbook, her father's journal, and Thomas's revelation that Eddie had taken the photograph of the lynching.

Junior reddened. "I may have let too much out of the bag early on," he admitted. "I told Eddie and one or two other people about discovering Thomas in California. At the time, I didn't connect him with the lynching."

"You told me it was to be kept secret, but it's done," Thomas said. "Now, let me tell you what happened to me." He told of Monk's revelation, of overhearing Paralee tell Pear that she knew 'what he and those white boys did'—but he did not tell them about the visit by Stovall and Judge Mabry.

"Do you think one of them might have frightened Uncle Dillard?" Poe asked, his habitual smile fading.

"I feel as if someone is playing a game with all of us," Justyn said. "A deadly game." She turned to Thomas. "Who do *you* think the falconer is?"

He looked at her sharply. "Perhaps it's Stubby," he answered, only half smiling. "I sometimes think it's as much his ghost wanting to set the record straight as it is my father's."

They ordered coffee.

"I think I'll do a 'flavor of the times' piece," Junior said. "I can look up some of those clippings Justyn saw in the scrapbook and create the 'party atmosphere,' using names. That should make some people uneasy."

"I think the thing to go with now is the fact that your father was apparently killed while still in jail, Thomas," Poe said. "That should come as a shock to a lot of people. I know that Uncle Dillard didn't realize it, or he would have talked about it."

"It sounds to me like you're capable of dealing with more than arson," Justyn said, smiling at Junior.

"And I'll add that Uncle Dillard died under 'mysterious circumstances.' "

"There's a detail that's always bothered me," Thomas said, his forehead furrowed. "One of the early clippings mentioned the bloody towels in my parents' house. The inference was that they were 'nice' towels that my mother must have stolen in her maid work. That inference made me so mad I didn't think straight. Now, looking back, suppose the towels weren't put there by my parents? Suppose someone brought them in?"

" 'Nice' towels from a 'nice' house?" Justyn said wonderingly.

$\triangledown$

22

"Do you realize, kid, that Stubby's been gone thirty years?" Chub smiled and tousled Eddie's hair. "Now, didn't you promise me you were going to make amends, straighten things out, put the lid back on? Haven't you pushed this just a little too far? Are you going to let me down on this, too?"

"Hon," Frank said, setting his suitcases down by the door, "where have you been? I called from Atlanta, and then from the airport." But before Justyn had time to answer, he continued happily, "The deal is closed. It all came together this morning, unexpectedly. And did we do well on it!"

She stepped happily into his arms. He was home. Something was happening in her favor, for a change. "I couldn't have done without you for another day," she said truthfully.

"Say, hon, what happened to you?"

She told her pyracantha-from-the-porch story, embellishing. He held her at arm's length to look at her, then pulled her close again. "I'm sorry I wasn't here," he said softly. "I wasn't meant to travel, hon. I've been homesick the whole time."

He sat down in his easy chair with a drink after dinner, and promptly fell asleep. She covered him with an afghan, then searched their bookshelves for a quaint lay history of Green Hills she had purchased years before. Its version of the Devil McKinner legend had bewitched her. Now she recovered it, settled on the sofa, and quickly gave herself to the story. The town's founding father trod again on moccasin-shod feet, his crow-haired sons and stolid Cherokee wife trailing single-file.

A dark view of Green Hills pervaded. She had always wanted to think of her town as a gathering of pristine little woodblock houses spread on a pastoral patchwork quilt, but she knew it wasn't. And in these pages the legend of a curse that settled after Devil McKinner's death seemed real. It was a curse of violence upon the men who murdered him, who divided his expansive holdings among themselves, who passed along to their heirs the tainted land, the tainted wealth. These men had established their own aristocracy and written their own history; continued to write it daily in the pages of the Green Hills *Mountaineer*, except that Junior and Poe were breaking rank . . .

The early-morning edition of the *Mountaineer* sent telephones ringing at an unheard-of hour. Not only Eddie and Ouida called Justyn, but also Monica Castille. She could hear in their voices that they blamed her for dredging up the old stories. It was almost as if old bones had been cast about, to go clacking like castanets in the unsettling long November dark. The sudden wind that came howling down from the Blue Ridge escarpment rattled the courthouse windows, sang a dirge on the barren railroad tracks, and made even Justyn's home in Primavera seem a cold and drafty place.

Thomas's room at the Ritzcroft faced east. He opened the blinds and stared at the lightening sky, the steeple-dotted skyline blossoming from gray to pastels. How much fretful sleep had he managed? An hour or two at best. And he had not been able to accomplish much writing or reading, either. He felt as if the erratic schedule, the beating, the stress he had been under ever since coming to Green Hills, were beginning to take their toll. The hot, dry room had him coughing, which made his chest and collarbone ache. And at the same time he felt an occasional chill. The idea of breakfast in the plastic restaurant downstairs was nauseating. He had to do something, go somewhere to take his mind off his misery. He dressed and, stopping at the restaurant only for a cup of carry-out coffee, made his way out its fire exit to the parking garage. No one seemed about, and his was the only car on Main Street at that hour.

But Paralee's children were already outside playing when

he pulled into her clean-swept yard. They clamored quickly around him, calling his name, touching him, making him long for the students he felt he had abandoned. But perhaps it would not take long now to get home to them, to Naja . . .

"You look like you're daydreaming," Paralee called softly from the porch as he stepped up.

"I hope not. I want it all to come true."

The cold fresh air was bracing. He was reluctant to go into the stale house, and followed her slowly through the room where the babies slept into the rank kitchen. Billie Holiday sang in the background, not a lullaby the sleeping children dreamed to, but men, black men . . . "Southern fruit" . . .

"You come to see if Pear's dead?" Paralee drawled matter-of-factly.

Thomas winced. "I came because I was lonely, I think. And"—he smiled—"where else can one go at this hour? Yes," he added seriously, "I suppose I want to know. Is he?"

She shook her head, earrings clacking, turban bobbing. "The children haven't eaten, have you?"

"No."

"Then talk to me while I cook us all up something. No, he isn't dead. He sent his driver again, but I said no, give me one more day. You know, I've been trying to make a baby, a boy, to name after him. Monk's sure doing his part, but I suspect Pear had them tie my tubes, the last one I had. He didn't like paying for them. I'm not too old," she said defensively.

"Paralee, let me have the letter."

"I hid it so good you can't find it, so don't start."

"I can't wait. I'm afraid."

"Don't wait, and you'll get yourself killed. What's one more life to those people?" She took a pan of biscuits from the oven and a half-dozen children swarmed in from the back door, grabbing all but the few she scooped up and set aside. "Out!" she ordered. "I'm making some cream gravy for *our* biscuits," she said, stirring patiently, finally placing a full and dripping plate before him. "I'm looking for a sign," she said. "I'll know it when I see it. I can't have a hand in sending him off unless I know it's the right time. If his soul got lost out there, they'd get him for sure."

Instead of entering his room at the Ritzcroft, Thomas stopped on the wide balcony that served as hallway and looked down into the vast atrium formed by the seven-story enclosure. A giant hot-air balloon bobbed in brilliant color beneath his midway room, while a thousand small balloons floated profligately above, ricocheting soundlessly from the glass-domed ceiling. The man-made climate was stifling. He undid his collar and leaned against the railing. For a moment, he felt suspended, dizzily, in time and space. The peaceful sounds of a fountain splashing lazily below mingled with a singer's scratchy notes as she practiced for the cocktail lounge's lunchtime jazz.

He dreamed faces in the vast space before him, felt a current building.

Justyn was no longer certain which gate in the large municipal cemetery was closest to her father's grave—it had been that long since she had visited. In frustration she parked her car and struck out searchingly under a lowering sky. Where did her father lie among the confusing and ever-multiplying stones? She remembered a white tower nearby—the Non-Denominational Prayer Tower, it was called, and hurried toward it as drops of rain began to fall.

The small circular interior, though chill, was peaceful. Its high roof made the rain seem far away. Narrow slits covered with dark grille served as windows, filtering light into a soothing dark mosaic. She sat down on a slab bench beneath a flickering icon and rubbed her arms and shoulders. She felt she would carry Chub's marks forever, as if she had been branded by the devil. Yet it was the remembered pain of her father's death that overwhelmed her. How she mourned that young face framed with an old man's hair, the clear twang of his voice that carried in its tone the flailing sound of a five-string banjo. There had always been about him some inconsolable air of country-come-to-town that embarrassed

Ouida and touched Justyn deeply. She knew he would have remained a player in Green Hills history. She mourned that loss, too.

She must have been sitting for a long time, when a familiar voice startled her.

"How did you know I was here?" The words seemed spoken close by, though she could see no one—spoken in Ouida Balantyne Orms's hoarse whisper.

Justyn stood up, confused.

"You told me you were coming. On the phone, remember?" A man's curt, strong voice answered. Buck Stovall.

"No, I don't remember," Ouida said drunkenly.

Justyn stepped silently from grille to grille until she found them, mere yards away. The rain had stopped. The sun reflected dazzlingly from a sparkling, dripping world. Her mother and Buck stood facing each other, ankle-deep in steam that rose from the shining brown grass. She saw her father's tombstone as a backdrop. Ouida swayed and Buck stretched a firm arm to steady her.

"I chose this spot because it was beside a tree, and Zach loved trees, and then they cut the damned tree down." Ouida laughed sorrowfully. "Now I feel twice a widow, losing you. I feel old. Please go away and leave me alone. I told you I never want to see you again."

"Yes, ma'am, you did. And, for the first time, you told me why. You told me the real reason you've turned cold, and then you hung up. Now, by God, you're going to hear my side."

"Go away."

"I don't know what you've heard, or imagined. I've been faithful as a rock."

"Eddie said women call you there all the time."

"*Eddie!*" Buck spat the name. "No woman has called me there, ever! Not even you," he reminded her. He stepped around the tombstone and pulled her to him so fiercely Justyn thought she could hear her breath escape in a soft *whoosh.* "*Eddie* . . . Eddie has tried to make me jealous, too," he said slowly, as if trying to sort his thoughts. "He tried to make me think that you were fucking that young Levity fellow."

"*What?*" She drew back as if he had struck her.

"He gave me those shoes of yours—the ones you said Justyn wore to that country club dance—and said he had found them in a Fricatown house Levity stayed in. When I saw Levity at your place, I thought . . . But then, he kept on suggesting things, too many. I saw he must be baiting me, just like he's baiting you. Babe, you've got to believe I wouldn't do anything to hurt you. I wouldn't take a chance on losing you."

Ouida looked away from him. "Poor Eddie," she said finally, but still disbelievingly, "it must have put him in a panic, realizing I'd marry you. It's not like him—"

"Yes, and I'm sure he's afraid I'll tell he was involved with the lynching."

"I know he took pictures."

"More than that. Oh yes, more than that. He and that pretty girl that married the judge were there, in the middle of it all."

"Ivey? Ivey Mabry was *there*? When I saw the implication, in the newspaper, I thought it was a lie."

"Oh, yeah. I wouldn't forget *her*. The prettiest, next to you. Loose as a coward's bowels, but a beaut. She and Eddie skirted around. Encouraged Chub. Encouraged us all."

"This is too much," Ouida said sadly. "I can't bear to talk about Eddie this way. Please, I need . . . I need to be alone. I need to think things out, alone. Why don't you go on to my place? I'll be along in a few minutes."

"Are you all right?"

"Of course I'm all right. I came to say goodbye to Zach. I never really have, you know. I never had reason to. I need to, don't you think?" She swayed.

"I'm not sure you should be driving, babe. Why don't I wait on you?"

"No. I'm not going to drink anymore, I promise. You go on. Make a pot of coffee. I'll be along in a few minutes."

Buck backed away reluctantly, leaving her standing in the

shimmering grass, her small figure scarcely taller than her husband's tombstone. The sound of Buck's mournful, plaintive whistling joined the birdsong around her.

Justyn thought of speaking, of joining her at a moment precious to both of them. But her mother, the lovely Ouida Balantyne Orms, as soon as her lover had vanished over the glistening hill, pulled the silver flask from her purse and began to drink.

Justyn stepped out as soon as Ouida started walking away. Somehow, she knew she would not look back.

ZACHARY CRAIG ORMS
DEFENDER OF JUSTICE
BELOVED OF FAMILY
REST IN PEACE

But he had not rested in peace, not in Justyn's heart. He had not come to terms with justice. Now she was trying to, at least for Thomas's sake, for his father's. But poor Zachary, lying beneath his stone, what could she do for him? Suppose she *was* pregnant, could she name a son for him? A pall hung over her father's name. It always would. She could not deny that.

"Well, Toots, what it all boils down to—he's dead, and we're alive."

"Mother!"

"I dropped my lighter. When I turned, here you were."

"Thomas is writing a poem about his father. I wish . . . I wish there was *something*," she said helplessly.

"You'd have to understand him better. And that's what neither of us can do." Ouida sighed, lit a cigarette, coughed.

"Mama, I want you to be happy. I'm sorry I don't like Buck."

"I love him, whether you like him or not."

"But what if he turns out to be involved in"—she waved her hands—"the old business of the lynching, more involved than we know? Eddie—"

"I don't want any more mention of Eddie," Ouida said

185

angrily. "Not by you or Buck or anyone. Eddie is my brother and I love him. He was all I had for a long, long time. You can't understand that."

Justyn sighed. She truly couldn't.

"I'd better get going. Buck is waiting for me. Are you going to be all right, Toots?"

How she wished she knew. "Right as rain." She smiled.

"Yes, it seems to have stopped," Ouida said naively. "Now we look for the rainbow." She laughed huskily, waving her small hand as she started once more down the hill.

23

T HE TIME HAD COME to make a move. Thomas could bear waiting no longer. He dialed Balantyne Hall.

Eddie, too, had been waiting. "If you want to find out what really happened, I can arrange for you to be told," he said. "But if you're after something else—revenge, prosecution, blackmail—I can fix it so you'll *never* know."

"I want to know what happened."

"All right, then. There are two other people you need to meet. Here, tonight. This will be strictly private, between the four of us. Eight o'clock."

Frank frowned when he handed Justyn the phone. It was Eddie.

"Jus," Eddie said, "I hope you're free tonight. I've got tickets to take your mother to the Little Theatre, but something has come up and I can't make it. Can you go in my place? I hate to disappoint her."

Justyn said nothing.

"I realize it's late notice, but—"

"What about Buck Stovall? Couldn't he go with her?"

"I doubt he could sit through a play," Eddie said sneeringly. "Besides, isn't it time you and your mother spent a little time together?"

"Oh, all right. If you'll call her back and tell her. Tell her I'll pick her up at a quarter to eight. Will you get the tickets to her? I'm going to be pushed."

Frank's frown turned to a scowl as she hung up the phone.

"I'd hoped for a quiet evening," he said.

"I know. But it's the Little Theatre. It will give us a chance to be together without having to talk. And you can have a quiet evening. Don't wait up for me."

* * *

Thomas had felt for a day or two that he was coming down with a cold. For several days he had been going on false, self-generated energy. Now that it seemed he was finally making some headway, the energizing force left him. He needed to be fully alert tonight, which meant he needed to rest now. He arranged for a wake-up call, ordered milk from room service, closed the drapes, and lay watching the room pale around him. Noise from the hall seeped through the hollow-core door, but gradually grew fainter. He dozed, thought it was Paralee's children he heard playing in the yard. Or was it his students at recess? He dreamed he went fishing with his father's shadow.

He woke abruptly, needing to vomit, and barely made it to the bathroom. Milk had been a mistake. Gravy and biscuits had been a mistake. He realized he was coming down with a virus in this damned cold, and now wet abominable, weather. He longed for Naja to tuck him in blankets or Paralee to swathe him in poultices . . .

He fell back across the bed and slept, woke shivering in the midst of a nightmare, crawled back under the covers, and slept until the wake-up call came. Seven P.M. Enough time for some juice, to collect his thoughts.

Again, Paralee unfolded the letter from her turban and read it slowly, sitting at the kitchen table with Joey as a lookout in case Thomas should appear. Not yet; not yet. As long as Pear breathed, his wish would be upheld. She promised him that. But the letter burned like a sinister presence. Thomas was not safe, not knowing.

She thought of Pear, the only family she had. Some of her brothers and sisters she barely remembered. Scattered and forgotten. Whatever Pear did, he was her brother. He stood by her, no matter what his wife thought. Even if she had a hundred children, he would stand by her . . .

My dear Thomas,
    I am having this letter typed without identification, date, or signature so that it may not be used against

me or my family, or as evidence in any case you may pursue. However, I hope that it may have positive meaning in your life and your determination to restore your father's honor and what you so naively call the "truth."

I am still amazed at how like a ghost you came out of nowhere to remind this sick man of his sins. I had almost forgotten! Tom Levity rising out of his grave, demanding his due.

When you telephoned me for a meeting, I panicked. I didn't know how I would react if you asked me incriminating questions, as I knew you would. I had forgotten how to deal with my guilty conscience, you see. I had a couple of my employees "rough you up." It wasn't supposed to turn out as seriously as it did. You put up too much of a fight, just as your father would have done.

And then I almost got you killed, through my own carelessness. I told someone where you were staying. Justyn had called to ask directions to your parents' house, so I figured that was where you must be. I heard about the shooting. I can't tell you how relieved I was to see you walking down my sister's lane. A ghost again.

Tom deserved a fine son, and he got one. You are right to believe in him as you do. He did not kill Stubby Balantyne, nor did your mother. The night they found Stubby Balantyne a car pulled into the alley behind my place. The horn summoned me. I thought it was slumming white folk wanting bootleg or a colored girl, but it was Chub Castille, Ivey Mabry (née Montgomery), and Eddie Balantyne sitting in the front seat of Stubby's big Cadillac. What they wanted was for me to keep my customers inside for a few minutes. It didn't seem much of a favor to do for influential white folks. I thought it was one of their pranks. Then Eddie gave me a wad of money. A *lot* of money.

When the body was discovered I didn't know what

to do. I had become an accomplice, though I never learned the details of Stubby's death. Things happened so quickly after that. They had arrested your father before I knew what to do. And then I kept quiet because . . . because. You had to be a black man newly off the chain gang to understand the way things were for me then.

There. A coward's confession.

I couldn't face you with this. I wouldn't tell you now, except for circumstances.

Now you know, to a large degree, what happened. I hope it is enough—that you will take the truth for what it is and leave our town. There is no good that can come of your remaining in Green Hills. Those people will kill you if you don't. I believe that. Go back where you came from, quickly and with my blessing.

Get married. Have children. Take pride in naming your first son "Tom."

When you read this, I will be your "late" friend.

Paralee rose, sighed heavily, and replaced the letter in her turban. She saw all of the children to bed, even the restless Joey, and stepped out onto the front porch. Floorboards creaked, a gust of wind howled. It was cold, but she had worked so long in the hot kitchen, her pores were so clogged with sweat and grease, she could not get cool enough. The moon was rising, bloody and full, a time, she knew, of birth, death, and madness. The emergency room would be full— young women's water bags bursting and young men dying of fresh wounds . . . It was a time she dared not leave the children, for fear Monk might reappear with the craziness on him, a knife in his hand.

What she was going to do if he did come, she had not made up her mind. It might be a relief to die, except for the children. Who else could prepare them for what it was going to be, this life? Work and wait, wait and work. Pear said Monk needed killing. Perhaps it would come to an end of its own somehow.

A fox barked. There, and again, right at the edge of the yard. There! She shielded her eyes and saw its red ruff reflect a shaft of light, bright as flame. How tame it seemed, sitting pert, no taller than broomstraw, watching her. How strange. They never came so close to town anymore. She raised her hand, called softly, and instead of bounding away, it barked back at her, a sharp, staccato "Ark! Ark!" that shattered the quiet of the forest surrounding. It sounded like Pear laughing.

Her breath caught. It was the sign.

And within a few moments she saw headlights bouncing along the drive. Pear's chauffeur had come for the packet of deceptively sweet-smelling herbs. It would not be long now. Then she would give the letter to Thomas, and he could figure out who his enemies were.

Eddie had been so busy preparing for his visitors he had not noticed how solidly darkness settled across the yard. He hated to have missed twilight, his favorite time of day, when shapes blurred and past and present mingled and the wide lawn seemed to shimmer in its own unchanging destiny. Resolutely he stopped what he was doing and without turning on a light stepped out onto the front porch to survey his holdings. The arc of the white-graveled drive, reflecting lightly, had been laid out a hundred and fifty years before, when progress made the old house at last turn its face away from the river—*about face*, Stubby would have said. Tonight, if all went as planned, he would be turning his life *about face*.

On impulse he stepped down into the darkness and walked along the house edge slowly, keeping his eyes away from the cemetery downhill. At the rear he stopped. He could hear the river, a gentle sound grown constant and necessary to him as his own pulse, and as taken for granted. Yet because of it, Balantyne life had come and gone here that resulted in his own life. Yet because of this not very remarkable stream called the Marshy River, the first Valenchat had decreed that he and his should flourish or perish here.

Eddie sighed. Unless it was his own, history bored him.

What would come of his stewardship of Balantyne Hall? How would the fourth Edward Valenchat Balantyne be remembered?

Strange, how clear his thoughts were under the vastness of stars, the brightening moonlight. Now that it was about to be settled, the loose ends of so many years seemed less frightening. He felt single-minded and philosophical about it. When this was out of the way, he would reclaim Ouida somehow, finish the refurbishing of Balantyne Hall. He would think of some distinctive way to leave a positive imprint on the generations. Perhaps he would marry. The girl with the horse teeth and coltish brother held promise, her mother rich as Croessus. The house was big enough to allow for more than one private life. Even if Ouida *did* back out, her apartment could become a suite for a wife . . . or brother-in-law. One thing was certain—the likes of Buck Stovall would never call *his* roof home.

A cat rubbed against his leg, startling him. "Jennie-Fur!" He bent and petted her. "I didn't know you followed me out. Bad cat! Come now, it's too cold." He had lifted the animal and started back, when the sight of something glowing and bobbing across the grass sent him scurrying. Strange how swiftly his mood could change.

Now the cat upset his balance and his nerves. He dropped it without apology. The night, its outcome, seemed less secure around him. He bolted for the kitchen door, but seeing Beesie still stirring within, stopped. The bobbing light might be Chub, jogging. Eddie struggled to regain his composure and walk back around to the front. Chub was nowhere to be seen, and Beesie had locked the door on him. Cursing, he rang the doorbell, and rang. Fumbling for his keys, he dropped them several times before finding the right one. Now he was running late. Now he must see that Beesie went to bed and everything went as planned. He knew his future depended on it. His very life might depend on it, he reminded himself, turning on the front lights and practicing the smile of a welcoming host in the foyer mirror.

* * *

Ivey threw her leg over the arm of the chair, exposing an amber-hosed thigh. "I'm so bored I could spit in the fire." She yawned.

Chub smiled. "Then, do. What's your pleasure?"

"My pleasure is pleasure, of which there isn't any."

"Don't be so pessimistic," Eddie said.

"But she's right," Chub agreed. "Nothing's fun anymore. Not like it used to be. For God's sake, let's think of something!"

Eddie shrugged and smiled. "Why do you think I invited you here?"

"Oooo," Ivey roused, "—why?"

"You'll see. Be patient."

"Remember the time Stubby got those shots for us?" she asked, laughing. "Pro . . . pro . . . what?"

"Testosterone?"

"Whatever it was, I've never been so horny. Remember? For *days.*"

Chub patted the sofa beside him. "Of course I remember. Come here."

Ivey sat up and kicked off her shoes, then bent to pick them up, her breasts swelling provocatively with the movement. "I'm getting wrinkles," she said dispiritedly.

"We all are," Chub said, patting the seat beside him more insistently. "And gray pubic hair. Say, kid, you look like death warmed over," he said to Eddie, noticing, finally, his pallor. "Burning both ends of the candle? Too many Dukes? Screwed by Wall Street again?"

Eddie held up his hand warningly. "I hear a car," he said.

$\triangledown$

24

As HIS HEADLIGHTS CUT like a scythe across the wide, forbidding lawn, illuminating, for an instant, headstones of the little cemetery down the hill, Thomas shivered despite the warm coat and sweater he wore. The porch lights of Balantyne Hall seemed to glow faint welcome as Eddie stepped out to meet him, waving him up the steps with a gesture more summons than greeting. As he took Thomas's coat he nodded him stiffly toward the living room, where Chub Castille and Ivey Mabry sat close together on a sofa, their handsome heads inclined in intimate-seeming conversation.

Eddie stepped to a tea cart that served as portable bar, where a chafing pitcher simmered. "It's so cold out, I thought apple grog might warm us," he explained. "Have a seat," he offered more civilly, "while I pour and strain this concoction."

Thomas chose a wing chair by a window and looked about him. Small damp logs steaming in the fireplace did little to warm the high-ceilinged room. The chill he felt seemed to deepen. Centuries overlapped in the furnishings like furls of the nearby river. Then Eddie poured hot cider through a sieve of pungent, sweet-smelling rootstalk into a crockery mug, and a tantalizing aroma of cinnamon and ginger permeated the musty perfume of evenings past. He added orange and lemon wedges, a jigger of rum, and presented the first cup to Ivey.

"Mmmm." She sniffed approvingly.

Eddie repeated the process with elaborate ceremony. "This one's for you," he said, bringing it to Thomas, who sat warming his hands on the cup while Eddie completed the servings. "Drink up," their host urged them, "the rum cools it enough to be palatable. To 'clearing the air,' " he added, as if in toast, though no one else raised their cup to him.

The drink *was* good, Thomas thought, an unusual bouquet of herbs, rootstalk, fruit, and good liquor. For a moment he felt warmed, as if in the company of friends. But there was no forgetting. The four sat drinking in silence, studying each other. "What is it you want to tell me?" Thomas asked finally of Eddie.

"What's this, kid?" Chub said. "Why *did* you ask him here?"

Eddie swallowed loudly. "He wants to find out what really happened. I told him we'd oblige him."

"You open your mouth and I'll shut it," Chub warned.

"Whatever we say stays in this room," Eddie argued. "Who'd believe it?"

"I'm warning you, kid. This is crazy."

"Did you want to tell me that a dead man was lynched? I already know that," Thomas challenged. "Or, that *you* killed him?"

Ivey came alert. Her eyes moved almost admiringly over Thomas's face. "How did you find out?"

"It doesn't take much to follow your trail, just a good nose, even if it *is* thirty years old."

Eddie flared. "And did you figure out where your father is reburied? Did your nasty nigger nose smell *him* out, too?"

Thomas emptied his cup and sat cracking his knuckles. "No," he said quietly, "but I finally figured out it had to be you who moved him, who spied when Dillard Beasley buried him. Once I learned you were there, at the lynching, I knew. But, tell me, did you go back the other day?"

"What's he talking about? Say, kid, take it easy," Chub said sternly.

"Down there in the cemetery!" Eddie said triumphantly. "That's where he's buried. The last mound in back of the slave lot. That's why I added the gravel, you fool!"

"*You're* the fool," Chub said angrily. "You can never leave well enough alone, can you?"

"Oh, let them talk," Ivey said, "this is fun."

"And if he persuades someone to dig up the body? Then what?" Chub turned an angry face to her.

"But, he won't," Eddie said confidently.

"But, how do you know?"

"Because we're going to bargain when all of this is over," Eddie said.

"If only the stupid train had run over Stubby, none of this would have happened," Ivey said.

"You would have been just another little black boy growing up with no shoes." Eddie smiled sardonically at Thomas.

"It was my idea. It would have worked," Ivey persisted. "I read it in a book. It would have worked." She sat forward eagerly—again, like a child.

Thomas was amazed. To him they all looked like children, bad children. A favorite line of Auden's poetry flashed and faded: *"Children afraid of the night/ Who have never been happy or good."* The chill intensified. He felt dizzy and desperate.

"If only Eddie had tested the goddamned guillotine like he was supposed to, none of this would have happened," Chub corrected Ivey.

"Eddie was supposed to check the block of wood that kept the blade from falling too far, to be sure it was strong enough," Ivey explained.

Thomas felt faint. Guillotine! Of course! Their voices chimed on excitedly.

"But, I did!" Eddie flared, defiant.

"Shut up!" Chub said, though it was obvious Eddie did not intend to. He chattered on, unburdening himself, sweeping his friends along with him in the narrative. Sometimes they interrupted him, correcting or embellishing details none seemed ashamed of, their voices sounding caustically youthful in the tired old room, while the hollow ticking of an ancient pendulum clock supplied a mortuarial accompaniment. . . .

"Why my father? Why did you have to bring *him* into all this?" Thomas asked disbelievingly. He felt weary, as if their talk were putting him to sleep.

"After our plan didn't work, we had to do *something*. We

had to distract the law, keep it away from Balantyne Hall. We knew about Stubby's argument with your father, everyone did."

"We went to Tom's place. He sent his woman out the back door as we drove up. By then everybody in Fricatown knew about the body. Tom thought we were the law. By the time he found out we weren't, it was too late. We had brought the towels we'd used for Stubby, and we smeared the place up . . ."

"What's the matter with him?" Chub asked.

The voices fanned and faded. Thomas imagined he was back at the Ritzcroft, that he had been dreaming. Someone must have cut his hair. The moment had come to wrestle the temple from its beams, but his strength-giving locks had been shorn.

"What's the matter with him?" Ivey repeated.

"I . . . don't understand," Thomas managed.

"There's nothing to understand," Chub said firmly. "You've said more than enough, kid. He's not a goddamned priest you're supposed to confess to. Do you want to read all this in the papers? What are we going to do?"

"It's already done," Eddie said. "I've poisoned him."

"Jesus God!" Chub moaned, putting his face in his hands. "You stupid little shit!"

"Nothing else worked. I followed him, found out where he was staying, almost got Buck Stovall or Judge Mabry to take care of him, but it didn't work. Now help me get him out of here."

"You're crazy! Ivey, come with me."

Eddie's voice rose. "Chub, don't tease me now. Help me get him out of here!"

"Forget your damned coat, Ivey. *Come with me.*"

"I want to know the rest," Thomas managed. "The rest."

"If you're wondering if *I* killed your father, the answer is yes. I got Stubby's gun and got the deputies to let me in, and I shot him. It was easy. There was so much confusion and so much noise. I couldn't risk someone listening to him. Someone might have listened to him, you see."

197

Justyn delivered Ouida to her door and watched her teeter safely to her steps. When she reached her home she was relieved to see the bedroom light already off. She had taken off her shoes and poured herself a glass of wine when the hall phone rang. She caught it before it rang again.

For a long moment, all she could hear was a faint keening sound. It was so full of pathos her heart seemed to stop. Then, "Justyn? Is this my Justyn? Mercy, come help us! Oh, help us, Justyn!"

The front door of Balantyne Hall stood open to the cold, its ancient light spilling onto the lawn. When Justyn stepped into the wide foyer she could see Eddie in the living room, standing in front of the fireplace, wringing his hands. Then she heard Beesie, still keening. She found her kneeling beside Thomas, who sprawled in a wing chair by the front window. His eyes were closed and his breathing laborious.

"They poisoned him, Miss Justyn. Those bad young people, they poisoned him."

Justyn could not find a pulse. "Eddie, what did you give him? Eddie! I'm talking to you!"

Eddie looked at her blankly.

"It was poison I got from Miz Bones, plant poison," Beesie said in so small a voice Justyn had to strain to make out her words. "Mister Eddie said it was to poison a cat."

"Well, whatever it is, it's killing him!" What to do? Plant poison! And what was the antidote for that? "Beesie, call my number. Let it ring until Frank answers. He's asleep, so it will take a while. Tell him I need him. At once. Tell him it's an emergency, Beesie!"

Eddie turned and looked at them.

"Eddie, can you help us with Thomas?"

"No. He's got to die."

"No. He's got to live! Can you help us? Beesie and I can't get him out to the car by ourselves."

"He's dead."

"He's not dead yet! Eddie, for God's sake . . ."

"Mr. Frank is on his way." Beesie had returned. She was so weak now she could scarcely slide her feet along in her scuffs.

Justyn helped her sit back on the sofa and covered her with a shimmering evening coat someone had left behind. Ivey Mabry? Monica Castille? Crockery mugs sat about, a tea service. What in the world had gone on here? Where were the others? Who had poisoned whom?

"Jus?"

Eddie called her name. She turned to find him staring, his head cocked sadly to one side. "Jus, I never meant to hurt him, you've got to believe that."

"Well, Eddie, then perhaps you shouldn't have poisoned him," she said as evenly as she could. The seconds seemed to stretch into hours. Thomas's breath rattled ominously in the quiet room.

"Not *him* . . ." Eddie said scornfully, "your father."

"My father? Eddie, what are you talking about?" His words took her breath.

"Jus, you know I'm not a violent man. I wouldn't hurt anybody, especially Zach."

The room reeled around her. "Eddie, you're not making any sense," she said, or tried to say. "Do you mean . . . ?" The sound of gravel flying in the driveway brought Beesie to her feet.

"He's here! Mr. Frank's here!" she said, even as Frank came running into the room in his robe and slippers.

"Hon, are you all right? You're pale as death!"

"It's Thomas. Eddie's poisoned him. We've got to get him to Miz Bones, the root doctor. She's the only one who will know what he's taken. Please, can we try to pick him up?"

"Let me try." Frank bent and put his shoulder to Thomas's chest, then lifted him like a feed sack. "Get the door, hon. And go open my car door. Then can you see to Beesie, and meet me there?"

Eddie had no concern now for Beesie or anyone else. He stood in front of the fireplace wringing his hands, studying abstractedly a faded oil of stag and hounds that had hung there unstudied all of his life. He did not answer when Justyn spoke to him. She went to the phone, started to dial Ouida's number, thought better of it, and looked up Buck Stovall's instead.

"This is Justyn," she said as civilly as she could. "There isn't time to explain. I'm at Balantyne Hall, but I've got to leave. Can you get Mother and bring her here at once? Beesie's sick and Eddie's not himself... On second thought, maybe you should call Dr. Wright to meet you here. I'll check by later. And, thank you, Buck. Thank you so very much."

Justyn had never driven up the lane to Paralee's, and she was not sure where it exited from Fricatown Road. She remembered a sign to the place years before, but as Miz Bones's reputation spread there had no longer been need and it had fallen into the grass. It was a corner glimpsed leaning in the broomstraw that finally directed her. Then she saw the small house ablaze with lights and Frank's car in the yard.

There were several small children clustered on the front porch, but no one came to greet her. Yet she knew the place so well from Thomas's description—the quaint house a clatter with chimes, the steep and creaky front steps—she needed no direction. She knocked on the front screened door; she could hear voices beyond. Finally she opened it and stepped in. The sudden sweet and sour odor of sleeping powdered babies almost made her cry out. She wanted to snatch one and run out the door. Yes, all was as she had expected: the babies, the phonograph playing softly.

Suddenly a tall, turbaned form blocked the light coming from the next room. "He's not going to make it," Paralee said, wringing her hands. "He's not."

25

JUSTYN THOUGHT THOMAS HAD stopped breathing. He lay
on his back on Paralee's bed, hands folded on his chest like
a corpse, his flesh tinged ghostly gray. A picture of him as he
had first appeared on the plane flashed painfully before her.
Green Hills had not been kind to Thomas More Levity, Jr.

"Where's Frank, my husband?"

"He's walked across the field to the pay phone, to call an
ambulance. I've done what I can do for him."

"Then I'll have to get back to Balantyne Hall. I've got to
find out from Eddie what's happened."

Paralee smiled. "Do *you* know what's happened?"

Justyn ignored the question. If Thomas breathed, she
couldn't tell it. She felt nauseated. "Paralee, I don't feel well.
May I use your bathroom?"

"Don't have no bathroom. I'll get one of the children to
lead you to the privy. Joey!"

Out the back porch past Thomas's sleeping mat, across a
clean-swept yard rich in moonlight, to the anachronistic
little shed, itself marked with the traditional half moon, she
followed the badly scarred boy. "Please leave me here," she
said. "I can see my way back."

Inside the privy she reeled from the stench. She would
have been violently ill no matter. Any thought she still might
have of being pregnant vanished. When she was able to step
back into the fresh air, she found herself still weak-legged
and queasy. She dreaded the room where Thomas lay, smelling, to her, like death. Instead, she made her way hesitantly
to the dark shed, swallowed in shadow, where pungent odors
warmed the night.

"Hon, where are you?"

She was thrilled to see Frank's shadow moving across the
yard. For a moment they held each other tightly without
speaking.

"Paralee gave me this, for you to give to Thomas, in case he makes it," he said, handing her an envelope. "She said it might be best for you to read it also."

The sound of a siren sent neighbor dogs howling.

There was a lump in Thomas's throat big as a fist that no amount of heaving would dislodge. Naja danced angrily just out of reach, her gold earrings casting a fire that blinded him.

"Am I dying?" he asked, opening his eyes.

A scar-faced boy eyed him woefully.

"Am I dying?"

"I s'pose so," the boy answered regretfully, adding, "My uncle already did."

It took about fifteen minutes for the attendants to steer the stretcher into Paralee's difficult surroundings, secure Thomas, and get him into the ambulance. Justyn left Frank and Paralee to explain as best they could what had happened. She knew the police would be called in, but they all needed time to think. Regretfully, she left Frank and hurried back to Balantyne Hall. Every light in the vast house seemed lit. Ouida must have been standing in the foyer waiting for her, for she was down the steps before the car stopped.

"Oh, Baby, what's happened? Eddie's gone! And Judge Mabry called. Ivey and Chub Castille took Ivey's jewelry and some clothes and whatever cash there was and ran away . . . He's beside himself and has called in a detective. Oh, Baby, what's happened? Where's Eddie? Beesie's out of her head. The doctor gave her a strong sedative, and you know I don't think she's ever had so much as an aspirin in her life. Where's Eddie? The El Dorado's gone. What in the world happened here tonight?"

"Mother, let's go up to the house and sit down. I feel like *I'm* going to pass out. Buck's still here, isn't he? Do you think you could make us some coffee? I'm so cold I don't feel like I'll ever get warm again. This house is like a mausoleum. Is there a space heater anywhere?"

Beesie lay snoring lightly on the sofa, warm beneath a pile

of coats. Justyn sat down in one of the wing chairs. Buck ceased his pacing to go in search of a heater. In her moment of solitude Justyn wondered wildly what she would say to them.

Ouida had calmed considerably when she returned.

"Where is Eddie?" she asked calmly, in a heavy tone that seemed to expect the worst.

"Mother, I wish I knew. Apparently he tried to poison Thomas. Chub and Ivey were here. They were involved in the lynching somehow, all of them—and in Stubby's murder."

"I'll get it out of Castille when he gets back," Buck said, returning with a heater.

"What makes you think they'll be back?" Ouida asked.

"The judge will see to it," Buck said. "That old man is vengeful as God. Look at all the men he's sent to the electric chair. He'll get his wife back, one way or another." He found a plug and arranged the heater at Justyn's feet. Then he unpocketed a clean handkerchief and wiped her face.

She had to fight a sudden urge to tell him about Chub; the rape. "If Thomas lives," she said, "he'll tell us everything."

Eddie Valenchat Balantyne's black El Dorado swerved along backcountry roads, kicking up gravel and dirt like a runaway phantom coach in the moonlight. Finally it wrecked, with considerable shock and afternoise, in a ditch not a dozen miles from Green Hills, just over the county line. Eddie sobbed. He had drunk half a bottle of bourbon, and still the edge had not gone from Ivey's and Chub's words. He felt that secret part of him, the self that was always afraid, was exposed. How could he ever face any of them again? It was always going to be as dark as it was now, the headlights gone, only the moon for a beacon, and it so far.

The sudden flashing of a blue light and the drawing close of a siren startled him. He dropped the bourbon and hit his chin soundly on the steering wheel when he tried to grab for it. The car sat at an impossible angle. He felt sick, tasting the trickle of blood on his lip.

"You'd better come out of there," a voice said as a flash-light raked him. The deputy's eyeglass frames glowed. His badge shone as gilt in the moonlight. "Having yourself a one-man party, my friend?" he asked. "Well, too bad for you, the party's come to an end."

Justyn fell asleep in the hospital waiting room. When she woke it was dawn. She sprinted down the hall and flung open the door.

Amazingly, there sat Thomas More Levity, propped up in bed, sipping from a glass held steady by a pretty nurse. Déjà vu.

"But, you're not dead!"

The familiar half-smile, half-frown altered his face. "That's not much of a greeting for one freshly back from the pearly gates."

"It's the best I've got. Oh, Thomas, I thought you were dead!"

"I hope Eddie and Chub and Ivey believe I am. It's been a night I wouldn't care to repeat."

"No, they've all disappeared."

He laughed. "I have sworn never to imbibe spices, apple juice, *any* ingredient of grog and/or leaf-of-tree or root-of-plant that has passed through Paralee's hands again."

"Speaking of Paralee, I brought you a letter from Pear. He's dead, you know."

"I thought I remembered Joey's telling me that, but it could have been a dream. Please, let me have it. You've read it?"

"Yes. And talked to Eddie. He said he hadn't meant to hurt my father—as if he'd killed him."

Thomas lay back and shielded his eyes to read the letter. Justyn pulled a chair to his side and sat holding his hand for a while. The room was so quiet she could hear the drip from the intravenous unit.

"I'm sorry I got you into all this, Justyn. I didn't know it would hurt so much. I don't mean the physical hurt, I mean . . ."

"I know what you mean. And it's not over. I've got to talk to Eddie, find out—well, find out all of it."

"Will you let Paralee know I'm all right? And I need to talk to your husband, find out what he told the police before I talk to them. I don't want to get Paralee in trouble. Apparently she told the medics that she had given me an antidote, but not that she had made the poison."

This time Paralee came out to meet her at the car, looking stately and concerned. Justyn brought her quickly up to date.

"If you haven't had breakfast, come in and eat with me. Or, at least, have coffee. I gets lonely for grown company, all these children around."

Justyn followed gladly, drawn to the house's rich aura of children. She could not get her fill of them, though they clung to her skirt and crawled into her lap in pestering fashion.

The phone was ringing just as Justyn walked in the front door. Frank answered.

"Frank? Buck Stovall here. I'm at Ouida's. Can you and your wife come over here, right away?"

"What is it?"

"I'm afraid I've got bad news. The police are here. There's been a—a tragedy. Eddie Balantyne was arrested for drunk driving last night, in the next county. Apparently he hung himself in jail."

"Eddie's dead?"

"Yes."

"Eddie's *dead*?" Justyn echoed.

Frank pulled her to his side. "Yes, we'll come. How's Ouida taking it?"

"She's sitting at the piano. She won't answer questions."

But when they arrived, the police were gone and the strains of "The Old Rugged Cross" greeted them. They let themselves in, not certain Ouida or Buck even knew they were there. She played, and he whistled, the melody a particularly poignant one.

"Eddie had a good tenor voice. He might have developed

it," Ouida said, as if to herself. "He never had a role model. Except, I guess, Stubby. Lord knows, he might have been different if he had had someone decent and wiser to love."

"He had you, babe," Buck said.

She smiled and laid her cheek on his hand. "You know, he told me just the other day that he had willed the house to you, Justyn," she said, acknowledging her with a nod. "He asked me if that was all right, or if I wanted it changed to me. I said no, leave it alone, never dreaming he would go before me. What in the world will you do with it? I can't imagine you living there."

The phone rang. Ouida moaned. "People will start calling, and coming. The body has to be identified." She looked up at Buck. "How am I going to stand all this, pet?"

"I'm right with you, babe."

"Damn the phone! Answer it, will you, Frank? Tell them I've gone to Balantyne Hall. Let's do go there, all of us. We can 'receive' there. That will give Beesie something to do. Damn, I hate this! Crying ruins my mascara."

News must already be spreading, Justyn thought as they drove onto the grounds. She dreaded staring eyes.

"Hon, do you realize what that piece of real estate is worth?" Frank asked.

"*Damnosa hereditas,*" she answered tiredly, over-whelmed. "How can we afford to keep it? But I sure don't want a family curse on my back, for selling it."

"It won't hurt to think about it."

"I could spend a lifetime just cataloguing the contents," she said, "or unraveling its history. If we tore it down, God knows what we'd find in the walls. Bodies. Treasure."

"How far does the property line go, behind the house?"

"To the river. It follows it a quarter of a mile or so. I'll show you, when we have time." She brightened. Any diversion to get through the interminable hours ahead, when gossipy people would be hugging her, shaking hands. The normally funereal air of the old house would be stifling.

And what would the town be saying about the Balantynes now?

Epilogue

THE FUNERAL WAS OVER, the crowds gone, the will read. Frank was back at work. Ouida and Buck had gone to Gatlinburg for the weekend to tour the Smokies. Justyn spent the morning at Balantyne Hall going through Eddie's things, hoping for a clue, she supposed, to the mystery of her father's death. Had Eddie killed him? It was difficult to believe that the kind-hearted young man she remembered from those days could have been capable of murder. Ouida, she knew, did not believe it, and was setting the past behind her. She envied her.

"Jus? Look now. I got dahlias for Mr. Eddie."

"They're beautiful, Beesie. I'll take them down in a little while. Can you fix us some lunch?"

She nodded, and looked approvingly at the pile of Eddie's belongings Justyn was readying for the Salvation Army.

"No, wait a minute, Beesie. I need to talk to you. It might as well be now. You know you're going to be here by yourself for a while?"

"I hope not."

"Well, you are. Mother doesn't want to be here now that Eddie . . . and I simply don't know what I'm going to do. Oh, I'll probably be here every day, I intend to go through *everything* to see what's here and what should be saved . . . Now, you can come to live with one of us, if you want."

"No'm, thank you."

"Well, Buck suggested he go ahead and finish the apartment, since it's this far along. He'll be here part of the time. Then you might want to stay in there for a while."

Beesie scowled.

"I know you love your room, but it's cold, Beesie, and dark, and so far from the bathroom. In the apartment you'd have your own little kitchen, and its living room would be such a good place to watch your soap operas—"

207

Justyn smiled, and Beesie smiled wanly back. At least she had not said no.

"I'll fix us some lunch now. And coffee?"

"Lot's of coffee, Beesie. I think that's what I'm living on these days."

There was time before lunch to take the dahlias down to Eddie's grave. Though a light rain was falling, the thought of being outside for a few minutes was tempting. Justyn put on coat and kerchief.

The funeral tent still stood over Eddie's grave. It might have looked almost festive if not for the dripping gray weather. She was almost upon it before she saw there was someone else there, standing on the far side, in the open.

"Thomas?"

"Justyn? For a moment, with your head covered, I thought you were your mother. I wondered what I was going to say to her."

"I'm glad to see you. I'm glad you're out of the hospital. But I didn't mean to disturb you. Beesie picked these flowers for Eddie."

"I've been down here a while. I came straight here. Eddie said my father's grave was the last mound in back of the slave lot. There."

She put her hand through his arm and they walked downhill. Even though the gravel gave traction, she could feel the mud beneath it shift. "I'm beginning to be quite sentimental about this place," she said. "I'm even thinking about having my father moved here."

"I'm thinking about having my mother and father moved somewhere together when I can afford to. I think she might want that. As far as I know, she never even dated another man. All those lonely years."

"When are you going back?"

"I've got to make a statement to the police, about everything. I don't think there's anything that can be done now, but it will be there for the record. I want to spend a little time with Paralee. One visit, but a good one. I love that lady. And then, I'm gone. I may not see you again, Justyn."

It must be perfect noon, she realized. The day seemed to have reached its zenith. It hung heavy and cold, but expectant. She felt she, too, must reach some point of perfect understanding. "I want to be sure I have the story straight," she said quietly. "Stubby was playing some sadomasochistic game with Eddie, Ivey, and Chub. It involved the guillotine, and it backfired, and Stubby died here at Balantyne Hall. They took his body to the railroad tracks, past Pear, who kept quiet. But that backfired, too, when the boys found the body before the train came, and so it was necessary for them to frame your father. Chub instigated the lynching, but they were afraid that might backfire, too, so Eddie talked his way into the jail on the pretense of taking pictures." She stopped the story there. She could not talk yet about her father.

"I think the facts are right. I don't know how much Junior and Poe will print, but they're excited enough that some of the truth will out."

"And you're going to write about it?" It started to rain harder. "Well, if this may be it, come and have lunch with us. With me and Beesie. She loves having company, even if she's not quite sure who you are."

For a moment he looked doubtful, then smiled. "That's what I like about the South," he said. "Hospitality. But, no thank you, Justyn, I never care to see Balantyne Hall again."